Also by Selene Simone in the Dragonfly Series

Available Now
Volume I: Dragonfly Deeds (2015)

Available 2017
Volume III: Dragonfly Visions

What the Dragonfly Saw

Dragonfly Dreams

VOLUME II OF THE DRAGONFLY SERIES

Dear Reader,
Happy reading and
I do hope you will want to
read Volume III due in spring 2017.
Cynthia Sandoval

Selene Simone
2016

Selene Simone

ISBN: 978-1-4834-5133-6 (sc)
ISBN: 978-1-4834-5134-3 (hc)
ISBN: 978-1-4834-5132-9 (e)

Library of Congress Control Number: 2015903754

Lulu Publishing Services rev. date: 5/12/2016

~ Dedication ~

To my husband, Kent, for his love and support.

To my two beloved bayou babies,
Rachal and Ross.

To my friend Lesley Walker,
for her challenge and leading me to
NaNoWriMo to help create this work.

To my artist, Juan Romero Rivas, for sharing his beautiful gift
and taking this journey with me.

And to my first readers and gentle critics,
Nichole, Andrea, Susanne, and Lily.

Lose another's heart and one day it may come back to you. But lose another's head, and you are no longer in their thoughts.
—Hyacinthe Delphine Drouin Danetree

Contents

Preface xi

Chapter 1   Something Old ... Something Older 1

Chapter 2   Anatomy of an Arrangement. 19

Chapter 3   Secrets in the Water. 37

Chapter 4   When Love Isn't Enough 53

Chapter 5   Three Does Not a Crowd Make. 73

Chapter 6   An Angel Gets Her Wings. 93

Chapter 7   The Heart Chooses Love. 111

Chapter 8   To Walk in Another's Shoes 125

Chapter 9   When Blood Is Thicker than Water 141

Chapter 10   No Calm in the Storm 169

Chapter 11   And the River Rolls On 191

Chapter 12   Sins in the Flesh. 205

Acknowledgments. 225

Suggested Readings 227

About the Author 229

# Preface

First and foremost, this is a work of fiction, although the dialogue and character attributes will most assuredly sound or seem familiar to some because I have written about human beings, and human beings must all follow certain undeniable basic patterns of growth and maturity until we cease to be. Our lives will either bestow or offer individualistic opportunities for us to think and behave differently from one another, but some experiences and conversations are commonplace regardless of culture, language, or race.

This novel covers many time periods and generations, each stitch of humanity, glory, and guilt weaving true patterns of life and love. I have written with great lust, and at times with loathing, and have spent each day of this adventure portraying perfect humans—perfect in their quests for flesh, finances, validation, and survival. This would not be possible without the historical references I chose that affected the decisions and experiences of my characters. No life, regardless of longevity or cognizance, can exist void of the paths of those behind us and the guiding lights of those on the path beside us and ahead of us. History trickles as blood through our veins, mutating with each birth and then being shaped by the scars, burdens, and triumphs we carry—some visible, some hidden.

I have chosen the region of southern Louisiana as the main geography for my novel. My own heritage there is as deep as the bayous and as rich as the soil. Its lands, peoples, languages, and dialects swirl like fine French brandy in a priceless snifter and survive to this very day. Though descriptive words such as "green," "moss-covered," "mysterious," "tropical," and "ancient" can be used often enough to give color and texture to any story involving the bayous and swamps of this beautiful world, I believe in my heart there are no proper words to describe the dangerous, seductive beauty. In my travels, I have found the bayous to be intoxicating, sensuous, and sinewy, capturing visitors like no other place I have known. It doesn't grow on you, it grows in you. Great cypress arms rock you while crickets and frogs croon you to dreamland. Yes, it is possible to fall in love with a place.

This book is my tribute to the visionaries: those who see with their own eyes and the eyes of others. The struggling ones. Those who persevere and survive in the face judgment. Those with their stories engraved on their flesh, penned on parchment, and painted on the fabric of history. Those with hearts as big as the sky and souls as vibrant as stars. May you find your character and live brightly and well in a place you have fallen in love with.

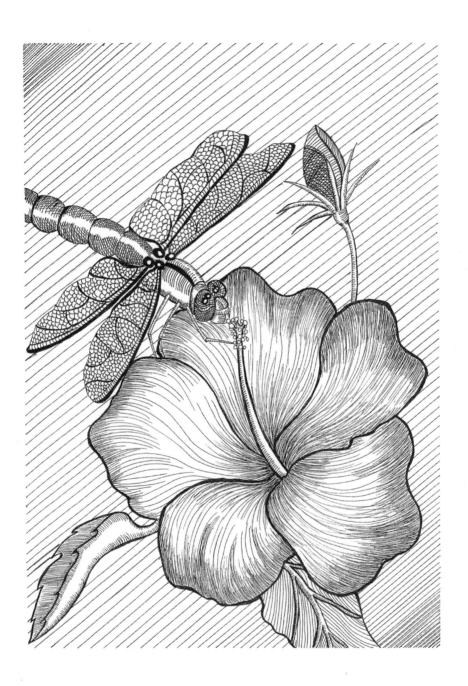

What the Dragonfly Saw

I saw it flit and flutter by
Over and over again
A vibrant orange-red dragonfly
I saw it sweep and spin
Then land atop a fragrant bloom
On the old hibiscus tree
At once I knew what the dragonfly saw
As I laid the body deep
Water water sink it slow
From bone to mud and brine
And cover well my scars and sin
From that ole dragonfly.

~ Belle Fleur ~

Chapter 1

Something Old ... Something Older

April 2013

The walls at Greyfriars held many things. They held the roof up, separated rooms, supported old portraits, exposed the weaknesses of those within them, and kept their secrets. In the parlor, Juliette had a captive audience as Honore Darden sat there seemingly attentive while she cut loose with anything she could or would talk about. She just couldn't shut up. She couldn't explain it, but she wanted to tell this handsome green-eyed stranger everything. Juliette started with the ridiculous amount of money floating around corporate legal cases and humorous water cooler stories from her office, and she then moved on to the fact that she could not really cook and hated most condiments, finally ending the show with a story regarding a makeup-sex weekend with someone she thought would be Mr. Right, despite their differences. Apparently Mr. Right had a change of heart and she was left at the hotel alone to wallow once again in singularity.

Honore watched in amazement as Juliette's facial expressions and body language changed with every memory and story she shared. She could go from serious to ridiculous in seconds flat. But he found her adorable. He didn't doubt or wonder about her accomplishments or intelligence, but it seemed to him she must be missing her girlfriends back in New Mexico, because he was beginning to feel she might expect him to start discussing hairdos and pedicures soon. He was about to try to break in with a question about the trunk when she put her coffee down.

"You see, Mr. Darden, at Greyfriars, the secrets are hidden in the walls, under the rugs, and in that damn old trunk that you are going to help me unlock. But I'm sorry, I'm probably boring you." She looked at her wristwatch. "I cannot believe I rambled on like this. I promise I don't normally do this with strangers." She blushed and continued. "I mean, well, people I've just met. Especially men. Not that I talk to a lot of men, really, like this." Her brain was screaming, *Please stop now before it's too late!* She composed herself. "Well, you probably have other jobs. I thought about bringing the trunk down, but it is so heavy. Are you ready to see it?"

He smiled. "It's okay. Your stories are very interesting. I hope there is a Mr. Right out there for you. He will never want for conversation. And I mean that in a good way." He put his coffee down, smiled again, and nodded. "Let's do it," he said, and he then squinted. "I mean, open the trunk. I didn't mean—"

Juliette blushed again and said, "Oh jeez, don't worry. I didn't think you meant ... well, you know ... *it*. I certainly didn't. And there is no Mr. Right presently. I mean, we don't even know each other, right?" There was too much smiling, too much blushing, and too many innuendos. "Oh God," Juliette said as she stood up, her hands on her hips. "I honestly don't know what is happening here. I'll show you the room, and you can go in there and just open it. Okay?"

Honore stood up and followed Juliette up the stairs. The whole time she climbed the stairs ahead of him, she tried to keep her hips from swaying too much. The whole time he followed her, he tried not to stare at her derriere, so he just kept looking down at the stairs. Well, except for that one time he had to look up to see how close to the top they were.

When they reached the second story, Juliette pointed to Aunt Pearl's room. "It's in there, next to the bed. I've got to do something across the hall." She was too nervous to go into the room with him. Something about the man made her feel silly, needy, and obvious all at the same time. She pointed across the hallway. "Just yell if you need anything."

2

He nodded. "Oh, okay then," he said. He went in and looked at the old steamer trunk sitting on the floor. He pulled out his small tool kit and surveyed the lock. This was going to be easy. He had it open in no time and lifted the lid, letting it rest against the bed. The smell was predictable—musty, old, with a hint of mothballs. Not like Juliette. He smiled. She smelled like gardenias. *Damn women. Why do they spend so much time trying to smell like that?* He found it intoxicating. Or maybe it was her. Almost the entire time she was talking in the parlor, he watched her mouth move—the way it curled up when she smiled. She had expressive eyes that danced while she spoke.

"Okay, H, enough of that," he whispered to himself. He saw a small wooden box and picked it up. It smelled worse than the old bundles of letters and books.

He put it back down just as Juliette entered the room and asked, "Did you say something? Oh, you got it open. Thank you very much." Then she got closer and sniffed the air. "Oh, Lord, that is unpleasant. I'm sorry you had to smell that." She found herself trying to think of anything to say just to keep him around. "Well, I guess that's that." She shrugged.

He put his tools back in his bag and stood up. They heard footsteps on the stairs. Esther entered the room. "Well, will you look at that?" She looked around. Her face looked sad. Memories of Pearl and the many conversations they had had over the years were flooding her heart and mind. "So many memories in here. You know, your aunt Pearl had the heartiest laugh. I still miss our card nights too. You play cards, Mr. Darden?"

He shrugged. "Why, Miss Esther, I haven't played in years. I wouldn't even remember how to hold them." They all chuckled. He was lying, of course.

Esther cocked her head. "You know, my sisters and I moved into the guesthouse here. I was going to talk to you about that." She looked at Juliette. "Do you think we should get new locks on the doors and windows?" She raised her eyebrows, and for the first time Juliette recognized the magical manipulation that was Esther.

She nodded to Esther. "Why, of course we should do that if you would feel safer." She turned to Honore. "What does your work schedule look like? Could you fit us in somewhere?" He was fine until she bit her lip. Then he was toast.

"Why, I believe I'm free the rest of the day. Is that something you want done today? Or we could schedule a series of appointments?" He looked from Juliette to Esther. The air was thick with anticipation. They were all on to one another, but no one was calling anyone out. It was too soon for that.

Esther clapped her hands together, and Juliette and Honore both jumped. "What are your dinner and supper plans today, Mr. Darden? I'm making gumbo, and there will be plenty. Right, Juliette?" She smiled at Juliette, and Juliette smiled at Honore.

"You heard the boss. Hope you're hungry."

He smiled and nodded. "Well, ladies, thank you very much. Ya'll are too kind. I hope I won't be imposing on you." Then he remembered his new young friend Julienne. "Oh, I may not be able to stay for supper. I have a guest at my house."

Juliette's eyes widened. *Oh my God*, she thought, *he has a girlfriend. I have been acting like a complete idiot.* She also immediately felt miserable. This strange man had gotten to her quickly. Within seconds after Esther's invitation, she was mentally deciding what to wear for supper. Would he like her in magenta, or maybe something black and lacey? *Stupid girl*, she thought. She spoke up. "Of course. Well, you can invite your lady friend also. That would be so nice. Wouldn't it, Esther?" The disappointment in her voice was unmistakable.

Honore laughed on the inside and smiled on the outside. He put his hand up. "Oh no, no. I don't have a lady friend, Juliette. I found a kitten this morning behind the house. Found his momma out on the road by my place. So it looks like I'll need to feed him. I could go home between dinner and supper, if that's okay. Or come back tomorrow if you prefer."

Esther took her cue and said, "Well, I'll leave you two alone to discuss your plans. Got something I have to cook up." She smiled at them and left. Juliette looked at Honore, and he looked at her. There was no denying that there was something cooking. And it wasn't Miss Esther's prize-winning gumbo.

"I feel so embarrassed right now, Honore, and I don't know why. Is this too uncomfortable for you? I'm sorry if Esther made you feel awkward in any way."

His voice was deep and soft. "I would be delighted to have dinner with ya'll. And I certainly do not want to disappoint Miss Esther. My momma taught me to be respectful and not turn down a home-cooked meal."

Juliette looked down and then asked, "Does she live around here too?" She noticed his green eyes change to a solemn gaze.

"No." He shook his head. "She passed when I was twenty-six. Long time ago. Not too far away from here. Teal Bend. Then I left." He sighed. "Crazy thing is, she made me promise I'd return around my fortieth birthday. I promised her, and here I am." He shrugged.

Juliette could feel the sting of tears in her eyes. "Poor thing. I am so sorry. My parents died when I was two, so I really don't remember them. Aunt Pearl raised me. No brothers or sisters. And now that she's gone, I reckon I'm orphaned."

He looked into her eyes. "Well, that makes two of us, Juliette."

She smiled and said, "Actually three if you count your friend Julienne. Suppose he wants to eat with us? Esther and her sisters are alone too. We could start a club?"

He laughed. "Yes I suppose we could. Suddenly it feels good to not be alone."

"I have an idea." She put her hand on his shoulder. "This might sound ridiculous, but I don't feel like you're a stranger here. I guess it's like a déjà vu thing. This cannot be normal, but I just feel so comfortable around you. Would you like to stay and go through some of the old family secrets with me? I can't imagine there's anything that terrible in here. If you're from this area originally, maybe we're cousins. There could be something in there for you, too. I'll go and get some lemonade. Make yourself comfortable, and I'll be right back." She was so happy that she didn't wait for him to answer and bounded out of the room.

Honore just stood there. This was going very fast. His momma was right. It was time to return. Maybe the treasure he was supposed to find had just left the room. He would stay. And if they were cousins, that would certainly change things. Or would it? Wasn't it first or second cousins are the no-no? They were not that, he was sure of it. He felt strange, excited, and nervous all at the same time. He shook his head quickly from side to side as if trying to regain his senses then sat back down in front of the chest, took the small box out again, and put it to the side while he waited. He then grabbed a bundle of letters tied up with a blue velvet ribbon. He noticed the corner of a small journal and pulled it out from another letter bundle. It was very old leather and had been disintegrating around the edges for years. Some of the edge crumbled off as he picked it up. There were initials on it: H. D. D. D. He was afraid to open it up. It seemed so fragile. He decided to wait for Juliette and put it down next to the box. As his hand brushed against a metal clasp, he received a shock like a static jolt. He jerked back his hand just as Juliette walked back in with two glasses of lemonade and offered him one.

"I see you've started already. So what do you think? Pretty old stuff, eh?"

He looked up at her. "Ah, the smell of history." She laughed and sat down next to him. "Well, what do you want to start with?" he asked.

She gave everything a once-over. Her eyes and her curiosity rested on the small chest. She reached over his lap and grabbed it. He smelled her hair as she reached in front of him. "I think maybe we should open this up. My Aunt Pearl left me this weird letter talking about family curses and family business. Esther said she was going on about a pouch. Get the pouch, don't let them find it ... Or no, wait, she was hallucinating about a caramel man with green eyes." As soon as she said that, she stopped talking and just stared into Honore's eyes. She laughed nervously. *Those beautiful deep green eyes and that olive skin ...* For a second her rationale went right out the window. "Well, Honore, that just might be you. I guess we're all crazy around these parts anyway, right?"

Honore looked at the box. "When my mother was dying, she said something about a pouch too. She was so strange. I thought she was just rambling because of the pain and medication." He looked into the trunk. "What do you think is in the box, Juliette? What else do you know or remember?"

She shrugged. "That's it. I mean, I grew up here, but I've been away for a long time, like you. I had another life in New Mexico. And now it seems like that life was a blur and my life is here. I didn't plan on coming back here to live. Aunt Pearl never told me anything odd about the family—just that we had family business to tend to. I figured she meant the stocks, royalties, and property. You know, normal estate things. What are you thinking?"

Honore looked at Juliette more seriously. "We are both orphaned, both of our families are from here, we've both been gone for a while only to return at the same time to the same place, and here we are. We were both given cryptic messages about a pouch. I have no idea what my mother was referring to about property and land, and it's my blood too."

They looked at each other. Juliette's voice took on a more concerned tone. "But this just gets weirder, doesn't it. I don't think I want to open this box, Honore. Now I am definitely not sure what's going on. Esther and her sisters Adah and Martha knew my aunt and grandparents for years—much longer than I thought. Apparently Esther watched me as a baby, and I only have vague memories of her being here every now and then as a child. I don't really remember her sisters so much. Isn't it funny how so many things and people in your childhood can go by the wayside and you just don't remember anymore."

Honore squinted and cocked his head. "Did you just say Martha?"

"Yes." Juliette answered. "Three adorable sisters bent on taking care of me and keeping me here. They don't want me to sell. I've already contacted a realtor. I'm still not sure where my life is going right now."

Honore shook his head a little. "I just got in yesterday. I met the sweetest little old lady at the bus depot, named Martha. All of a sudden, I had a place to live and this locksmith job. She even knew my name before I told her. Said it was on the bus roster when I bought my ticket, but I paid cash. They just sold me a ticket and never asked my name for any roster. And she kind of looks like Esther." He put his head in his hands.

Juliette put her hand on Honore's knee. It was so close to hers. "Hey. Let's just not freak out while we're ... *wow* ... we're freaking out, aren't we?"

He nodded and said, "Yes, I believe we are being set up, and I don't know why. We don't know each other, but it feels like we do, and it seems like we should be here doing this right now, and I am trying to be reserved and strong and logical."

Juliette got on her knees and took his face in her hands. She leaned into him as he rose to her, and their lips met. The world around them disappeared. It felt as though they were melting into each other—as though the kiss itself had been waiting all of those years just for this moment. Everything felt natural and the way it should be, and then Juliette pulled away. They sat there for a few seconds just breathing and staring into each other's eyes. They were caught like lightning bugs in a jar spinning round and round, except they weren't looking for a way out. There was no more innocent chatter, polite conversation, or awkward silence. They both knew what they wanted—each other.

Honore put his hand up and spread his fingers. Juliette raised her hand and rested it against his. He began to gently feel her hand, tracing her fingers with his, then moving softly down and around her arm and to her shoulder, stopping to caress her cheek. This time he reached over and kissed her. She slowly leaned back while they kissed until she was lying on the floor and he was over her, in one fluid movement. It felt like magic. Enchantment. It was sweet and slow, like honey dripping from a spoon.

Esther smiled when she could no longer hear them talking. She put her driving gloves on and put her purse on her arm. "Juliette?" she yelled up the stairs.

Juliette and Honore stopped and quickly resumed their sitting positions. "Yes Esther?' Juliette said, trying to control her breathing and a heart that was ready to pound out of her chest. "I have to go make grocery and then to the Rexall. I may be a while. Ya'll gonna be okay?" They both answered yes at the same time and then smiled. "Okay, then. I'll make dinner when I get back."

They heard the front door close. Juliette jumped up and held out her hand. Honore took her hand and rose from the floor. She led him out of Pearl's room and into hers. It took them only minutes to shed their clothes. They began to kiss again, running their hands over each other. Honore lifted Juliette up by the waist and laid her on the bed. Again everything was natural and perfect and smooth. She guided him into her, and each thrust captured more and more of her until he consumed everything she thought she had and everything she was.

They just lay there afterward, holding on to each other. Honore's hands were in constant motion until he was ready again. He smiled. "I must say I thought I came here to pick another lock." He was kissing her ear and nuzzling her neck.

"Why, Mr. Darden," she said, putting on her best southern belle accent, "I do declare you are the handiest locksmith this side of the Mississippi." They laughed and made love again, after which they lay in each other's arms exhausted but satisfied.

Esther returned home sure she would need to slam the door pretty hard. If she and her sisters had done their jobs successfully, then the young people upstairs were probably getting to know each other just as Mother Nature intended and time allowed. It was time to end this ridiculous family trouble, and now all three families were together under one roof. She wanted to depart this life with a clear conscience. She brought everything into the kitchen, took out her gumbo pot, and put her Elvis CD in the player.

Honore and Juliette jumped when they heard the front door slam. They both panicked and jumped out of bed. She whispered to him, "Okay, you go to the bathroom down the hall on your right. I'll go into Aunt Pearl's and get dressed in there. Then meet me back in Pearl's room, okay?" They both started giggling. He grabbed her and kissed her, and he then picked up his clothes and looked down the hall. He made a quiet run for the bathroom. Juliette watched him go down the hall. He had a very nice butt. She picked up her things and went to the top of the stairs. "Esther, is that you?" She heard a metal spoon clanking against a pot and, just barely, Elvis's "Don't Be Cruel" playing in the kitchen. She was relieved. They'd have to be careful to keep their tryst a secret from the sisters. Honore met Juliette back in Pearl's room, and the two resumed their original positions by the trunk. They drank the lemonade, which was now watery since the ice cubes had melted, and kissed again. "We are never going to get to any of this, are we?" he asked.

"I could not have predicted what just happened. I don't know if I even care about all this anymore. Hold on for a second, okay? I want you to read Aunt Pearl's letter and then let me know what you think." She got up and picked up the empty glasses. "More lemonade?" She smiled.

"I don't know if I can trust your lemonade anymore, Juliette. You sure you didn't slip me any green M&M's when I had the first glass?" They both smiled again.

"I'll be right back." Juliette winked and left. She popped back in to toss him the letter she had retrieved from her room, and she then went downstairs to get refills.

Esther was whistling to the music while she stirred the gumbo. Juliette felt so happy at this moment, but she wished Aunt Pearl were there to talk to her and advise her. She found herself hoping that maybe one day Esther and her sisters could be the elders she could bond with and go to for wisdom and guidance. She didn't even have any close female friends she could call and share with. Esther turned to see Juliette open the fridge. "Well, Juliette, how's the treasure hunting going? Did your young man get inside that thing yet?" Juliette turned with a flustered look. "Esther, how you could ask such a thing. We have just met, and he is only here to do a job. I mean his job with his tools." Her brain was yelling for her mouth to shut up. "I was just getting us more lemonade."

Esther smiled. "Well, I was talking about the trunk, sugar. What were you talking about?" She kept stirring.

Juliette shook her head and started to fill the glasses. "Oh yeah, right … that *is* exactly what I was talking about. Sorry, Esther. That smells wonderful. You figure about another hour or so for dinner?"

Esther winked. "Oh, about one and one half, I think." She put the spoon down and put a lid on the pot. "I'm just going to finish a few chores before I start the rice. Oh, I was wondering about getting a groundskeeper. Maybe Martha could put another ad on the bulletin board at the bus station?"

Juliette raised her eyebrows. After what had just happened with the locksmith, she thought maybe they should try the local church. "You know, Esther, I think I'll handle that one. But thank you anyway. I'll let Honore know when to expect dinner." She left to go upstairs.

Esther waited until she was sure Juliette was out of earshot and called Adah and Martha, letting them know things were going as planned.

Juliette sat down next to Honore. He handed her the letter back. "Wow. I don't know what to tell you. My mother gave me a letter too. I kept it, but I never did open it. I know my father didn't have anything. There's really nothing on the reservation that I don't have access to. I don't feel like I'm missing out on anything. Well, maybe we can figure this out together. Do you think we should spend more time together?"

Juliette took his hand. "I don't know what to say. What we did doesn't feel wrong. I know I want to do it again. Do you? I mean, you're not on the lam or anything, are you?"

Honore smiled. "No. I am not on the lam. But I say we keep this on the down low from the sisters. I have to say I was not looking for anything or anybody when I came back here, but if getting to know you better is part of this homecoming, I'm in."

Juliette kissed him on the cheek. "Good. Then I'd say, sir, that you picked the right lock today—in more ways than one. And I agree about the sisters. We won't let on about anything regarding us. We're just friends. And because you're helping me sort through this mess, that will be our alibi for your constant presence here. I wonder how much they know about all this. I know they are from here too. I am starting to have a feeling Aunt Pearl and the Henderson sisters have their own secrets. And if they're trying to set us up, maybe we should try to get information out of them? I think it's time for Esther to teach you how to play cards." She winked. "And you should probably read that letter from your mother when you get home."

Honore smiled and answered, "Yes dear."

Juliette jumped up. "I know. Let's take a walk around the property. I'll show you the crypt and the infamous hibiscus tree. Legend has it, it is haunted by restless souls. But I see it as having beautiful ancient blooms and hovering gorgeous orangey dragonflies."

They left Pearl's room and went downstairs. Passing through the kitchen, they complimented Esther on the aroma.

"I'm just going to show Mr. Darden the property, Esther, and the crypt, so we will be a few minutes," said Juliette. "Is that okay as far as dinner timing?"

Esther smiled. "Why, of course. Ya'll take your time." She looked at Honore. "And as soon as we get a grounds man, the yard will be more presentable."

Juliette gave her an "I can't believe you just said that" look.

Esther shrugged. "The gumbo will be ready whenever you get back. Now ya'll have a lovely walk."

"Thank you, Esther," Juliette said, and she opened the side kitchen door for Honore.

Juliette spoke as they began to walk the grounds. "Now this is what I remember about Greyfriars from my Aunt, so the tour might be brief. Anything else we will probably have to get from that trunk. The house was built around 1740, maybe 1742, by my fifth great-grandfather, Philippe Danetree. He built it for his wife, Hyacinthe. They had two children, and from there it's been in the family until now. It ends with me. I am thinking of selling though. I talked to a realtor, and she thinks I might get $900,000 to maybe $1.3 million for it, depending on the market and demand. It is a historic site, so that might have some bearing on any buyer. Of course I'll keep the tract with the crypt on it. Wait till you see that. Greyfriars should have a family in it, don't you think?"

Honore nodded. "Well yes, it is kind of large for just a couple of people. So you'll never marry or have children? Shouldn't you wait to make that kind of decision?" They had reached the hibiscus tree. "What if you find your Mr. Right and want to fill those rooms up?" He had his back to the tree, and just as he finished speaking, a dragonfly landed on his shoulder.

Juliette looked at the dragonfly and then to Honore, and then something happened inside of her. She felt as if she were losing her balance, as though the ground were rolling under her.

He kept talking like nothing had happened. "You never know."

Juliette said, "Did you feel that?"

"Feel what?" he asked.

She shrugged. "Maybe it's just the heat. You have a visitor on your shoulder." She nodded to his right shoulder. He tilted his head just enough to see it and then blew a breath at it, and it flew off. Juliette grinned at him. "My Aunt Pearl said there was one for everybody in the family."

Honore cocked his eyebrow. "Well then maybe we really are cousins." He leaned over to her and kissed her on the lips. "Kissing cousins now."

She smiled and slapped him on the arm. "Watch it. Esther might see. Now back to this tree. It was brought from France as a marriage present to Philippe and Hyacinthe, and so was that." She pointed across the yard to the large, weathered birdbath. They walked over to it. "I understand many a Danetree has stood by this very site and pledged undying love." She decided to change the subject very quickly. "Let's go to the dock."

When they got there, she resumed the tour. "Not the place for a long walk off a short pier. Supposedly Philippe Danetree drowned after his boat sunk during a storm and is buried over there." She pointed across the Teche to a large, tall white marble monument with a cross at the top. "He watches over the property from there."

Honore was having a hard time keeping his hands off of her. "If we don't keep walking, I will not be responsible for what happens next, ma'am." He smiled.

Juliette giggled. "Okay, okay. Come on." She started to walk toward the house. "We'll take my car to the crypt and the creepy burned-down chapel." He followed her out the front. She ran in to get her purse, and then they put the top down, hopped in her Morgan Aero, and took off.

It was just a few minutes by car to the family plot. Honore was surprised to see a large dollhouse-size replica of Greyfriars with a locked iron gate in front of the entrance. She put her hands on her hips. "And these are my people. They sleep in bunk beds in there, and back in the day every year on Mother's Day and Father's Day, we held tea parties right here in front and brought them cookies." She waited for Honore's response.

He stared at her. "I must say you are looking crazier than me right now. I don't have a story to match that one. Your own chapel, eh?" He looked over at the chapel ruins.

"Yes, but it was built and burned down a long time ago. Maybe there are pictures somewhere. I don't know. Aunt Pearl didn't say much about it either." She held her hand out and took his, facing the crypt again. "Family, this is Honore Darden."

"Honore Francois Darden," he said.

She smiled. "Honore Francois Darden it is. And apparently he has his own dragonfly. Maybe he'll have tea with us someday."

He pulled her to him and kissed her. "I hope they find me acceptable."

She reached up and brushed a curl from his forehead. "I sure do. Now it's gumbo time. Let's go."

When they arrived back at the house, it was about one in the afternoon. Esther had set a beautiful table in the formal dining room with the good silverware. "Oh, Esther, this is just lovely. Thank you." Juliette said, complimenting her.

Dinner was leisurely, delicious, and filling. Honore put his napkin down. "Well, Miss Esther, that was excellent. Thank you again for the invitation. Now, if you ladies will excuse me, I must return home. I can make an estimate regarding the doors and windows when I get back, if that's okay."

"Why, of course, Honore. That will give us some time to evaluate what we need done. And thank you for everything today. I hope we can work this all out. Would you like me drive you? It wouldn't be any trouble."

"Oh no, Juliette. Thank you, but I think I'll walk. Thank you again, Miss Esther. I can see myself out."

"Why thank you Mr. Darden but I'll clear the table while Juliette walks you to the door. There's a bag of kitten food by the door for your friend."

There were smiles all around as Juliette walked him out. "I wish you'd let me drive you," she said. She took her cell phone out of her pocket. "Is this we exchange cell numbers?"

Honore shrugged. "Honestly I have never owned one of those things. Just really never needed one and the land lines work just fine." He could tell from the way her eyebrow went up that maybe it was time to invest in some modern technology. He held up his right hand. "I swear on a stack of Bibles I do not have one of these things but I am not opposed to checking into it for business purposes, and one private one. I'll be back real soon okay?"

She pouted. He looked around and then kissed her. With that he smiled, turned around, and left. Juliette watched him walk away. He had this swagger when he walked that made her tingle. She went back inside.

"Esther I'm going to go back to Aunt Pearl's room," Juliette called from the hallway. She had a lot of reading to do.

When Honore got home, Julienne was sleeping on the front porch, warmed by a hazy stream of sunlight. When he unlocked the front door, the kitten yawned and arched his back as he stretched. "Look what Miss Esther got you, buddy—crunchy seafood special. Yummy. I'll be right back." He went inside and got two dishes—one for milk and one for food—and put them on the porch. He gave the kitten a pet on the head and then went back inside. It was hot and humid, so he turned on a couple of fans and opened up windows to get any breeze that decided to visit. He went into the bedroom and took an old sealed, creased envelope from his top drawer and then sat on the bed and opened it up. It made him feel melancholy to hold the letter and see his mother's handwriting. He began to read.

> My sweet son,
>
> I love you so much, and it makes me sad to think I will never hold you again until it is your time. There are so many things I want to say that I didn't tell you. You have always been loved and wanted. You are the best thing in my life and always will be. I wish I could have seen you get married and have children. Maybe one day you will have a family. I hope you find true love. That is my wish for you.
>
> There are other things I want you to know. Things your grandmother Nena told me I should share with you when you got older, but I thought it was just strange

old elder talk. It didn't make sense to me. There was something about a curse, a witch, and a very wealthy family in a plantation house. She said that their blood was our blood—that we were half-breeds and we had rights too. She said we should be living in that big house. I swear I didn't know what she was talking about. I just thought she might be crazy. Then I started having dreams, Honore—bad dreams full of blood and a brown lady and a white lady and a body.

The dreams stopped the day I found out I had cancer. That's why I am writing this to you now. I don't have much time left, and I don't want your memories of me to be dreadful ones. I do not believe we are cursed. But I think that plantation family has secrets they don't want discovered. I cannot confirm that we are of their blood, but I do know green eyes run in the families. That's all I have, Honore. I am sorry. Maybe I should have just taken this to the grave. But what if Grandma Nena was right and you could have that kind of life? It would be better than the one I raised you in. I love you so much. I want you to have all good things.

Love, Momma

He put the letter back in the envelope and stared at the floor. Her letter read much like the strange letters and journals in the trunk at Greyfriars. He had a sick feeling. "Oh my God. It cannot be Juliette's family. No, this is all wrong. It has to be another house. I can't show this to her. What the hell is going on here? I don't think I can go back there." He stood up and went to get some brandy. "Damn middle of the day. What am I going to do? Think, H. Think."

He jumped as the phone rang. It was Miss Martha. He knew exactly what he wanted to say to her, but she spoke first. "There was a man that called from St. Louis inquiring whether you had arrived or not. I told him you had, and then he wanted your phone number. Said he had something important to tell you. His name is Mack."

Honore forgot what he wanted to confront her about. "Did he leave a number?" Honore asked.

"Oh yes, let me look here. I wrote it down. Yes, here it is." She gave him the number.

Yep, that's Mack's home number. "Miss Martha, when does the next bus leave for the airport?"

"Well, it's two thirty now, and the next bus coming through here going there will be the three fifteen."

"Okay, thank you. I'll call you back. I may need a ticket."

Honore hung up and dialed. It was good to hear Mack's voice again. "Hey, it's H. What's wrong?" He listened to Mack's story. "Okay, I'll be there as soon as possible. Just sit tight, Mack. It'll be okay. Just try to keep it together until I get there, okay?"

He called Martha back. "I need that ticket, Miss Martha. I'll be there soon."

He then grabbed a few things, locked up the house, and made sure to leave a big plate of cat food on the porch. He got to the bus station just as the bus was pulling up. He knew he had a few minutes while the driver checked in and went to grab a cup of coffee.

Martha smiled when she saw him and handed him his ticket. "I hope all is well with your friend, dear. I noticed you didn't get a round-trip ticket. You can't be leaving us already. You just got here. How did that locksmith job work out for you?"

"It went just fine, Miss Martha, just fine," he answered. "Oh I … well, a kitten showed up at the door this morning, and I think it might belong to the house. I hate to ask, but if you have time, could you look after him? His name is Julienne. I've locked everything up. I'll probably be gone a few days, but I am coming back. Could you call Miss Esther at Greyfriars and tell her I'll be back in a few days, maybe a week, and that I'm sorry I will have to delay the other jobs until I get back? You know Miss Esther, don't you?" It was at this time he once more regretted not having a cell phone.

"Well, I believe I do know Miss Esther. I will let her know. Have a safe trip, Mr. Darden."

With that, he left and boarded the bus. Part of him was almost afraid to come back, but Juliette had gotten to him. So many things changing so fast. He would try not to think about her until he got back, and then some things would need clearing up.

Martha called Esther immediately to give her the news. Esther frowned. It was certainly a kink in the plan, but she had to tell Juliette. Juliette's response was predictable. "You're kidding me, right? Oh, Esther, I hope everything is okay. Do you think he'll be back? What am I going to do now? He'll be back, right?" Juliette folded her arms across her chest. Esther could tell Juliette needed a sounding board more than answers. She could see there was some kind of attraction, otherwise, Juliette wouldn't have been so worried. She continued. "Maybe I scared him off showing him the family crypt."

What she was thinking was much more damning. She had engaged in sex with a stranger in her home who was there to work. *Oh my God*, she thought, *I am a sex-crazed monster.* She shook her head. *No. He engaged in it too. It was mutual, right? Tom was right. I should have handled all of this from New Mexico. Must be some kind of Danetree curse.* She wondered if the mess in the trunk would confirm her assessment.

Esther could almost see the wheels turning behind Juliette's grey eyes and said, "Oh, I think he'll be back, honey. Now let me get you some tea."

Juliette gave her a hug. "That would be very nice. Thanks, Esther. I just don't know if we can find another locksmith that can do what he can do around here."

"Of course, dear. I agree wholeheartedly. Now, would you like chamomile or something spicy?"

Juliette blushed. "Why, Miss Esther, I think I'd better have something comforting just now. I'll be upstairs going back in time to find out what I'm doing wrong."

Esther watched her leave the room and shook her head. *So many things she should know.* Esther looked up pointing with a scolding finger. "I told you, Pearl. If the past ain't done, it keeps the future on the run. Too many ghosts in these old walls. Now the poor child has to find out the hard way." She turned the radio on and drank her tea.

18

Chapter 2

Anatomy of an Arrangement

Winter, 1763

The winter of 1763 was full of wedding plans at Greyfriars, which kept Hyacinthe and Cecile very busy. It was understood that Marc, once he and Cecile were married, would take charge of Greyfriars until Charles was of age and could handle the responsibilities. Marc was now included in all of the functions of the business, along with Charles. They worked together well, and Charles thought highly of Marc and his military experience. Charles had even let Marc light the Christmas bonfire to welcome him into the family. Everyone was happy. Comfort had a special gift for Hyacinthe as well. She had made a sketch of Hyacinthe and then used it as a template for an oil portrait she had given her on Christmas Eve. She had started it in September, but it had taken a long time to dry. The family was stunned at her talent, and Cecile made her promise to paint a wedding portrait for her and Marc. Hyacinthe was very complimentary about her talent and style, but she still seemed to keep her at a distance.

Comfort and Charles had few moments together and cherished them, but they were ready to take their secret relationship a step further. It became all too consuming, but they had to wait for the right time for both of them.

Hyacinthe was very happy during this time. She was glad to see her daughter happy with her beau and looked forward to grandchildren.

19

After the wedding, she would focus on Charles. Maybe Marc could help him. He was sixteen now, though he'd had to grow up a little faster after Philippe's death. He hadn't shown any inclination to join the military, but Hyacinthe had written to her father about him working toward a commission in the military, like Marc. It would be good for him, and when he returned he would be ready to settle down and run Greyfriars. She noticed Comfort seemed to have taken her words of guidance to heart and started a new life. Hyacinthe was hoping she would find a husband soon, but felt confident that she had been successful in preventing any mistakes with Charles. Her world was running smoothly, and she finally felt in tune with her surroundings and with herself.

The wedding date was set for Sunday, April 8, with Father Warren presiding, and invitations went out in February. Comfort helped to design the announcements and began to feel like part of the family again. Cecile included her in as many wedding activities as possible—even in placing an order for baguettes and pastries for the wedding dinner after the ceremony. Willie and Florine were excited as well and kept busy with plans and arrangements.

Charles had been in charge of delivering invitations to friends and business associates in Teal Bend. As he approached Petit Coeur, it began to sprinkle and then pour. But instead of galloping home, he went to Comfort's cottage instead, hoping she'd be there. And she was. He got off of his horse and approached quietly with the rain helping to cover his arrival. He brought his horse to her barn and tied him up next to a hay bale, and he then came up to the front door and banged on it three times. "Woman, open up. I'm wet and I'm cold!"

Comfort froze and ran to get her kitchen knife. "Comfort, *it's me!*" he yelled, and he started laughing.

She flung the door open, forgetting she was in her nightdress. "Charles, I could have killed you. You cannot startle me like that." She was furious. Then she realized she was in her bedclothes. "Oh," she said, and she ran to get a robe.

Charles came in and stood by the fire.

Comfort came out with a blanket. Charles had already stripped off his coat, his hat, and his breeches. She looked up and held the blanket out. "Cover yourself, sir." He walked up to her, took the blanket, and then dropped it on the floor. He pulled her to him and kissed her on the lips. His shirt was damp, and she could feel his arousal growing against her stomach. She looked up at him, half nervous and half excited. "Are you sure, Charles? I am if you are."

He picked her up and carried her to the bedroom, where he laid her on the bed. He took off the rest of his clothes, and she did the same. She stared at his body and stopped at his groin. His part looked so strange and funny sticking out. *Very much like a two-day-old baguette,* she thought. She was nervous and trying not to laugh. Charles had seen the street ladies in New Orleans and heard stories about "the act," but neither one of them had any kind of experience, nor had they seen the opposite sex unclothed before.

"Will it hurt, Charles?" Comfort asked as she instinctively spread her legs. He could see her chest rising and falling quickly in anticipation.

He positioned himself over her. "I don't know, Comfort. All I know is we love each other. I want to, you want to, and right now we can. I'll be very careful not to hurt you. I'll just put it in a little. If it is bad, then we'll stop, okay?" She nodded. Her chest heaving with a little fear and a lot of anticipation. "All right then, let's do it."

And they did. And it hurt. She cried, and he held her and took care of her until she wanted to do it again.

It was getting late. Hyacinthe asked Willie to go and get Pierre. It was raining, and Charles had not returned when she thought he should. Just then the front door opened, and in stepped a soaking wet Charles. He saw his mother at the top of the stairs. She came down. "You gave me a scare. You are back late. Go and dry off in the kitchen by the hearth. It is still warm. I'll bring you a blanket."

He kissed her on both cheeks. "Mother, I am a man now, not your little boy anymore. I was going to stay at the apartment in Teal Bend because of the weather but decided to take my chances. Are you not happy to see me? Should I have stayed there tonight?"

"No, no. You are right to come home. But you will always be my little boy. Now go and get warm. I'll get your nightclothes."

"Yes, Maman." He laughed and headed for the kitchen. Everything looked different: Maman, the house, the rain, the world. He felt different. He felt great. The feelings and sensations he had experienced with Comfort were above and beyond anything he had felt before. Now he knew he could not live without her. He would never marry unless it was to her.

Comfort lay in her bed alone but not lonely. She could not stop smiling even though she felt sore. She looked over to the empty space next to her and stroked it, remembering Charles lying there. Her whole body still tingled and desired him. She got up to wash herself and then sit by the fire until it went out. It was a cold and rainy night, but her body was hot, and her thighs still burned and shook slightly from their lovemaking. It had been worth the pain. It would probably be a while before they could be together again, but she wanted to make love every chance they got. Life was beautiful, and the anticipation was delicious.

With one month before the wedding, Cecile was driving everyone crazy. Marc had gone to New Orleans with Monsieur Rieu on business, and Pierre and Charles were out in the field checking on the cane and the crews. Monsieur Rieu told Charles that some planters were smuggling or supplying the North with sugar shipments because the British were interfering with the sugar trade coming out of the British West Indies. He wanted to make sure that everyone knew Greyfriars business was legitimate and not compromising French and British commerce and politics. Charles really wanted no part of the politics but realized that it was part of business and that sometimes taking a side was unavoidable regardless of treaties, agreements, and favors.

He missed Comfort but tried to stay busy while they waited to be together again. That chance came when he went to pick her up the day before the wedding so they could bring the breads and cakes over to Greyfriars. She had given him a key to come and go when he pleased. He walked into the front room and could hear the sound of someone throwing up in the bedroom. He entered. Comfort was doubled over a bucket on the floor. She pointed a finger to the bedroom door, and he knew it meant he should wait in the other room. When she came out, he had a cup of water for her. "Are you okay?" he asked in a soft voice.

She didn't quite know how to tell him. He noticed she was putting on weight, but she had such a small frame that he noticed it only in her face and accused her of eating too many of her own cakes. That earned him a punch in the arm. She looked at him with tears in her eyes. He placed his hand on her belly, and she placed hers over his. "It's okay. I will take care of you. I know we are young, but we will make it through all of this, I swear."

She started to cry. "Your mother will kill me if she finds out."

"She'll kill me first, then she'll kill you." He hugged her. "I'm sorry. I didn't mean to mock you. We are both in this. We will have to be careful now. We must act naturally around the family. We will come up with a plan. But right now we have breads to deliver. Do you want me to do it alone?"

She shook her head and smiled. "No, I should be okay now. It's usually just in the morning that I feel sick. Let's go." They packed up and headed over to Greyfriars.

It was a beautiful day for a wedding. Cecile looked radiant, and Marc was very handsome in his uniform. Hyacinthe cried. Florine cried. Willie cried. Pierre swore he didn't cry, but no one believed him. Monsieur Rieu proved to be an excellent cohost. He had loosened up over the years and become more social, making the house more jovial and light. Hyacinthe was glad to have him around but knew that as soon as Marc took over, he would return to Paris. She wanted to return with him but knew she could not leave her children, and she wanted to be around for the grandchildren. She often felt guilty that her parents had been denied that privilege with her being so far away. She was never well enough to travel and in her heart knew she would not see her parents in this life again. She spent the day visiting everyone attending, making sure they had enough to eat and to drink. It was quite the celebration.

She noticed Comfort sitting in a chair with her sketch pad and walked up behind her. She could tell it was a drawing of Cecile and Marc under the wedding arch. "My. That is beautiful, my dear. You have such talent. One day you will be sketching Charles's wedding portrait as well, I hope." She put her hand on Comfort's shoulder. "So have you met any young men in Teal Bend? Surely you must have a few suitors?"

Comfort continued to sketch. "I have one. He is from New Orleans and wants to marry right away. He is a fisherman and often gone. I was thinking that maybe later in the year I could live in New Orleans and learn how to paint properly and maybe make my baguettes there as well?"

Hyacinthe smiled and walked around to face her. "That would be a wonderful idea. Of course, I will see you have everything you need, and we will be fine here. Maybe you will enjoy the city and be happy there. It can be a very beautiful place, and with the port so close, you can travel. I fell in love with Martinique once. I am sure it is even more exciting now. Well, I must visit our guests. We'll talk later." She turned and left, smiling all the way around the yard. Comfort smiled too. Even though Hyacinthe had gotten under her skin, she stayed strong and played along. Charles would be proud.

By June, Marc and Cecile had taken over the master bedroom, with Monsieur Rieu occupying Cecile's old room. He had expressed his desire to leave for Paris around March of the next year. With no new plantations starting up and few French settlers coming down, things stabilized and Greyfriars was considered a major producer of sugar loaves and indigo, with a strong reputation and secure profits. Monsieur and Marc were both aware of what a Spanish presence might have in the south, but they were confident that French culture and influence would remain strong for the next few years.

Comfort was now four months pregnant, and she thought maybe it was time for her to not spend so much time at Greyfriars, as it was getting harder for her to hide her baby bump. Charles agreed to her plan about going to New Orleans to stay for the birth. "Are you thinking the convent?" he asked.

She smiled and said yes. "Wouldn't it be nice to have our baby born where I was born?"

Charles nodded. "I like that idea. It is a safe place, and you would be taken care of. I could visit you there during business trips and not raise suspicion from my mother. I am sorry we have to sneak around. I do love you and wish things could be different."

She touched his face. "I know. But this is perfect. Your mother thinks I have a gentleman friend that wants to marry. When I return with the baby and the sad story of how his boat did not return, well, you see how it goes." She shrugged.

"You are a very clever girl." He kissed her.

"It will be okay. You'll see. Willie said she would watch the house for me."

Charles's eyes grew large. "Willie knows?" He looked shocked and worried. "She has known for some time and is happy for the both of us. She said she hopes the baby will have your eyes and my skin. Everyone else will think I have been deserted."

He nodded and said, "I hope you are sure about her. I guess we have to trust her now. Let me know when the time will be right so I can take you. I will divert my mother's attentions from you when I can. Time to return home. I will see you later."

She watched him ride away and thought about their baby and smiled.

As Christmastime drew near, Charles grew nervous and tried to schedule visits to New Orleans throughout the month. Hyacinthe was happy that he was taking such interest in the business. She tried to talk to him about the military, but he would have none of it. Marc was a fine officer, but he had no interest in wearing the uniform. His place was in the fields and in the business. Hyacinthe gave up. She knew he was too young to marry. He was only seventeen. She just didn't see him meeting anyone around their area. Maybe she would leave him alone for a while. He had been a good boy and deserved a break from his ever-plotting mother.

Estelle Charlotte was born December 16, 1764. She was seven pounds eight ounces with a healthy appetite. She had a head of beautiful black curls, hazel brown eyes, and the loveliest caramel skin. Charles had arrived in the city on the seventeenth and told the sisters he had come to check on a member of his household staff, being concerned about her well-being. They welcomed him, remarking how much like his father he had become. His father had made the same visit years ago, just as concerned about a young girl that worked at Greyfriars. They remembered him as a kind and caring employer. They must have been thinking of Belle. Charles just smiled and made a generous donation. They had no idea how much like his father he was.

When he returned home on the twenty-fourth, Marc and Cecile were building the bonfire on the levee and Hyacinthe was up in her room doing needlepoint. He stood outside her door to collect himself before he backed up Comfort's fisherman story. He was sure she would believe it. He knocked.

"Come in," she said. She got up and hugged him. "I was afraid you wouldn't be home for Christmas. How was your trip? Have a seat, and tell me everything." He sat down and put on a sad face. Hyacinthe looked at his reaction. "Is something wrong, Charles?"

He nodded. "I do have some unhappy news, Mother, but I do not want to upset you." Hyacinthe stopped her needlework to give him her full attention. "Please, Charles, what is it?"

He tried to seem melancholy. "Well, I stopped in at the convent to make a donation, and one of the sisters recognized me and told me there was a young girl there that had mentioned Greyfriars asked if I would check in on her. So of course I did. It was Comfort, Mother. And she was holding a baby girl."

Hyacinthe crossed herself. "Ah, *Mon Dieu*. What happened? What about her husband? She did marry in in New Orleans, did she not? She never told us about her wedding. Was he there?" she asked.

Charles shook his head and looked down. "No, Mother. Apparently he went out to fish and never came back. She thinks he drowned, and she was too ashamed to come home with a baby and no husband."

Hyacinthe seemed truly sympathetic. "Poor thing! Of course she can come back. It's not her fault. Oh, she must be suffering. I certainly did not wish anything like this on her—a drowned husband, like me. I only wanted her to have a good life. You and Pierre can go and fetch her after Christmas, and I'll have Florine tidy up her cottage. I believe I still have Cecile's old baby clothes. Maybe she and I can go through them and find something for the poor baby."

Charles mustered a half smile. "Thank you, Maman. She was very worried about how you would react."

She reached over and touched Charles's hand. "What did she name the child? We didn't even get to meet her husband. How sad."

Charles panicked. A major glitch in the plan surfaced, as they had never thought to give the phantom husband a proper name. He had to think fast. "She named the baby Estelle Christmas."

Hyacinthe sat back and furrowed her brow. "Christmas? What a name for a baby."

Charles shrugged. "Yes. I know. But the child was born near Christmas, and her husband was Maurice Christmas. I believe he was from the West Indies. She is terribly sad. Apparently she loved him very much and swore she could never marry another." He watched as his mother clasped her hands together and brought them to rest on her lap. A look of determination crossed her face. "Well, it is settled then. We will bring her back and have Dr. Boudreaux check in on her. She is a poor widow now."

Charles nodded, quite pleased with himself, and asked, "Are you going to the bonfire, Maman? I see Marc and Cecile have set it up. Are we to have guests?"

She shook her head. "No, not this year, my darling. Just family. I'll be down soon. Now go and help your sister."

He kissed her on the forehead and left. After he shut her door, he thought about the reaction he would surely get from Comfort after he told her what he had named her departed husband. "She'll be punching me in both arms," he whispered to himself. He went outside to help light the fire. It was the best Christmas ever. He had become a father, mother and baby were healthy, and his mother would never know. It was perfect.

Comfort arrived home with Estelle on January 3, 1765. Charles was there, as were Cecile, Florine, and Willie. They all wanted to hold the baby and were there to make sure Comfort was not alone, being newly widowed and all. Willie winked at her while the others pulled out baby clothes and brought her tea and biscuits. "And this is my christening gown." Cecile held up a beautiful cream lace gown that was about two feet long.

"You don't think it will be too long, do you?" Comfort asked. She absolutely hated lying to them, but her love for Charles and their daughter was stronger than her urge to tell the truth.

She was fawned and fretted over. Even Madame Hyacinthe thought Estelle had the most beautiful eyes and held her every now and then. She thought nothing of it when Charles held and rocked her. She believed that now Charles and Comfort had gotten over their infatuation with each other, they could be friends again. And it would be good practice for when he became a father himself. Comfort had begun to work in the household part-time and resumed her baking business. Cecile would babysit every now and then. She and Marc had decided to wait to start a family. Everyone fell in love with baby Estelle, and in March she was christened at Greyfriars in Cecile's gown with Cecile and Charles as godparents.

Monsieur Rieu bade adieu to Greyfriars that May. It was a sad time. He had come to mean so much to everyone. Hyacinthe begged him to stay, but he could not. He told her he could send another associate from Paris if she liked. She declined the offer. He had been the one to save her family, and no one else could fill his shoes. The family left for New Orleans to see him off. Charles would soon be eighteen and was accomplished enough to assume more responsibility, along with Marc.

It was 1765, and Spain had not yet sent a Spanish governor to its new bayou colony, and Acadians that had been ripped from their homes in Canada had started to arrive in New Orleans to settle outside of the city, in and near the Attakapas and Opelousas Post—not too far from Greyfriars. They were free to practice their Catholicism and speak their language. Although a Spanish territory, French was still the most widely spoken language in their new home. It was a somewhat unpleasant time in New Orleans, with a lack of a military presence, and the outer areas were not untouched by those who would take advantage. Charles and Marc decided to grant an arpent of land to any of the Acadian families who contracted for at least six years to work on the plantation. They had been devastated by their removal and treatment by the British and told horrific stories of children separated from their mothers and shipped away in death traps in which many perished. They had been stripped of their farms, houses, and dignity. Some were exiled to France and forced to live on filthy land where many died from poor sanitation and hunger. Others that had landed in northern colonial states chose to relocate to the southern territory when given the chance. Then they began to come by the hundreds. One of the families that chose to work for Greyfriars was the family of Alexandrine Marguerite Broussard.

The first time Hyacinthe met the Broussard family, she saw an opportunity for an arrangement between Charles and the lovely Alexandrine. The fifteen-year-old daughter of Jean and Sylvie Broussard was not only quite lovely but also carried herself with an air that somehow made her appear manor-born. Hyacinthe thought the only thing lacking in the beauty was wealth or a title, and those could be easily acquired through a good marriage. The young lady worked just as hard as any in her family, but her hands remained soft and graceful. Hyacinthe put her plan in motion. She always made sure to include Alexandrine in her conversations with Charles and sometimes invited her to the house under the guise of "another helping hand" necessary to run a proper household. Hyacinthe invited her mother, Sylvie, over for tea to get a feel for what plans her mother had for her.

Hyacinthe chose the back sunroom with the tall glass windows to provide a lovely view of the bayou and the back of the property, which always looked very peaceful and pleasant. It was May, and the lawn was green and lush. The moss hung perfectly off the ancient oaks, and the hibiscus tree was in full bloom, adding a brilliant red showing. She wanted everything to be as perfect as possible while she broached the subject of a possible union between their children.

Hyacinthe waited until after Willie left the room to start their conversation. She poured a cup of tea for Sylvie. "You know, this tea is actually made from the petals of that very hibiscus tree over there." She glanced quickly to the direction of the tree. "Willie calls it her special bissap tea. I do hope you find it pleasant." She handed Sylvie the cup and then poured herself one. They each took a sip.

Sylvie smiled. "Oh, this is quite delicious. I did not know you could use the petals like this. I do want to thank you for this invitation. You are most kind. The opportunities you have given my family are a blessing we will not forget."

Hyacinthe smiled. "You are most welcome. We are pleased to have your family here with us at Greyfriars and hope your accommodations are adequate for your family. Your daughter Alexandrine—she is happy to be here?"

Sylvie nodded energetically. "Oh yes, madame. She is happy. She has adjusted well to our new home. Thank you for your concern."

Hyacinthe smiled warmly and said, "I must share with you that when I arrived here, I was only happy that I was married to a capable husband. I do not believe I would have survived those first years here without being cared for. Such a primitive land. I was pleased when my Cecile married Captain Marc. I feel she has a good future with him. I was concerned at first because there were so few prospects for her in this land. But I am sorry I am going on just now. I am sure your Alexandrine had many suitors. She is quite beautiful and such an agreeable young lady."

Sylvie blushed. "Oh, you are very kind, madame."

Hyacinthe smiled and said, "Please call me Hyacinthe, Sylvie."

Sylvie nodded. "Of course, Hyacinthe. I too am concerned about what Alexandrine might face when she is of the age and mind to marry. She has still several more years before she must consider her future as a wife and mother."

Hyacinthe saw her opportunity. "My concern now lies with my son Charles. I believe he will be ready to marry in a few years and run Greyfriars as well. He has been working very hard and taking good care of the business. I think he should marry a girl that will complement his heart and his mind. Of course she should also have some understanding of what we do here. Wouldn't it be nice if we could arrange a future for our children together? But forgive me for thinking out loud. Would you like some more tea?"

Sylvie felt a surge of pride rise up in her and straightened her back. If her daughter could marry this well, then she should pursue the option.

She held out her cup. "Yes, please. This talk of an arrangement sounds like something that might be beneficial for us both, yes?"

Hyacinthe smiled. Sylvie smiled. They gently clinked their teacups together as the sun lit the room with a warming glow.

In the coming months, Hyacinthe made sure that Alexandrine's father, Jean, was included in decisions regarding the planting, detrashing, quality, and harvest of the cane. She invited the family to the Christmas Eve bonfire as well. Every now and then she required Charles to bring the Broussard daughter to Greyfriars and assist her with her needlework or sewing, as Hyacinthe's eyesight wasn't what it used to be and Comfort was so busy with her baking and a toddler, along with other tasks. What she was really doing was grooming the young lady to become Mrs. Charles Philippe Olivier Danetree.

Sylvie always made sure Alexandrine was picture perfect when these arrangements were made. Alexandrine enjoyed the short time in transit when Charles picked her up and dropped her off. She told her mother she found him to be very easy to talk to, polite, and pleasing to the eye. Sylvie was quick to report these observations to Hyacinthe, which delighted her to no end. On the other hand, Charles, when asked about the task of chauffeuring the young lady, would shrug and say he didn't mind doing this task for his mother and found Alexandrine to be a very pleasant girl that he could easily talk to. Other than that, he expressed no opinion about her physical appearance, nor did he hint at any attraction to her. *Oh well*, thought Hyacinthe, *these situations take time.* Not everyone could have a love like her parents. Sometimes an arrangement was more comfortable—getting on with the business of marriage, both parties knowing their roles and what was expected of them. However, if one fell in love, then the heart could quickly upend the head and leave a swath of chaos, uncertainty, and wounds that had to be either healed or buried.

Hyacinthe's attention to Alexandrine did not go unnoticed by Comfort. She would often get a sick feeling when she knew the girl was coming to the house or when Charles could not spend time with her because he had to pick her up or bring her home. She knew exactly what was unfolding. Charles did not agree with her, and this became a source of discord between them when she addressed her fears.

One day they were in the carriage, having just arrived in Teal Bend after the market. Willie was at the cottage with Estelle. "You must know what is going on Charles," Comfort said.

He continued to look forward, guiding the horse. "Comfort, please, not again. I really do not understand you women sometimes. I try to make you as happy as I can. I try to make Maman as happy as I can so she does not focus on us. I try to make sure investors are happy—and the overseers and the field hands. Can you not make this time together pleasant so that I can he happy?"

She put her hand on his arm. She was afraid of losing him to a more socially acceptable female, and equally afraid of driving him away. She knew she was right. Now it was just a matter of time. At that moment she decided to spend some time with Alexandrine herself. Maybe once the new girl saw how Charles was devoted to Estelle, she would come to an understanding of the relationship between her and Charles. Surely she would not want to marry a man knowing he was already involved and might be the father of a child out of wedlock. She decided to be quiet the rest of the ride.

Right before Christmas that year, Hyacinthe received a letter from Paris. Her father had passed away after a short illness.

September 1765

My darling daughter,

It is with great grief and sadness that I must write to you of your father's death. He is with the angels now. He only took ill last Friday. He had a fever, then he was speechless by the evening on Saturday. On Sunday morning he did not wake. How I wish you could grow wings and fly to my side, my little girl. I do suffer terribly even though the house is full of people at this time. By the time this correspondence reaches you, we will have buried my dear love. I can tell you that half of my heart is there with him and the other half with you and my darlings Cecile and Charles.

Monsieur Rieu keeps me informed as to the situations at Greyfriars. He tells me that you are well and Cecile and Marc are happy there. But what of Charles? How is our handsome young man handling affairs? Has he married? I cannot imagine he has time to socialize properly. I hope you are helping him to find suitable girls that may be considered for marriage someday. Have you taught him to waltz? A mother's steady hand may sometimes need to gently guide her young to reason when it comes to the matters of the heart.

If you are well in the spring, it would please me greatly if you were to visit and stay for the summer. It would be lovely to see you, as we have not been together in many years. Letters and packages are food for the eyes but are not a substitute for an embrace or the sound of a beloved voice. I do not think I would do well to voyage at this age, but you are still young. Please think on this. Though there can be much tension in the city, since the price of the war has emptied many pockets, Paris perseveres through it all. You would love the businesses selling restoratives. You might call them soups and sauces. They are delicious places and help keep the spirits lively for travelers.

I am sending enough cloth for a few dresses for you and Cecile and Florine. I also send some of your father's personal items for Charles. I understand Amelia has gone away with her husband. I do hope she visits when she is able and is treated well by her new love. I will close now. I love you so very much. Please give my love to the children. May God bless you all.

Love always,
Mother

Hyacinthe cried most of the week. She loved her father very much and felt guilty she had not visited her parents once in the previous years—and especially now, when her mother needed her more than anything. She would travel in the spring. She had to. She could not bear it if her mother left the world before she saw her one last time. She would have Charles make the arrangements.

Charles had been instructed to pick Alexandrine up; however, Pierre was hard at work on a wheel, and only one horse was available. With a sigh, Charles mounted and rode off to get the girl. He was not especially happy with this, since it would make the ride uncomfortable for them both, and surely Comfort would treat him poorly if she found out they had ridden on the same horse. He decided he would walk and let her ride. When Sylvie saw what Charles had planned, she raised a fuss and did not stop until Charles was on with Alexandrine firmly wrapped around him. As they rode away, she smiled. They did make a lovely couple. How fortune had smiled upon her family after the horrors and brutality they experienced during le grand derangement when they were forced from their homes in Nova Scotia. She never thought a life like this all would be possible. She and Hyacinthe predicted them to be married closer to Charles's twentieth birthday. And the time was going by very quickly.

For Charles, the ride back home was not uncomfortable at all. In fact, he thought it was quite nice. It didn't take as long as it did with the carriage, and Alexandrine was as light as a feather. When they got to Greyfriars, he dismounted and then raised up his arms to take her by the waist and help her down. She grabbed one of his hands and then slipped just slightly and fell into his arms. He was quick to hold on to her, and he then let her go when he felt her feet on the ground. Their eyes met.

"Thank you, Charles," she said with a smile. "I am sorry if I am a bother to you."

He shrugged and took the reins in his hands. "You are no trouble. But I will have to talk to my mother." Alexandrine was scared. "But what have I done, Charles? Please tell me!"

He laughed and turned around. "You barely weigh anything at all. I think you need to eat more. One of these days the wind will take you right off of the horse." He laughed, and then she did too.

She rolled her eyes. "Thank you, Charles. I'll see you later." She headed into the house. He watched her walk away. The blue ribbon in her hair matched her blue dress and coat. He normally did not notice what she was wearing.

Another Christmas bonfire went by, as did another wet, cold, muddy winter. They managed to make it through the season without illness. Hyacinthe noticed they also made it through without any sign or word of pregnancy from Cecile and Marc. There were a few times of possibility, but they were followed quickly by Cecile's monthly cycle. Hyacinthe began to think maybe she and Sylvie should think about speeding up the arrangement process with Charles and Alexandrine. Sylvie agreed. She and Jean were agreeable to their daughter getting married at seventeen. They believed Charles, at nineteen, was mature beyond his years and would be a responsible husband for her. The sun again warmed the land, and spring of 1766 was in full force at Greyfriars. The conspirators would make sure more than flowers bloomed in its gardens.

Chapter 3

Secrets in the Water

Spring 1766

Louisiana had its first Spanish governor, but things remained somewhat normal for most of the families already established there. Hyacinthe did not leave for Paris as she thought she might. Just as Charles began to prepare her voyage plans, Cecile announced that she was pregnant and due around January of the next year. Hyacinthe did not want to take any chances that might cause her to miss out on the birth or first months of her grandchild's life, so she sent her mother word that a great-grandchild was on the way and that a later time would be better to leave on such a trip. She knew her mother would understand. Her focus had now switched from Charles and Alexandrine to Cecile and the pregnancy. She was overjoyed.

Cecile seemed nervous about the changes going on in her body but seemed to be okay. Her morning sickness kept her in the bedroom for the first two months, and several times she swore she was going to throw the baby up when the vomiting became intense. Marc was constantly worried but glad there were enough women in the house to tend to her. He was happy and hoping for a son. He had ended his service with the military and helped in running Greyfriars with Charles.

Sylvie and Hyacinthe's plans for a wedding had to wait. Comfort was happy that Hyacinthe was no longer pushing Charles and Alexandrine together so much. This gave her time to get to know her rival. She decided to invite Alexandrine to her cottage to visit and have coffee and pastries. They had worked around each other casually at Greyfriars, but that was all. Alexandrine was happy to accept Comfort's invitation.

There was a knock at the door, and Comfort knew it was show time. Of course everything tasted delicious, and the two spent quite a bit of time talking about baking and techniques. The conversations were polite and civil.

Alexandrine liked Comfort and was amazed at her accomplishments, wanting to hear all about her experiences as a young mother, widow, and businesswoman. Comfort shared stories of her, Cecile, and Charles growing up together. Alexandrine could see Comfort's eyes light up when she spoke of Charles. The longer they talked and laughed, the more Comfort realized she actually liked Alexandrine and didn't have designs on Charles at all. She said she found him likable but her ideal husband would not be a planter. She would rather not marry at all until she was ready. She wanted to marry a sailor. She loved the sea, and she wanted to move back to Nova Scotia, where she had been born. She told Comfort that she suspected her mother and Madame Hyacinthe of trying to arrange a marriage between her and Charles, but she would rather pick her own husband if she wanted one at all. She didn't think Charles had a clue. Comfort could not hate her now, and she was relieved. Maybe they could be friends after all. Just then Estelle began to cry and came out into the front room looking for her mother.

"Oh, she is so beautiful, Comfort. How fortunate you are. I am sorry you have to raise her alone. It must be very hard. If at any time I can look after her for you, please consider my offer."

Comfort turned Estelle around to face Alexandrine. "Look Estelle Charlotte. We have a new friend that has come to visit us. Isn't she lovely?" She reached over and gave a small pastry to Alexandrine. "Here. Hold this and maybe she will come to you."

Alexandrine took the pastry. "Come little one. Come to me. I have a sweet for you, yes?" Estelle looked at her mother and then to the pastry. She took her thumb out of her mouth and headed for Alexandrine's hand.

Comfort laughed. "Watch your fingers, now. She has teeth coming in. I found out the hard way." Estelle leaned in to take a bite and fell. She began to cry, and Comfort got up, but Alexandrine had already picked her up to hold her.

"Oh, poor baby." She stroked her head. She had beautiful, silky short black curls. Estelle looked up. "Oh my, Comfort, and she has the most beautiful eyes. They look light brown from a distance, but up close you can see the greenish color. Did her father have green eyes?"

Comfort froze. She had been caught off guard. "Yes, he does. I mean ... he did. He did." She took a deep breath. "Well, I suppose we have kept you long enough. I have chores to do and a dinner to prepare. Maybe we can have coffee again. This was very nice." She rose, as did Alexandrine, who handed Estelle back to her. "Yes, that would be very nice, Comfort." She kissed Comfort on both cheeks, and then they walked outside. She mounted her horse but turned one last time. "You know, Comfort, you and I might have something in common. I just hope he appreciates us both. Good-bye." She smiled and trotted off to return to Greyfriars. Comfort stood there and watched her leave. She felt Alexandrine was most certainly onto her, but not in a threatening way. Of course there would be inferences and suggested scenarios, but she felt this girl would not be her enemy. Time would tell.

Alexandrine rode at a comfortable pace, surveying the land and village around her. On the way, she pondered those little greenish-brown eyes and the name Charlotte. *Isn't that the female opposite of Charles? Oh my.* Maybe life here wasn't going to pass her by without incident. This was something that required careful timing. She had to make sure her suspicions were confirmed. Until then she would be the unassuming daughter of the overseer, whose planter she was being maneuvered into marrying.

In August the Danetrees and others were outside enjoying a picnic at Greyfriars. Marc, Charles, and Jean Broussard were fishing off of the dock, while Hyacinthe, Cecile, Sylvie, and Alexandrine sat on blankets laughing, talking, and discussing baby names. "I thought we would name a 'him' after Papa," Cecile said. "If it is a girl, then of course she will have your name, Mama, and Marc's mother's name." She smiled and rubbed her growing belly.

Hyacinthe laughed. "Oh, that will be lovely. Gertrudis Hyacinthe. No, Cecile, I forbid you. She must have a lovely name."

Cecile stood up. "I believe that I will go inside now. It is a bit warm, and I feel the need for a rest."

"Very well then," said Hyacinthe. She stood up too. "I will take you up and then rejoin our merry group here." She took her daughter's arm, and they walked away. Several minutes later, they heard a scream coming from the side of the house. Hyacinthe came running back. "Marc! Marc! Hurry! Cecile has fallen. Everyone help, please!" She was crying as she turned around to run back to Cecile.

That night Cecile suffered a miscarriage and almost bled to death. Hyacinthe wrapped the tiny form in a silk scarf and set it aside. She felt her heart break with the loss and then break even further as she thought about how she could have lost her daughter as well. Charles had ridden to Teal Bend to fetch a doctor there. Their regular doctor, Dr. Boudreaux, who had seen the Danetree family through many an illness, had moved to New Orleans. When the new doctor arrived the next day, he gave her a checkup and found her able to survive the ordeal, but she would need time to recuperate and would need those around her to be understanding and nurturing. She had lost quite a bit of blood but was showing no signs of any further hemorrhage.

Cecile and Marc decided that the baby boy, Marc Philippe, should be buried in the crypt with Philippe and Olivier. When Cecile was well enough, they had a ceremony. Pierre had carved a tiny box. They placed it on a small shelf inside of the crypt. It was a solemn time at home, and everyone made sure that Cecile knew she was loved and the baby was mourned.

This also meant Hyacinthe and Sylvie would, in time, resume their plan for their single children. Charles and Alexandrine still seemed to be at the "getting along" stage, with each of them using the word "pleasant" to describe the other. The mothers certainly saw this as a positive. They thought that maybe a spring ball would help to show them off as a couple. Hyacinthe offered her blue silk gown with robe for Alexandrine. "They will match her lovely blue eyes. I also have a matching parasol. We must not tell Charles. I will have him wear blue also. Everyone will look at them and marvel how they match." It was agreed. They were pleased with themselves, and all passed the winter of 1766 relatively happy.

By the next spring, Cecile's body had fully recovered, though her heart had not. Hyacinthe gave her many tasks to help distract her from her from becoming too melancholy: planning a menu, going to New Orleans for material for a gown, deciding which decorations should go where. This seemed help greatly, and soon she was smiling most of the time, laughing, and singing throughout the house. The rest of the household seemed lighter also, and spirits were high as all were anticipating the party. Hyacinthe had hired musicians from New Orleans to perform music for dancing. She had even forced the household to take part in ballroom dancing lessons led by herself. She seemed truly happy being able to share the lessons she grew up with up. Comfort was hired for breads and pastries. Willie made delicious meat pies. There was shrimp, crab, oyster dressing, and turtle stew. What Hyacinthe didn't know was that the delicious casserole Willie made was actually possum baked with sweet potato. It was a recipe she had learned from her momma, who had learned it from her momma, and so on. During all her years at Greyfriars, the family had always loved it and never questioned the contents. They thought it was delicious chicken, so Willie didn't tell them anything different. She had been keeping the chickens safe from the possums for years and figured it a just punishment for raiding the coop. Willie thought it best that what they didn't know wouldn't hurt them.

With music in the air, laughter, and conversations on anything and everything floating about, Greyfriars was alive and celebratory. Hyacinthe and Sylvie heard many compliments about how handsome Charles was and how he had become quite the young man, and how beautiful Alexandrine looked and that they would make a nice couple. Hyacinthe even requested they dance the first dance. Of course she had taught them both separately, but they made her proud when everyone saw them so graceful together.

Later, when Charles got his mother aside for a little talk, he let on that he knew what she was about.

She tried to look shocked. "But Charles, what are you saying? I had no idea she would choose that dress. She had several to choose from. Who knew you both would wear blue for the party."

Hyacinthe took a sip of brandy and looked around the room. He cocked his eyebrow. "And the dance? I am sure you had nothing to do with that as well?"

She shook her head. "Really, Charles. Must you be so suspicious? It was a simple dance, that's all. Look around. Everyone is dancing now. I am sure none of them will remember who started the dance off tomorrow or the next day. Now I must go. We have guests." She kissed him on the cheek and walked away.

He watched his mother move around the room, in and out of smiling groups of friends. She was truly happy tonight. He almost felt guilty about accusing her of setting him and Alexandrine up. Comfort had fortunately decided to stay home with Estelle on this evening. She would have been miserable. Especially during the dancing part.

Sylvie saw that Charles was standing by himself. She called Alexandrine over and handed her a cup of punch. "My dear, I promised Charles this cup of punch. Could you take it to him? I must go to the kitchen quickly."

"Of course, Maman." She took the cup from her mother and headed for Charles. She stopped in front of him and held the cup out and smiled. "My mother lied to me and said she was getting you a cup of punch and that she couldn't finish the task because she had to go to the kitchen quickly. Now you will smile and take the cup from my hand. Then we will pretend we are enjoying each other's company. We will laugh and smile while our mothers plot from the kitchen, as I am sure your mother is a part of this as well. Do you understand what I am telling you, Charles?" When he took the punch, smiled, and began talking about the beauty of cutting a stalk of cane on a slant and watching as the sugar crystals oozed out glistening in the sunlight, she knew they were going to get along just fine. The afternoon and evening was a great success. Morale was flying high, and even after the guests were gone, the singing and dancing went far into the night.

Alexandrine decided to visit Comfort the next day. Charles had picked her up, and instead of going to Greyfriars, she asked if he'd take her to Comfort's cottage first, under the guise of having something for Estelle. He hesitated at first but gave in, thinking it would be strange if he denied her this favor. Comfort was in her vegetable garden when they rode up. She looked up and seemed quite shocked to see them together visiting her. She raised her eyebrows at Charles. He shrugged to her.

Charles helped Alexandrine down, and she went over to Comfort and kissed her on both cheeks. "I hope you do not mind. I forced Charles to bring me here. I know it is unannounced, but I had to see you. Where is that sweet Estelle?"

Comfort smiled. "Oh, she is napping just now," she said. "Well hello, Charles. Always nice to see you. Let's go inside, and I'll make coffee or tea if you like."

"That sounds lovely, as long as we do not wake the baby," Alexandrine said.

Comfort waved a hand in the air. "She'll be fine. Anyway, Charles is here, and she adores him. If she wakes up, he'll take care of her." It made her feel good to say that.

Comfort led them into the house. She was somewhat confused and apprehensive about what the visit entailed. Charles and Alexandrine seated themselves while Comfort made coffee. Charles spoke first. "Alexandrine has a gift for Estelle, but I cannot imagine where she is hiding it. In your petticoats, mademoiselle?"

"Charles!" Comfort scolded. "You do not discuss what a lady may or may not have in her undergarments." They all laughed.

"Yes, he is quite the cad, is he not?" Alexandrine added. "My gift for Estelle cannot be contained in a petticoat or parcel. It is a different kind of gift."

Comfort served coffee. "What do you mean then?" she asked.

"Well"—Alexandrine looked at Charles and then Comfort—"I am sure we are all painfully aware of the 'arrangement' that Madame Hyacinthe and my mother are plotting between Charles and me."

Comfort said nothing.

Charles stood up. "What is the meaning of this kind of talk, Alexandrine? Why do you bring this up here? I am sorry, Comfort. I will take her home. I hope we have not upset you."

Comfort put her hand up. "Have a seat, Charles," she said. She was perfectly calm. He sat.

Alexandrine continued. "As I was trying to say, it has become obvious to me that a marriage arrangement, although commonplace, is not what I think I would care for." She looked at Charles. "I do like you, Charles, and find you easy to be around, but I have no desire to marry you, and I think you feel the same about me. Are we agreed?" He nodded. She continued. "Yes, we are agreed."

Charles could only sit there in wonder. "But why would you come here to tell me these things?" he asked. "What has Comfort to do with this?"

Comfort looked at Alexandrine and then Charles and said, "Because she knows, Charles. She knows everything. Don't you?" She looked back to Alexandrine. Charles was shocked. He started to panic inside.

Alexandrine raised an eyebrow. "Calm down, Charles. Your secret is safe with me," she told him. "Although if I could spot the green in Estelle's eyes, I doubt that I am the only one who has an idea that she might have a sliver of Danetree in her. I understand these types of relationships are seen as somewhat acceptable in the world, but I have a plan for the three of us." She noticed Comfort's hands were bunching up her apron, and she reached over to take one of them. "My dear, we are young, but we are not stupid, as they would think us. My plan will keep you and Charles together forever, and Estelle will always have her mother and father close by. Do you want to hear more?"

Comfort could feel tears in her eyes. Charles got up, pulled his chair next to Comfort, and put his arm around her shoulders. "Please." He kissed her forehead and looked at Alexandrine. "What is your plan?"

She smiled. "We know that a marriage between the two of you would not be accepted and would cause the family to lose any credibility it has. You would have to live on the run or go so far into the bayou Estelle would not have the quality of life she deserves. We will go along as usual, with you picking me up and bringing me home. At the Christmas Eve bonfire, we will announce our plan to marry at Christmas next year. As far as affection is concerned, we will remain a reserved and proper chaperoned engaged couple." She stopped to roll her eyes and take a breath. "Our mothers will be satisfied, our families will be happy, and this innocent child will have her father available to her whenever she pleases. What you do not know, Charles, is that I care deeply for Comfort and Estelle and that the love you all share is something that should be preserved. See? I am much more than a young, unassuming country girl. I was schooled and read everything I could get my hands on as I was growing up. These sorts of intrigues can often be satisfied very diplomatically without dangerous battles of the heart. What do you both think?"

They looked at each other and then back at her. Charles's mouth was hanging open. He did not know *this* Alexandrine. She smiled. "You look very much like a cod stuck in a net, Charles."

Comfort got up and hugged her around her neck, crying. Alexandrine held her. "But why are you sad? I thought you would be happy?"

Comfort used her apron to wipe her eyes. "Oh, I am. I am. You hold our lives in your kind and gentle hands. I thought I was going to hate you, Alexandrine. I thought you would be the one to take everything away from me, but you have given me everything. I do want to be your friend."

Alexandrine began to cry as well. "But we are friends, Comfort. We will be good friends forever. I hope you will trust me."

Charles smiled and looked at the two of them crying and hugging. Another cry came from the other room, and he turned his head. Little Estelle waddled into the room. She went to Charles with her little hands up in the air to show she wanted to be picked up. He felt full of hope, full of love, and the future was now full of promise.

It went just as Alexandrine said. While the flames rose high into the winter night from the levee for Pere Noel, Charles and Alexandrine announced their intent to marry. The mothers cried. Cecile, Marc, Willie, Florine, and Pierre were overcome with smiles and happiness, and Comfort and Estelle joined in the festivities as Hyacinthe called for a round of apricot brandy. Charles, Alexandrine, and Comfort looked at each other and toasted to the upcoming arrangement.

The date for the wedding was set for December 20 of the next year. In the following months, Hyacinthe and Sylvie spent every chance they could together, planning and sewing. Hyacinthe had written to her mother about the upcoming wedding, hoping her mother might change her mind and sail to Louisiana and live at Greyfriars with them. Marc and Cecile were sailing for France in the spring with hopes of bringing her back with them. Hyacinthe remained hopeful that her mother would accept the offer.

During the summer of 1768, Charles and Pierre had come back from a meeting in New Orleans with troubling news. The Spanish governor announced that he was concerned about the security of the territory, and word spread that he would end trade with France and its possessions. Without Marc there to share in discussions regarding the crops and the business, Charles was under pressure to make sure Greyfriars and the family stayed secure in the current political atmosphere. He had also heard that some of the colonists were planning to show their displeasure at the restrictions that were being placed upon them and their movements. The governor had made many enemies in Spain's new colony, as it was still French dominated. France and Spain shared common religious practices and legal systems, but Spain's denying its subjects the freedom to settle their families on land of their own choosing had been a mistake. Charles made it a point to speak to the Acadian families that had accepted employment with Greyfriars to get a feel for their sentiments and to make sure he was not harboring any plotters. He thought this would be a good business decision.

Marc and Cecile were due back October 19 with or without Grand-Mere Drouin. But it was not a safe time traveling to and from New Orleans or even doing business in the city itself. It was a terrible waiting game. Charles thought about taking Pierre to meet them in the city but didn't want to leave Greyfriars without any male protection, so they stayed at home and waited. They were relieved when the coaches and escorts arrived, and Cecile Drouin was the first person Charles helped out of the carriage. Hyacinthe began to cry immediately. They thought she was going to hold on to her forever.

Once they moved inside, Hyacinthe and her mother's conversation was all in French and was very fast as they tried to squeeze years into moments. Hyacinthe had moved a second bed into her room for her mother, planning on keeping it there until they decided how to move the household around. Her bags and wardrobes were placed in the smaller room next door. Madame Cecile was happy to finally see the house where her daughter had been living her life. Hyacinthe had done well, and young Charles Philippe had proved himself time and time again as a capable man. Her namesake, Cecile, had married well, and soon she would meet Alexandrine. She knew the elder Charles and Philippe were looking down from heaven and watching over their family.

Nine days later, riots broke out in New Orleans, and the Spanish governor Ulloa and his pregnant wife were put on a ship that was to leave November 1. When those at Greyfriars found out, they were thankful their family had made it to safety in time. But not everyone was safe. Charles learned that Alexandrine's father and brother had been involved with the new governor's ousting and the riots. He and Marc were very angry but did not know what to do, especially with Charles and Alexandrine's wedding coming up so soon. They were assured by Jean and his son that Sylvie and Alexandrine knew nothing about their deeds, and if there was to be a punishment meted out, they alone would be the ones to suffer and not the women. The men decided not to tell the women about the situation until after the wedding or until they absolutely had to.

Charles and Alexandrine Danetree were married December 20, 1768. Alexandrine had Estelle for her flower girl and to carry the rings. It was a chilly December night, but they made an early bonfire and kept the cider and brandy flowing. Hyacinthe noticed how jovial Comfort had been with all the preparation and ceremony and knew she had made the right decisions for Comfort and her son in avoiding any involvement between the two. When she caught a glimpse of Alexandrine and Comfort standing next to Charles, with Estelle holding tightly onto Charles's neck, she could not help but notice the level of comfort between the two and the child's seemingly strong attachment to her son. And those little ears seemed to stick out just as Charles's had when he was little. She watched Alexandrine on one of Charles's arms and Comfort holding on to the other, looking up at him adoringly, and suddenly her focus seemed to blur out Alexandrine and she saw something for a second that surely must be a result of too much festivity and brandy— some odd memory of another couple in front of a bonfire long ago. Her head began to hurt, and she had to excuse herself and retire early. She had not had the head pains for quite some time and could not explain their return. She only hoped they would not stay, especially as she had just gotten her *Maman* back.

Marc and Cecile's gift to Charles and Alexandrine was the master suite. They moved in across the hall and spoke of actually returning to Paris with Grand-Mere Drouin in the spring. Hyacinthe was dreading that time, for she did not wish her mother to leave and had been trying everything she could to persuade her to live out her remaining days at Greyfriars. But her mother's wish was, when her time came, to be buried in Paris next to her husband. She could not bear to think of being away from him on foreign soil, even after death. She cried when she first saw the hibiscus. It brought back such beautiful memories of Paris, as did the birdbath. She was glad to see these things still in the family and being passed on to another generation.

It saddened Hyacinthe to see her mother looking older. She had beautiful silvery-white hair and a few wrinkles here and there, though she seemed so peaceful—almost as if she were just waiting to die to be with her husband. It made her think of Philippe and how much in love she thought they were at first. She thought it unnerving now how her mother was drawn to the hibiscus tree and the birdbath, while she hadn't been able to stand to be near them since Philippe disappeared. She couldn't explain it. Those very items at one time were precious to her, too.

The time went by too fast for Hyacinthe. She could not convince her mother to stay, and her mother could not convince her to return to Paris with her. Young Cecile had made a tiny braided wreath with strands of hers, Charles's, and Hyacinthe's hair and put it in a locket. She had then presented it to the elder Cecile at a bon voyage party they put together. Hyacinthe rode with Pierre, Marc, and the younger Cecile to

New Orleans. This time only Marc would be escorting the elder Cecile back to Paris. He had made arrangements to meet with investors there and to bring ledgers for review. He wanted to visit his own family as well.

Hyacinthe knew this would be the last time she would see her mother. They looked into each other's eyes, and then her mother smiled. "I love you forever, my darling. We will see each other again. You have a full house and many beautiful grandchildren to look forward to. I expect letters from everyone regularly. Maybe next year you will come home, yes?"

Hyacinthe lovingly embraced her mother. "Oh Maman, I love you so much. Yes. Of course. Next spring it is, then." This made them both feel much better. Somehow discussing future plans pushed the thoughts of death and absence further away, allowing for a more tolerable parting. Hyacinthe cried uncontrollably most of the way back home.

It was not long before Hyacinthe began to hint about grandchildren with Charles and Alexandrine. It stopped when the young couple spoke about moving out of Greyfriars and building their own home. That seem to quiet Hyacinthe for a bit. She did not broach the subject with Cecile without Marc there. In October of 1769, Jean Broussard and his son Luc went into hiding when it was learned that conspirators in the rebellion the previous year were being executed and imprisoned. Thousands of Spanish soldiers had arrived earlier that year to enforce Spain's holdings and to root out those who would oppose the crown. Sylvie was beside herself, as was Alexandrine. They had no idea of any involvement of the husband and brother they loved and now feared for, but the men knew they had made the right decision in not telling them previously. They had heard that some prisoners had been sent to Cuba. Sylvie sought solace in Hyacinthe's friendship and spent more time there than at home. She would sleep in the room next to Hyacinthe's as an overnight guest.

One night she heard Hyacinthe talking. She tapped on her bedroom door and then let herself in. Hyacinthe was still asleep but was tossing and turning. Sylvie thought it was almost as if she were having fits of some kind. "No. No, Philippe. How could you with that girl?"

Sylvie thought she should wake her up, but she got nervous. "Ma tête. Où est ma tête? Belle. Qu'avez-vous fait?"

Where is my head? What have you done? Sylvie was scared now. She ran across the hall to Marc and Cecile's room and banged on the door.

Cecile answered. "Oh Sylvie, what is wrong?"

Sylvie looked very worried and was wringing her hands. "It's your mother, Cecile. I believe she is having night terrors. She is talking strangely. Please come."

Cecile ran past Sylvie to her mother's bedside. Hyacinthe was breathing quick, shallow breaths. "What did she say, Sylvie?"

Sylvie told her, "She was saying something about Belle. 'My head. Where is my head? What have you done?' In French. Before that she was saying, 'Philippe, how could you with that girl.'"

Just then Hyacinthe sat straight up in bed, startling both Sylvie and Cecile. She looked as if she were not quite awake. She looked Cecile in the eyes. "I had to do it, you understand. He made me do it. He had to be punished. She had to be punished. Their child will take everything from us." She blinked a couple of times and then grabbed her head, closing her eyes. She lay back and went back to sleep.

Cecile looked at Sylvie. "We will not speak of any of this, Sylvie. Her head pains have returned, and her mind is turning strange again. Do you understand? No one must know what she said. I will send for a doctor tomorrow. *No one must hear of this.* I will stay with her now. Thank you, Sylvie. I am glad you were here. Now good night."

"Good night, Cecile." Sylvie left, closing the bedroom door behind her. What was torturing Hyacinthe so? She decided she would ask at another time.

The next morning, Hyacinthe went down to the kitchen to get a cup of coffee, thinking it would make her head feel better. She had not gotten dressed yet and remained in her dressing gown and robe. Willie noticed she wore no shoes. This was not Madame Hyacinthe's normal behavior.

Charles had come downstairs with Alexandrine after smelling coffee and biscuits. They also noticed Hyacinthe's strange behavior. "Mother, are you all right?" Charles asked.

She looked at him almost as if she didn't recognize him. "It's my head, you know. I swear it feels as if there are demons in my head trying to fight their way out."

Willie spoke up. "There is porridge on the table in the dining room, and oranges, if you are hungry."

"Thank you, Willie. We are." They left the kitchen.

Willie turned her attention back to Hyacinthe. "Madame, are you sure you are all right?" Hyacinthe smiled and nodded. "Oh yes. The morning is lovely, isn't it? Everything under the sun and bright." She walked through the kitchen, approaching the door to the side yard, and stared out of the door's window. "Look how green the grass is, and it looks so soft." She went to put her cup in the sink, but it slipped and broke on the floor. "Oh, I am so sorry."

Willie smiled. "It's all right, Miss Hyacinthe. Willie will make it clean. Don't you worry. Why don't you join Charles and Alexandrine in the dining room now?"

"Yes. Of course." She left the kitchen, but when she passed by the dining room, she kept going and quietly slipped out of the front door. Hyacinthe looked up at the sky and then began to walk around the side of the house toward the back. She smiled at everything she saw, felt the velvety soft grass beneath her feet, listened to the birds sing, and felt the sun's warmth on her shoulders. When she reached the back lawn, she walked over to the birdbath and ran her fingers along the top. She stopped and looked down and saw Philippe lying there. She smiled sweetly and said, "What are you doing there, my darling, lying down? Come walk with me." Philippe got up and took her hand. They strolled over to the hibiscus tree. Hyacinthe reached up to touch a bloom. "Aren't they quite beautiful, Philippe? Are they not the most wondrous things in the world?" She turned to look up at him.

He smiled at her and said, "You are, my love," and caressed her cheek with the back of his hand. She closed her eyes, and when she opened them back up, Philippe was gone. His body was on the ground at her feet, and his head was gone. "No. No, Philippe!" she screamed. His arm lifted away from his torso, and his finger pointed to the bayou. She screamed again when she saw his head in the water. She knew she had to bring it back so she could fix him. "Poor thing, Philippe. I am coming. I am coming. Wait for me!" She ran to the edge of the grass and jumped toward the head, flinging her body into the bayou with a great splash.

Willie looked up when she heard screaming from the backyard. She had a sick feeling in her stomach. She went into the dining room and saw Hyacinthe was not there. "Oh Lord, oh Lord! *Charles, hurry!*" she yelled. She then ran back into the kitchen and out of the side kitchen door toward the bayou. Charles and Alexandrine looked at each other and were soon running just seconds behind Willie.

The screaming woke Cecile up. She had fallen asleep in the chair in her mother's room and spent most of night staring at her in case she had another night terror. She noticed her mother was gone from the room. She got up and ran to the window just in time to see Willie, Charles, and Alexandrine running toward the hibiscus tree. Then she saw Charles jumping into the bayou. "Oh my God, no!" She ran from the room. "*Marc, Sylvie—hurry!*" She raced outside.

Marc and Sylvie arrived just in time to see Charles going back under the water. In a few minutes, Charles resurfaced at the dock, climbing up the ladder while pulling something heavy out of the water. They ran to the dock to help him. Willie and Alexandrine were crying. Cecile ran to Charles. He was shaking and sobbing, holding their mother in his arms. "I couldn't save her, Cecile. She was stuck. I couldn't save her. Why did she go in the water, Cecile?" Cecile held her brother. Sylvie and Alexandrine held each other, and Marc tried to console Willie. Life as they knew it was over.

A black wreath was placed on the door at Greyfriars. Cecile and Sylvie prepared Hyacinthe's body and dressed her in her blue gown with her pearl earrings. She looked almost angelic. Many people came to the wake, and a rosary was said. Father Warren performed the service. The family told everyone she had slipped and fallen into the bayou. It was too painful to think she may have wanted to leave them on purpose. No one really noticed the brownish striped female dragonfly that had joined the orange males on the hibiscus tree. They would be the first of many souls bound to Greyfriars and trapped between worlds.

Chapter 4

When Love Isn't Enough

Spring, 1775

By the spring of 1775, Marc and Cecile were still childless. Cecile feared that her miscarriage had rendered her barren. Marc felt helpless. He loved Cecile very much and made sure to remind her it did not matter if they never had young ones. He would love her and stay by her side forever. Charles and Alexandrine began to feel the pressure of producing an heir to the Danetree fortune. Sylvie had returned to living at home since her husband had returned from hiding. Unfortunately their son had been killed shortly after they fled the rebellion in 1768. They also eagerly waited for a grandchild from Alexandrine, since she was their only remaining child. That's when Mrs. Charles Danetree came up with her next plan.

Estelle was eleven years old now. There was no doubt that she belonged to Comfort and Charles. Marc and Cecile never brought it up and loved having Estelle around. They were comfortable with the situation, and they could see Alexandrine and Charles were too. Everything seemed to be going smoothly at Greyfriars, and they all wanted to keep it that way. Sylvie thought it sad that both young couples remained childless as time went going by. These sentiments did not go unnoticed by her daughter.

On a sunny afternoon, Alexandrine had Comfort over for tea with her and Charles. "The way I see it," she said, "is that Charles and I must produce an heir. Marc and Cecile, unfortunately, cannot do this, so we must." She looked at Charles. "We have gone this long without having to worry about people questioning our union, but all is lost if we have no child. My mother even occasionally asks me how we are doing with her worried look. This is my solution." She looked at Comfort and could tell in her eyes she knew what was coming. Comfort nodded.

Charles held Comfort's hand as if reassuring her they would be all right no matter what. "From what I have learned, it only takes one time to produce a child. We will hopefully have a boy. He and Estelle can grow up together. This is my plan. What do you both think?"

Comfort glanced down at the table and then back to Alexandrine. "You are right. It will be the only thing to save what we have here. I agree. Oh, what it is to be a woman in this world. So many things are unfair." She sighed.

"I agree." Charles added. "If it helps, Comfort, I'll rub alligator grease all over my body and make it as unpleasant as possible." He smiled, and they all laughed.

"Surely you jest, Charles. You are terrible," Alexandrine chided. "Do you both agree?" She asked them.

"This is acceptable to me," Charles said.

"I agree," said Comfort. "Hopefully Estelle will have a brother."

Alexandrine pursed her lips and nodded. "Good. Then tonight it is, Charles. You can bring the cognac. And I do mean the good stuff. Oh, and bring a bottle for yourself." They parted ways, and Alexandrine cleared away the tea service.

Charles took a walk around the grounds, thinking to himself. It wasn't the thought of coupling with Alexandrine that bothered Charles so much. He had always found her pleasing to look at. They had been sleeping next to each other for years without consummating their marriage, per the agreement. It was the look in Comfort's eyes that tore at his heart. But he knew deep down this was the best decision for all. He would do his part. He also knew Alexandrine had a lover—a sailor from Canada. She had fallen in love with the boy before they were forced to leave their homes in Nova Scotia. Charles scheduled lengthy business trips to New Orleans when they knew he was in port. That way she could travel with him and have her trysts while he was free to sneak back to visit Comfort in Petit Coeur.

Alexandrine returned to the sunroom, sat in the rocking chair, and looked out toward the bayou. With one finger, she looped a loose curl over and over again as she pondered the situation at hand. She was sure her plan was going to work. There had been several times during her marriage when she felt natural carnal urges, and she knew that if she made all the right moves, Charles would not be able to resist her. But she wanted to make love, not just have sex. And so she longed for her Ambrose. She remembered feeling crushed when her father returned from hiding with a surprise for her. He had been in touch with Ambrose Landry—a name she repeated in her prayers and a love forever etched in her heart. If she had held out only a few more years, she would be married to him and not in this arrangement. But how was anyone to know what the future would hold.

It was hard at first reconnecting with him. He had reservations about their affair, even though Charles allowed it. But he could not resist her. Alexandrine smiled to herself. She had always been one to know her mind, but in this world her opportunities were somewhat limited, and the fates had dealt her a very challenging hand—one she could not afford to throw away. And so tonight, after much good brandy, Charles would become her Ambrose, the man she really longed to be with, and she would become his Comfort. She would deal with the explanations, if necessary, much later. She was sure Ambrose would understand.

Marc and Cecile had left for New Orleans earlier in the day. Everyone else had gone home, leaving Charles and Alexandrine alone in the house for the night. Charles grabbed from the study a bottle of Remy Martin—a gift from Gran-Mere Drouin for the newlyweds. They had never opened it. It was time. He opened the bottle, took a few swigs, and picked up a cognac glass for Alexandrine. Charles headed up the stairs. He was slightly nervous but didn't think he'd have any trouble producing the necessary instrument to satisfy the task. When he entered the room, he looked around in the darkness, squinting, but did not see her. "Where are you, woman? Your husband demands your presence and your services." He began to laugh. "Oh Alexandrine, please come out, come out, wherever you are." He heard a door creak, as she stepped out of their rosewood armoire.

Alexandrine walked up to him wearing nothing but a black velvet ribbon around her throat. There was just enough moonlight coming through a slit in the heavy draperies to allow a stream of light to illuminate her breasts and the smoothness of her skin. He handed her the glass and poured as she held it. She put it to her mouth and in one shot emptied the glass before holding it out for another drink. "Well, Mrs. Danetree." Charles smiled as he poured. "May be this won't be so mechanical after all."

She smiled. "Would you like to play a game?" She slammed the second drink, already feeling the warmth from the first.

She walked over to the bed and picked something up. Charles liked the way the light shone across her derriere. She had a heart-shaped rear.

She held up silk scarves in each hand. "Would you prefer red or pink?"

He walked over and chose the red one, raising an eyebrow, and asked, "Is this some high-seas intrigue your sailor lover has taught you, my dear? Shall I disrobe, or would you have your way with just the breeches at the ankles? Shall I bend you over?"

Alexandrine stood with her hands on her hips. "Do you talk this much with Comfort? I cannot imagine what she sees in you if all you can do is cluck like a hen. My sailor knows how to handle his mainmast in the fiercest storms. I'm sure you're probably only as capable and comfortable as a skiff on a calm creek." She looked at his pants and smiled, watching as he took another swig of cognac from the bottle and began to take off his clothes. She had pushed the right button. *That was too easy.* Now he was out to prove himself, and she had challenged his manhood by comparing him to another. When his breeches hit the floor and he stepped out of them, she noticed he was more than ready for the task at hand. And she was not disappointed. Her thoughts flashed to her lover Ambrose. He was an exciting lover and had taught her many things in their time together. She did not ask where he learned them, and he did not tell. Now she would try them with someone new. She would teach Charles a few things.

Alexandrine walked up to Charles and placed her hand on it. She looked up into his eyes. They were glazed and wild. She knew she had him. She leaned forward to get close to his ear and whispered "Checkmate" as she gripped him tighter. His back stiffened, and he drew in a deep breath. He reached around her, placed one hand at the small of her back, and pulled her to him. He did not expect to feel this way. He did not want to desire her. But now, at this moment he knew that he wanted her—to be on her and in her. He was going to let her do anything she wanted.

She pulled away and got the scarves. She wrapped one around his eyes and led him to the edge of the bed. She picked up the cognac, took another drink, and then tied the pink scarf around her own eyes, feeling her way back to Charles. She put her hands on his shoulders and forced him down on the bed and climbed on top of him. She leaned over and felt for his mouth with her hands and kissed him gently on his lips. They were full and soft, and the smell of cognac was intoxicating. He placed his hands on her thighs and caressed them until he reached her hips. He gripped her buttocks in his hands and pulled her forward. She raised her hips and lowered herself onto him. When she moaned out loud, he sat up and wrapped his arms around her, pulling her tight to him as she rode him. He reached up and took his blindfold off, and hers as well, without breaking rhythm. They looked into each other's eyes. This was becoming more than just sex. They had real feelings for each other, and they both knew it. Their moans and sighs filled the halls of Greyfriars with sounds that hadn't been heard since Philippe and Hyacinthe first made love in that very room.

The next morning they were awakened by the smell of bread and coffee. They woke up in each other's arms. Alexandrine looked away and pulled the quilt up to her neck. Charles raised himself on one elbow and took her chin in his hand so she had to face him. He said nothing. He kissed her on her forehead and then her nose and her cheeks. He looked into her eyes and then kissed her lips. He was ready in seconds, and she did not deny him.

They ate breakfast around nine thirty, as usual. They took their coffee in the back sunroom. Charles lit a cigar and passed it to Alexandrine, then he lit another for himself. "You know," he said, "I am leaving for New Orleans tomorrow to meet Mark and Cecile. I do not know if your Ambrose will be in port, but you may come if you like. What do you say?"

She looked over to him and smiled. Everything was different now. Her love and desire for Ambrose were certainly not lessened by the passion she and Charles had shared, but now she felt something for the man she had married. In other words, there was a slight complication. She had seen and felt his passion. And shared it. "Charles, I do not know what will happen to us now, but I can tell you I wish to stay here while you are gone. We were just there three weeks ago, and I don't want to travel just now. Besides, it is too soon for him to be back, I think." She looked off toward the bayou, taking a puff from her cigar. "Maybe a game of chess before you go?" She smiled with an eyebrow raised.

Charles smiled. "Oh madame, you are a vixen. I would say you have me quite at a disadvantage with your moves. I should never have taught you how to play chess."

Alexandrine stood up and held out her hand. "Come with me. I believe it is an old tale, but three times produces a boy. We cannot disappoint the family, now can we?"

He rose and took her hand. "Alexandrine, are you sure about this? I don't know about you, but last night and this morning … well, it didn't feel like I thought it would. It wasn't like a chore. I rather enjoyed it, and I think you did too."

She looked up at him. *He has such a soft heart*, she thought. "Yes, Charles. It was good, very good. I will admit I did not expect to feel anything either. Maybe we should keep these feelings to ourselves and not share these moments with Comfort and Ambrose. There is no need to hurt them. We have always been comfortable with one another, and we are both in love with other people. What danger could there be? Now let's go upstairs." She smiled and led him away.

In June of that year, Alexandrine was sure she was pregnant. She was actually happy. Charles was happy. They told Comfort privately. She was as happy as she could be and let them both know she would help with everything necessary for the pregnancy and birth. They waited until she was four months along to announce it to the rest of the family. At that point she had just started to really show. They decided to have a family meal and announce it then. Sylvie and Cecile cried happy tears while Jean, Marc, and Charles lit cigars and opened a bottle of brandy. It was a splendid evening, and everyone was filled with good spirits. Alexandrine looked around the room at the faces of everyone around the table talking, drinking, and laughing. She felt truly happy, as though she were a part of something much bigger than herself and her arrangement with Charles. She looked at him. He, Jean, and Marc were having a lively discussion. He was quite handsome. She watched him smile, and she felt warm—and something else. They were connected now in the most intimate way. They shared a child. She felt her stomach and considered that maybe it was more than a life growing inside of her—maybe it was a love as well.

Sylvie, Cecile, and Comfort were all present when Paul Jean Baptiste Danetree was born during the afternoon of January 20 of 1776. The birth went very smoothly, and the infant boy exhibited a very healthy set of lungs very quickly. As soon as he was cleaned up and the bedding changed, Charles was allowed into the room. Alexandrine was weak but doing well. Comfort watched as Charles kissed his wife on the forehead and picked up his son. She could see a tear on his cheek. She felt as if she were watching her world become like a thin porcelain teacup perched dangerously on the edge of an unstable shelf. She went to Alexandrine and took her hand. They looked at each other and knew their agreement now had to change. Comfort excused herself, gathered Estelle—who was desperate to see the new baby—and went to get into her carriage. Just as she put the reins in her hands, she heard Charles's voice.

"Comfort, wait." She stopped, looking down at him. "Oh Charles, I feel like I cannot breathe. I have to go home."

Estelle said nothing. She looked so tired.

Comfort looked at Charles. She needed to be strong for all of them. "I will be fine, Charles. Don't think of me. Your place right now is at her side. We will be fine." She forced a smile. "Now say good night to Estelle and me. We will see you tomorrow."

Estelle yawned. "Good night, Uncle Charles."

Charles looked at his daughter and smiled. "Good night, little one." He looked at Comfort and knew she was hurting. He was glad she didn't know everything. He wasn't sure if it was possible, but he felt as if he were in love with two women at the same time. And his heart had enough room for both. "Tomorrow it is then, ladies."

Comfort tugged the reins, and the horses took them home.

Little Paul Jean stole everyone's heart at Greyfriars. He was spoiled rotten. Sylvie had stayed the first month at Greyfriars. She couldn't bear to be away from her daughter and grandson. Jean was fine with her there, because it allowed him to hunt and fish whenever he chose to without worrying about coming home too late or smelling like fish. There were certain concessions everyone had to make in a marriage. He stopped in every now and then to have a smoke with Marc and Charles and to see his grandson. Babies were a wondrous thing, and he was proud to see his line continue for another generation.

When the time came for Alexandrine to rendezvous with Ambrose, she was unsure how he would take the news about her child with Charles. She had explained to him the benefits they were able to share because of her marriage and he had agreed, but the talk of children and heirs from this marriage had never been part of the discussion. Ambrose met her at a private apartment where they always stayed. He had a key and let himself in. She was sitting on the bed when he entered. "Ambrose." She smiled nervously. We need to have a talk." Normally they would start making love at this point, but his face was frozen as the minutes went by and Alexandrine told him everything. "Please Ambrose, you must understand. We could not continue this way if Charles and I had not produced an heir. Please tell me you and I will be all right." She stood in front of him and began to lift her skirts.

He took her hands, and the skirts dropped back to the floor. "How do you know the child is not mine? We were together only weeks before you and Charles. This could be mine. Now that he is born, who does he look like, Alexandrine?" He gripped her hands tighter.

She pulled away, massaging them. She had not expected this reaction. "But what are you saying, my love? It was almost a full month between you and Charles. I am sure it is his. Please let us just be together here and now. Things are going as they should, Ambrose."

He stood up. "I must see the baby. You must bring him to me, and we will see who the father is. If he is mine, then we will leave this place and go back to Canada."

Alexandrine had to think fast. Greyfriars could not risk the scandal and turmoil if this agreement should come to light. All would be lost, and everyone would be thrown to the cold. She dropped to her knees and began to cry. "Oh, you are right, Ambrose. We must make this right. I will tell Charles, and he will see you are right as well. I will take care of the meeting. Please forgive me, my love. I will make this right. I promise you."

He knelt in front of her and took her face in his hands. "My prayer is that he is mine. Then you must leave Charles, and we will leave this place." He kissed her and started to remove her clothing.

As he undressed her, the only thing she could think about was that if he didn't come around, she was going to have to either end their relationship or end him. Both were painful and extreme choices. She kissed him back. She felt removed and sad. She could allow no one to come between her Jean Paul and what could belong to him—even if that meant sacrificing her love for Ambrose.

They lay in each other's arms after, and she listened to him speak of things happening in other parts of the world. He did tell her of the war in the colonies. He said that the Spanish, French, and American colonies were banded together against the English and that he might make port less frequently in the future, depending on the dangers and restrictions affecting the shipping lanes. He was thinking of joining the Continental Navy. It would be hard on them as a family, but he wanted to see they were taken care of. He had also been training when he could to practice his shooting skills. He hated to waste bullets and wanted the enemy to fall with the first shot.

Alexandrine just let him talk. And with every plan he made for them "as a family," she knew what she had to do. There were too many to protect. She knew Marc and Cecile would be gone another two weeks, and then it would be just her, Charles, and the baby. It would be easy to dismiss the household staff early. "You will be here for another week, yes?" she asked him.

"Yes," he answered. She wanted to cry. "In three days' time, you must come to Greyfriars. And tell no one. Do you understand?" He nodded. "I will arrange a meeting for us all, and we will decide from there what we all should do, my love." Ambrose smiled and slept. Alexandrine could not sleep. She knew she must handle this alone—and that Charles must not know either.

The ride back to Greyfriars was somewhat quiet but not unpleasant. They spent the night in Teal Bend, and Alexandrine persuaded Charles he should spend the next couple of days with Comfort and Estelle. She would have her mother come over and stay with her and Paul Jean. He agreed, and the plan was set in motion.

Ambrose arrived as planned and knocked at the door to Greyfriars. Willie was gone for the day, Pierre and Florine had gone to visit Amelia, and Charles was with Comfort and Estelle. Alexandrine had never intended to ask her mother to stay with her, so it was just her and Paul Jean. So far everything was going according to plan. She asked Ambrose to take his horse out back and said she would meet him there. She let him in the side kitchen door and led him to the back sunroom. She could tell he was very nervous and offered him one brandy and then another. The she went to get the baby. She watched Ambrose as he held Paul Jean, who was now four months old. She could see he had the same large dark brown eyes as Ambrose, as well as the same nose. Then she saw a tear on Ambrose's cheek. She touched his shoulder.

Ambrose looked up at her. "You have your proof now. You know in your heart he is ours. I will make preparations for you both. We will sail within the week." He was so happy.

Alexandrine was so crushed. Nothing in life had prepared her for what she must now do. "Here, let me put him down and we will talk." When she came back, Ambrose had gone outside and was standing by the hibiscus tree. He had left his hat and coat on the table. She knew he always carried a pistol, which she found as she rummaged through the inside coat pockets. It was small enough for her to handle. Her father was a hunter, swamper, fisherman, and skinner. There was nothing he did not teach her. She had to make the first shot count. There was a small horn of black powder and a small box of lead balls. She poured the powder in to the barrel carefully and then carried the flintlock pistol to the kitchen. She took a dab of grease from Willie's grease tin and smeared a tiny amount on a small patch of cloth she tore from her petticoat. She put it over the top of the barrel and then placed a ball on it and shoved the ball into the barrel until she was sure it rested against the powder. She primed the flash pan and gently closed the frizzle. She then tucked the gun into the back of her skirt and headed out to meet Ambrose at the bayou side.

He heard her coming and turned around. He loved her so much, and now they had a family. He could not have been happier. She walked up to him and stood behind him, placing her hand on his shoulder. "You know," he said, "I cannot give you a fancy house like this or a privileged life like the one you now enjoy. But I do know we will always have love and each other. You'll be happy, Alexandrine. I promise you." She looked past him at the bayou. "The bayou is beautiful, isn't it? It seems so peaceful today, Ambrose—like you could almost lie on it like a bed and float away from everything."

Ambrose watched the water. She stepped back and took the pistol out from her skirt, cocked the gun, and pointed it at him. He turned around. "Mon Dieu, Alexandrine. What are you doing?" There was a look of disbelief and horror in his eyes. He took a step toward her. "I am protecting what I love, Ambrose. And though I love you"—she could feel tears streaming down her cheeks—"I love my son more. One day this will all be his, Ambrose. And when I die, I will have many sins to answer for. But you—you will go to God, my innocent darling. I am sorry, my love—so very sorry." Before he could get another word out, she pulled the trigger.

Ambrose just stood there stunned, and then he looked down toward his chest as a small crimson spot grew until he dropped to his knees, his white shirt becoming wet as the blood escaped from his body. Alexandrine stood there very numb, the gun at her side. She kept watch until the man she had once loved, took his last breath. Then she dropped the gun, walked over to him, and knelt by his body. She closed his eyes and brushed the thick brown hair from his forehead. "My angel." She kissed him on the cheek, stood up, and rolled his body toward the bayou until he dropped over the side into the water, and then she watched as the gentle current carried him away until he went under. She went back for the gun and threw it into the water. When the ripples stopped, it was as though nothing had disturbed the surface at all. Something inside of her snapped, and she remembered the hat and coat in the house. She retrieved them and threw the powder horn and box of balls into the bayou, along with the buttons from his coat, and set the rest on a trash pile ready for burning. She watched the flames consume the remnants of Ambrose Landry and send his essence into the heavens.

She walked over to his horse, guided it to the front gate, and hit it hard on the flank, sending it snorting and galloping away, and she then went back into the house to set everything right. She washed her hands and brought Paul Jean into her bedroom, where she curled up next to him and fell asleep. It had been a very long morning. She would go to get her mother later. Right now she just wanted to hold her son and protect him—Danetree or not.

As the fall approached, Marc and Charles spent more time in New Orleans. They were aware of what was happening in the American colonies, but their Spanish governor Galvez seemed reluctant to get involved just yet. He was more concerned with increasing Louisiana's population. This was fine with Marc and Charles, who saw this as an opportunity to increase their production and labor force. One thing that did not escape Charles was Alexandrine's moods. She would be very easygoing most of the time but would occasionally fall into deep depression. He also noticed she did not want to accompany him to the city to see Ambrose anymore. He did not want to see her become like his mother had when the moods and head pains struck her, so he made sure her mother, Sylvie, was there often. They would lie in bed at night, and sometimes she would let him hold her. It was all he could do.

Paul Jean was a happy baby that grew into a happy toddler. Estelle loved looking after him, and all seemed to be going well. In the world away from Greyfriars, Governor Galvez had finally been given permission from Spain to declare war against the British, and battles were being fought in succession, with the British surrendering to Galvez at Baton

Rouge, Natchez, Mobile, and Pensacola. With the turmoil in the gulf, sugar and molasses shipments from Greyfriars were affected, but they managed to keep it together until things settled down.

Whenever Alexandrine looked into the face of Paul Jean, she saw Ambrose. Since Charles had never met the man, it was easy for her to compare his dark, brooding eyes and thick brown hair to her father's side of the family without anyone questioning his origins. But she knew. She decided to talk to Charles about having another child.

Comfort mentioned to Charles that she was nervous because apparently Alexandrine's lover had not been in the picture for quite some time. Charles told her that he had probably deserted Alexandrine after finding out she and Charles had a child.

Alexandrine's idea for another child went well with Charles, and in February of 1782, the Danetree family welcomed Jean Charles into the world. It was another healthy birth, and Alexandrine knew he was a true Danetree. Paul loved his baby brother and doted on him, as did Estelle. She seemed to be the happiest of everyone. She would be turning eighteen that year, and the young man Estelle had met in Teal Bend at the market did not escape Comfort's protective senses. She liked him well enough and wanted to make sure her baby was choosing well. She would have him meet Charles too.

Charles was impressed with Estelle's young man, Christophe, after having him checked out. He had a successful bakery in New Orleans and could provide well for Estelle. The only obstacle Comfort could see was that Estelle would have to move to New Orleans. Comfort did not trust that city. It always seemed to be on the verge of chaos, only to survive until it came to that edge again. She wanted her daughter safe and near her. Any mother would. Charles had a different take on the situation, as he was a constant visitor to the city. He told her many families had survived there for decades and that New Orleans would always have challenges—but then any port city would. He also reminded her that even small settlements had to sometimes address the very same issues and that Estelle had to see the world. This did not make Comfort feel better, but she realized she had raised a beautiful, intelligent, confident young woman who had a chance at a life that had escaped her mother's grasp. Estelle would be a woman married to a man she loved, and they would have the life she had only dreamed of. She consented to the union. Charles and Alexandrine insisted the wedding take place at Greyfriars. After all, Estelle Charlotte Christmas was a Danetree.

It was a lovely summer wedding, and Comfort, Charles, Alexandrine, and the rest of the family watched as Mr. and Mrs. Christophe Marleau slipped their rings on. Estelle was stunning with her cream lace gown gracing her slender, olive-toned figure, and her green eyes were unmistakable. She wore her "aunt" Cecile's ivory comb for her long black hair. She carried an arrangement of hibiscus flowers from the tree, laced with jasmine and honeysuckle. "Uncle" Charles had provided Estelle with a sizable dowry to help bolster the bakery in New Orleans. She would be living out the childhood aspirations of her mother and father, and Comfort and Charles knew they had made all the right decisions with their only child, who had been born out of love and was now going to marry for love.

Comfort hated living alone and spent a great deal of time at Greyfriars helping Alexandrine with the boys and Willie with the kitchen. Willie was in her seventies and expressed a desire to go back to the Sea Islands off the South Carolina coast to be with her sisters for her final years. Life would be much harder there, but she wanted to be near her family.

One night after supper, Cecile pulled Charles away to the study. She had some things to discuss with him. He poured them each a brandy. "Charles, I am having the hardest time with my conscience anymore, and there are things I believe you need to know. I understand we have become quite comfortable with our lives and situations here at Greyfriars, but …" She stopped and handed him a small journal with the initials H. D. D. D in gold on the front. "It was Mother's diary. I found it when I cleaned her room after she passed, but I wasn't sure you would want to see it." She waited for Charles to say something, but he just held it and said nothing. "I think you should read it, Charles—and only you. There is something else. Sylvie knows too. Something Maman said that night. She wasn't right. You know that. It was about the other boy. You remember. I know you do. Our brother, Belle and Papa's son, Tomas."

Charles looked up at her and tossed the diary onto the desk. "That was a very long time ago, Cecile, and no one cares anymore. What do you think remembering is going to get us? It will only bring up bad things that should die with us, Cecile."

She shook her head. "It's worse than that, Charles. If what I heard Maman say and what she wrote is true, then the curse will be passed on to our children—*your* children. As sad as I am without any, maybe I should be grateful that when it is my time, my worries will go with me. You have two beautiful sons, Charles. Read the diary, I beg you, and then destroy it. There is another thing we need to talk about. Marc and I are thinking about moving to Paris for good, to be close to his family and to Grand-Mere Drouin. Monsieur Rieu has offered him a position there. He will talk to you about that himself later. We would not be leaving until next year—if we go." She stood up and handed him her brandy. "You can have mine, too. You will need it, my brother." She patted his hand, kissed him on the forehead, and left the study.

Charles looked at the journal and thought he should just burn it in the fireplace now. Mother was gone. He didn't believe in curses and felt he wanted to damn Cecile for bringing up the other boy. She knew he did not want to hear about his father's indiscretions. They had made his mother lose her mind. He was young when these things happened, but he wasn't stupid. His father had lied, his mother had gone mad, and he had a secret brother. He stopped for a moment to reflect on his own decisions about his own life. He had just married off his illegitimate daughter while enjoying the company of two women. He considered that maybe he should read and not judge. He felt that perhaps he had become like his father after all. He had just never had to face it—until now.

The next day, he and Marc had a nice long discussion in the study while the women cooked and sewed and the children played. "I have decided not to accept the position in Paris just yet, Charles. But Cecile and I will travel to Paris next year and stay for the summer as we have done before. What are your thoughts?"

Charles and Marc had run the business of Greyfriars together for so long now that Charles could not imagine doing it without him. "You are my brother, Marc, and as much as I want your and Cecile's happiness, I wonder how I could do this all by myself."

Marc smiled. "I know. I think of you as a brother as well. I will write to Monsieur Rieu and ask about sending some new agents we can train. Will this work for you? I do want to make Cecile happy, and she wants Paris. Women—we love them too much sometimes, yes?"

Charles smiled. "Yes, you are certainly correct. Marc, I know you understand about Comfort and Alexandrine, and I—"

Marc put his hand up. "Please, Charles. You do not owe me an explanation of your personal arrangements. Things seem to have gone quite well for you. The children are all happy. Your women seem happy."

"Thank you, Marc. Though I must say I did not think my life would be like this."

"Do we ever really know?" Marc asked. "Our generations each grow with their sets of troubles and successes. We are no different, my friend. We will be fine. What we really need to do is survive this Spanish governor and pray the world will always need sugar and molasses." They both laughed. Charles felt much better. Maybe he would read the journal after all—just not now. It was a beautiful day, and he wanted to spend time with his children. There would be more days, weeks, and months like this when life seemed normal.

Time passed. They ate, they slept, they cried, they laughed, and they lived each day with vigor. It was a good life. Marc and Cecile had come back from Paris in September 1783 with sad news that Maman Drouin had finally gone to heaven to be with her husband. They did a rosary for her and shared what memories they had. It was decided that Marc and Cecile would move into the Paris home the next year.

Monsieur Rieu and Marc had secured several agents willing to travel to Louisiana and learn the business from the working end, as they primarily had seen to the paperwork and ledgers only when they arrived in Paris. On a short visit, Marc and Cecile had brought back a few mementos from Grand-Mere Drouin for Charles and Alexandrine, along with bolts of brocade and velvet, and of course a case of cognac. There was also news of France's financial troubles due to its participation in the American Revolution and the division of territories, with Spain claiming a huge portion of the New World. It was two months after Marc and Cecile left for Paris when the new agents arrived, making the transition easier for Charles and Greyfriars. It was a sad time with all of the changes, but Charles and Alexandrine promised to visit Paris with Comfort and the boys within a couple of years.

There were more changes to come. Pierre and Florine moved closer to Amelia and her husband, and Willie left for the Sea Islands and her family. Charles hired several new people to staff the household. It was a period of adjustment for everyone. He put the new agents, Monsieur Levert and Monsieur Dugas, up in a house next to Jean and Sylvie and had a cabin built for the new house and grounds staff—Hubert and Anne Vicknair and their ten-year-old son, Emile. They had been recommended by Jean and Sylvie as part of a later migration to southern Louisiana of displaced Acadians. The Vicknairs were happy to relocate to Greyfriars. They finally felt they had a home after all of the uprooting they had experienced.

As Paul Jean and Jean Charles grew, they received the same schooling as Charles, Comfort, and Cecile had, except music lessons for Paul Jean went by the wayside and were replaced by crop studies with Charles and fishing and hunting adventures with Pawpaw Broussard. As he and Jean Charles got older, their physical differences became more pronounced. Paul still had his handsome, brooding dark eyes and a pronounced nose, while Jean Charles looked like his father with green eyes, black hair, and a more aquiline nose, and he was and longer in the leg.

Comfort heard from Estelle when the post was delivered but wished she lived closer. There were still no grandchildren, and their bakery was very successful. But all of that would change on March 21, 1788. A great fire swept through New Orleans, destroying most of the city's wooden buildings. The only thing left standing from the bakery was the brick ovens. They had saved their cash box and some ledgers but had had no time for anything else. It was utter devastation. Governor Miro set up a tent city for those displaced, but Estelle and Christophe headed back to Petit Coeur. When they arrived, Comfort and Estelle cried until they could cry no more. Comfort got busy fixing up a room for them and then got on her horse and rode to Greyfriars to tell the family. It was a bittersweet reunion for everyone.

Estelle met all of the new people in the Danetree household, and she couldn't believe how fast the Danetree boys had grown. Paul remarked that Estelle looked like his father and his brother and wondered why he didn't have green eyes too and how come his nose was bigger than everybody else's noses. Estelle had realized in her teenage years that Charles had to be her father. She knew he had always taken care of her and her mother whenever they needed anything, and after living in New Orleans for so long, she was well aware of the arrangement between certain men and certain women. But she could not hate him or her mother for their love. And Aunt Alexandrine? She loved her too. Together the three adults had managed to keep their civility, and Estelle never doubted their love for her or her stepbrothers. She had seen families torn apart and was grateful hers was surviving despite the inequities. She and Christophe had been fortunate to see Willie, Marc, and Cecile before they started their journeys leaving through New Orleans, but she had missed Pierre and Florine's parting.

Charles and Christophe spoke about rebuilding the bakery, except with brick this time and not wood. He and Estelle would stay in Petit Coeur for a couple of months, but they had to get back and claim their business and rebuild. Charles would help with whatever they needed. He was also glad the Ursuline Convent had been spared in the fire. Christophe told him about Governor Miro's plans and how they would rebuild the city and that they were hoping things would be improved. New Orleans wasn't the cleanest or safest place to be, but it was their home, and they wanted to help save it by keeping their business there. Charles admired their resolve. He understood what it took to survive in the business world. It could be a constant fight just to make it through the natural hazards and the unnatural politics—especially in a territory going through growing pains.

By July a new bakery stood next to the brick ovens that had survived and Marleau's Boulanger was back in business. Paul Jean was twelve and Jean Charles had turned six. Charles, Alexandrine, and Comfort teased each other mercilessly about their grey hairs and achy knees and hips.

Every now and then Charles would pull his mother's journal out, but he could not bring himself to read it. He didn't know when that time would come. Everyone seemed to be doing just fine. They had even survived a smallpox epidemic. He thought back to his mother dying as a madwoman. He assumed her journal was full of scribbled ramblings. He would put it back in the small drawer under the desktop and put the key in his vest pocket, always for another time.

In November of 1788, Charles received a letter from Marc. It was not good news. France's financial troubles were dire. They had lost credibility in the banking world, and he was to attend a meeting in the spring of 1789 with other representatives from various classes to discuss the reformation of the government to consider all classes as equally as possible. Crops had not done well either. He wrote that the only thing to harvest in France was sour grapes and civil unrest. There were rumors of revolution, but he was sure it would happen regardless of the outcome of the meeting. Cecile was nervous but doing her best to stay busy around the house and volunteering in the city with the poor. Of course this also meant there would be no visits for a while until safety could be assured. He sent their love to all and hoped the families were in good health. Charles posted his letter to Marc and Cecile the next day in Teal Bend, not knowing whether or not it would reach them.

Chapter 5
Three Does Not a Crowd Make

Politics at home and abroad got Charles to thinking about other planters in the area. There had been seasonal meetings over the years where they discussed business techniques, transitions, and trends. There had also been stories of slave unrest, abuse, and murder on other plantations, leading to riots and plots. Rations, clothing, fair pay, and time off for personal planting had always been the policy on the Greyfriars plantation. Charles made it a point to visit and meet with his overseers and representatives of the enslaved that lived and worked on his family's land. But he also knew that the need for a sense of freedom and dignity was a powerful one and hoped in the current tumultuous economic times that he would be seen as approachable, reasonable, and trustworthy. He chose to keep the status quo of using slave labor and knew fully well that his head could wind up at any time on a pike in front of his great house.

One of the planters that shared Charles's concern was Thomas Berwick. He brought his family to the area in the 1770s and owned about 1,600 arpents on Berwick Bay. He was someone Charles could look to for advice. Thomas's family had really wanted land in Mississippi and had petitioned the West Florida Council for land close to Natchez, but at that time Governor Galvez needed his organizational skills in Louisiana, so he wound up in Opelousas, surveying while he established his crops. He was seven years Charles's senior and had children close in age to Paul Jean and Jean Charles.

Charles thought it a good idea to ask Alexandrine if they could host the Christmas bonfire and invite the Berwicks. If his sons and Thomas's daughters could meet, maybe one day the two planters could solidify their land holdings for their future generations through marriage. He thought it ironic that he was entertaining the same thoughts that he and Alexandrine had fought when they were arranged.

He would invite the Christopher O'Brien family as well. Christopher had secured a Spanish land grant and settled 1,900 arpents on Tiger Island across from the Berwicks. He grew indigo and had a lumber mill that processed and sold cypress planks. He was a widower with a number of children—mostly sons older than Charles's—that helped him run the business on their plantation. Charles needed to get his sons closer to the Berwick girls before the O'Brien boys could snatch them away. He would let Alexandrine handle those delicacies. She had proven herself to be a master negotiator and manipulator in the business portion of the affairs of the heart. Charles had become so accustomed to his French agents and New Orleans connections that he sometimes forgot how important local alliances could be. Alexandrine's response was one of excitement and was in full agreement that the house should be full of young people for Paul and Jean to socialize with, and she wanted to meet the other wives.

Charles and Comfort had managed to spend quite a bit of time together since Estelle had gotten married and moved to New Orleans. They had the privacy and freedom to spend hours together without having to worry about getting caught. Sometimes Charles even arranged to spend the night with her as long as he wasn't needed at the house. Their lovemaking had become smooth and natural over the years, with a little daring thrown in—especially when Charles tried the same techniques Alexandrine had taught him during their times together. He would just tell her he had thought of something new they could try, but she knew better. What he didn't know was that Alexandrine had spoken to her of a few things as well—naughty party gossip and rumors about the delightfully uncivilized behavior in candlelit rooms on other plantations and in the city at special parties where anything and everything was accessible and acceptable. She kept those conversations secret from Charles. After all, what he didn't know wouldn't hurt him.

One rainy night, Alexandrine was feeling blue and Sylvie was staying with her. Charles had left for New Orleans, and she figured he had probably stopped at Comfort's on the way out. She decided she wanted to visit Comfort and keep her company, allowing her to talk to someone closer to her own age. And they did have Charles in common. Her mother didn't care for her leaving the house in the rain by herself, but she was her father's daughter, and Sylvie knew she could not stop her. Alexandrine took her heavy dress off, leaving her clad in her petticoats. She slipped on one of Charles's heavy shirts, slipped her legging knife into her stocking, and donned her cloak. She grabbed a bottle of brandy and a couple of cigars from the study, packed them in an old leather bag, and then headed for her horse.

When she arrived at Comfort's cottage, everything was dark except for the lively flickering from the front-room fireplace. She knocked on the door. No answer. She felt bad about waking Comfort, but she knew Comfort would understand. The rain had let up but it was chilly. She knocked again.

"Who is it?" Comfort said from within.

"It's Alexandrine. Open up. It's cold."

Comfort ran back into the bedroom and whispered, "Charles, it's Alexandrine. I'm going to let her in." Charles rolled his eyes as Comfort closed the bedroom door. His horse was in the barn, and he knew that if Alexandrine had put her horse there, she already knew where he was. If something was wrong at home, he could get there easily. If not, then he would just stay in bed and leave them to their girl talk.

Comfort slipped her nightdress on, wrapped a blanket around herself, and then opened the front door. "Alexandrine, is everything all right? Do you do know how late it is? And you shouldn't be out by yourself like this. What were you thinking? Come in. I'll put another log on." Comfort stood aside and let her in, then she closed and locked the door. *Maybe she won't be here that long.*

Alexandrine put the leather bag on the floor and threw her cloak on a hook by the door.

Comfort laughed. "Oh my. Is this the latest fashion from Paris? Is that Charles's shirt?"

Alexandrine pulled the brandy and cigars out of the bag and held them up. "Voilà, mademoiselle. I bring fashion, fine cigars, and the most fabulous brandy this side of the Mississippi. I am afraid I suffer from melancholia and need medicine."

Comfort frowned. "Are you still sad about Ambrose? I am sorry, my dear. It is so late, and I was sleeping. But do you want to have a drink and we can talk about it?" She walked over to a cupboard and took out three glasses. She raised her eyebrows and nodded toward the bedroom.

Alexandrine grinned. "Oh yes," she whispered. "Do you think he might join us for a drink and a smoke?"

Comfort grimaced and whispered back, "he doesn't know I have smoked a cigar before. I haven't told him about our secret visits or other intrigues." Again the whispering.

Alexandrine asked, "Do you want to invite him out here with us? I thought he would have left for New Orleans by now."

Comfort smiled and went to the bedroom. When she returned, Charles was with her. He put his hands on his hips. "My dear, you know this is my time with Comfort. You girls have the daytime. And what are you doing dressed like that? So you wear my clothes when I am away, I see." He smiled.

"I think she looks better in that shirt than you do, Charles." Comfort said. They laughed.

Alexandrine held up the brandy. "Maman is with the boys, and if you put my horse in the barn, you may have a drink."

"Fine. Fine." He headed back into the bedroom, threw his nightshirt and boots on, and then left to put her horse away.

Alexandrine shrugged and said, "I am sorry, Comfort." Comfort noticed the woman took a drink of her brandy, not a sip. And then she took another. She sat down across from her on the rug in front of the fireplace. Alexandrine had teary eyes. She looked at Comfort. "I feel so alone, Comfort. So alone. You and Charles have had each other most of your lives, but I have no one."

Comfort reached over and brushed damp strands of hair from her face. "I am so sorry. Believe me, I do care about you, Alexandrine, and I know Charles loves you in his way. I am sorry this whole arrangement is turning out to be a trying one for you." Comfort took a drink.

Charles walked in. "Well, ladies, I see you have started without me." Comfort poured him a brandy and gave it to him. "May I join you?"

Comfort looked sternly at him. "Please, Charles. This is serious."

He looked at Alexandrine and noticed she was wiping her eyes. "I am sorry. Have I done something?" Alexandrine began to cry. He sat down next to her and put his arm around her. "What shall we do then, ladies? We will not be drinking and riding tonight. You two can have the bed, and I'll sleep out here." He shrugged and looked at Comfort. Alexandrine held out her glass.

The bottle went around until there was but a drop left in the bottom. Everyone was laughing, and the fire had become mere embers with a few straggling flames. Comfort stood up on wobbly legs and held out her hand to Alexandrine. "Come on now. Bedtime for you, madame." Alexandrine took her hand and pulled her down onto her and Charles. More laughing ensued. Charles propped himself up on his elbows as Comfort rolled off to one side and Alexandrine to the other. He was feeling very good right now. The two most important women in his life were at his sides, he was drinking very good brandy, and there was a fire in the fireplace. What more could a man want.

Alexandrine and Comfort sat up. His wife leaned across his body and kissed Comfort on the lips. He noticed Comfort neither flinched nor seemed repulsed. They looked at Charles with his confused smile. Comfort smiled. "She has been telling me things, Charles. Naughty things." She looked back at Alexandrine.

"Well then," he said sarcastically, "maybe I should go to bed and leave you two alone to your dirty deeds. Just what has she taught you? Hopefully it is not chess. She is quite the tricky player, Comfort."

It was Alexandrine's turn to smile. "I guess it's time to show you my queen-takes-queen move, my darlings. Charles, if you care to watch, you may be seated on the chair." She looked at Comfort. "I'll need a long piece of twine or rope, and that sheet from your bed. I'll get that jar of peach preserves I see in the cupboard, and a spoon."

Charles watched as they strung the twine across several of the rafters and then threw the bedsheet over the twine in front of the fireplace, like a curtain. His head was swimming, and his eyesight glazed, but he could make out their two bodies as they stood between the sheet and the glow. He thought it quite beautiful the way the firelight caressed their shapes. He was both curious and pleased by their theatrics.

In their small space, Alexandrine winked at Comfort and whispered in her ear for Comfort to follow her lead. Comfort giggled. Goosebumps freckled her light brown skin as Alexandrine took her by the waist. They began to move together, dancing and swaying slightly. Alexandrine hummed a tune to give them rhythm while spinning Comfort around. She released her, and they stood apart. Alexandrine reached over slowly with her hand and brushed her fingertips over Comfort's shoulders, breasts, and stomach. Comfort mimicked the movements as Alexandrine closed her eyes. It felt good to be touched like this—softly and playfully.

Charles was mesmerized. Drunk and mesmerized. He called out, "I shall name this play 'Seduction of the Shadow Fairies.'" They both shushed him, and he smiled. He could tell Alexandrine was opening the jar of preserves, as she exaggerated her movement to enhance the drama. She spooned some into her hands and then placed her hands on Comfort's breasts. Comfort began to moan. She was lost in the brandy, the flames, and the flesh. She shuddered when Alexandrine leaned over and placed her mouth over a nipple, gently flicking her tongue, taking in all of the sweet preserves. Charles could see the movement of Comfort's chest, and she breathed deep, giving herself to the moment. Comfort teased Alexandrine back in kind. Her head was swimming in her newfound freedom, her body alive and willing.

Charles had heard stories from some of his business associates in New Orleans and France about lavish parties in some of the big houses where the sparkling Champagne flowed freely, along with the courtesans. Just like this. And it was all his to enjoy—Charles, the voyeur. His concentration was broken by the half-empty preserves jar falling to the floor and the tightness of his own breeches. He swallowed hard. Sensations began to rush throughout his body, pumping his brain full of primal urges. He was determined to take them now—both of them—invitation or not.

Just as he stood up and began removing his clothing, they took the sheet down, walked over to him, and placed it over his head. It was warm from the heat of the fireplace and felt good draping down against his skin. He stood there as they caressed his body through the material. His breathing quickened as he felt hands lightly rubbing against his already hardened member. He pulled the sheet off and with one movement grabbed both of them by their waists, pulling them close to him. He looked into their eyes. There were no words to be spoken. It was his turn now. This world was his stage, and everything act would be played out to perfection. Their passion became a rhythmic passage of gasps and sighs and the sounds of wet, wild bodies reveling in and on each other. It was a celebration of flesh and frenzy, and the full moon was watching from its balcony high in the heavens.

When they woke up, they were cold and huddled together under several blankets in front of an equally cold fireplace. Streams of light through the draperies, clothing everywhere, an empty brandy bottle, and Alexandrine's headache were clear indicators that it was time to get up and get home. She rose first, shaking and searching for anything that looked like hers. She began to dress. Charles was next. "I will start a fire," he said.

Comfort got up and slipped on her nightdress. "I am going to get stockings and shoes on." She smiled at them both and left.

Charles watched Alexandrine get dressed while he pulled on his breeches. "You know Comfort was right."

She looked at him, one eyebrow raised. "Why, whatever do you mean, husband?"

He grinned. "You *do* look better in that shirt than I do. And whatever is your mother going to think when you get back to the house wearing my clothing?"

She laughed. "I was never the conventional daughter she dreamed of. She really wanted another son, but I am glad to be a woman. I don't know if I'd be able to ride as well as I do if I had a silly dangling thing between my legs." She stood up and put on her gloves. "Charles could you hand my knife to me then fetch my horse, please?"

He got her knife from the mantel and watched as she slid it into her stocking and then left to get her horse.

Comfort had returned. "You are leaving before coffee?" she asked.

Alexandrine kissed her on both cheeks and hugged her tightly. "Yes, my peach. Please come to dinner, yes?" Comfort blushed and nodded. Alexandrine took Comfort's chin softly in her hand. "What we did last night may never happen again, but always know how much I care for you. You are in my heart." Just then Charles came back into the house.

"How did I get to be so fortunate a man?" He asked as he entered.

Alexandrine walked over and kissed him on the cheek. "Obedience has its rewards, my darling. I will see you in a week. Safe journey." She smiled and left.

Charles turned to Comfort. He had to smile. "You have been keeping secrets, madame."

She smiled back. "Come inside. It is cold, and I need a fire."

"Of course," he said. "Obedience does indeed have its rewards."

March of 1793 arrived. Thomas Berwick had passed away the previous winter. Charles allied himself with the eldest son and namesake, Thomas, and the other O'Brien sons. These alliances and the established French agents helped to keep Greyfriars solvent in the changes they were to face together. Estelle and Christophe had left New Orleans and moved back in with Comfort. Times were growing more dangerous in New Orleans and the surrounding areas, and Christophe wanted Estelle to be safe, especially since a baby was on the way.

Comfort was beside herself with joy. She and Estelle spent long days talking, baking, and planning. Comfort made sure that if anything happened to her, her daughter and family would have the house and property. Charles helped Christophe set up a bakery in Teal Bend and made sure all finances were in order where his daughter was concerned.

Back in France, Marc and Cecile were living in a different world than the one they had arrived in. The power of the monarchy was dramatically reduced, and France was on its way to becoming a republic. Marc wrote to Charles to let him know that he was fine and surviving the sometimes violent changes going on but was not sure Cecile was doing as well. At the onset, she had gotten caught up in the revolution with other women. He wrote,

> ... You should have seen her when she arrived home. Her gown was ripped and she carried a pike in one hand and her parasol in the other. She was a glorious mess for the cause. My concern now, is since that time she has become like a fugitive in our own home. Afraid to leave, afraid to be seen. She was one among thousands Charles, but she believes we will have to suffer with the other aristocrats. If it were up to the Jacobins I believe all of our heads would be on pikes. We have managed to go along smoothly here and are working diligently to see a new and equal France, but Cecile will not listen to me. This has not changed. Sometimes I am afraid for her health. She wrote you a letter as well. It is enclosed with this one. She speaks often of you and worries for you as well. I am tempted to return to Greyfriars but she wants to remain here. She says she cannot be at Greyfriars again after your mother's death. Adieu mon frère.
>
> Marc

Marc's letter brought smiles and concerns with it. Charles wondered if Cecile was suffering from the same melancholia that had affected their mother. He remembered her trying to tell him things about their parents. Then there was their mother's diary and letters. He had gone all of this time without reading any of it and was doing perfectly fine. Cecile's letter was very different from Marc's.

> My dearest little brother,
>   There are no words I can write to explain what is in my heart. I miss you all dearly and hope all is well with you and our family. I know Marc will probably write

81

to you of things that men write about, such as politics, planting, and silly wives' hysterias, but I tell you I am far from hysterical and even farther from what our poor mother suffered from. Here we are torn between the guilt of having too much and the plight of the poor. I cannot tell you which is worse. Poor in spirit or poor in pocket, but damned either way. Please tell me you have read the things I gave to you. I tell you, Charles, life will change after you have done this. I am afraid you will have to carry these burdens, for I have no children.

Mother said many strange things the night before she died. I listened until I was too weary to hear any more. I blame myself for her death, you know. Had I not been sleeping that morning, things might have turned out very differently. Marc says the guilt I feel is natural for a child that could not save her mother, but he does not know everything. I have never told him my dreams. But I will tell you.

Remember, when we were little, the night Belle came to us with the little boy, Tomas? You know he is our brother, Charles. Belle and Papa's child. That night there was a storm. I heard screams and yelling, and so I got up. The voices were coming from the back property. I went to the windows and looked down to see Maman and Belle, and there was Papa, lying on the ground. There was a lot of rain, and it was dark, but the lightning flashed, and I saw them. Papa's head and neck were red, like blood. Maman held something red and shiny in her hand, and her nightdress was red like Papa's head. Believe me, after the violence I have seen here, I know that which I speak of. Maman and Belle looked up at me. I pounded and pounded on the glass, but Marie forced me away from the window, took me to bed, and gave me her special tea she made for Maman when she had her head pains.

Marie poisoned Maman, and she tried to make me forget what I saw. She said I dreamed it and that I was walking in my sleep. She said Papa had left for the city. I was so confused, Charles. We were so young. There was no reason for me to discount her. We had seen and heard things we shouldn't have all those years ago. Monsieur Rieu, Florine, and Pierre knew Marie was evil as well. She was trying to get control of our house and our lands. I heard Pierre, Francois, and Monsieur Rieu talking one night in the study about her. They sent her away from us, and then Maman got better. Charles, you must remember all of these little things. As for Comfort, this does not make my love for her any less. She will always be my sister, and I know she will always be in your heart and in the eyes of your daughter Estelle. Don't worry. I am sure Maman did not know. I must close now, my darling Charles. I do not know that we will see each other again in this life, and I pray that our souls will be judged fairly when we leave this world. We must all atone for our transgressions—even the innocent. I can hope that the loss of my baby somehow paid the evil debt left to us by Marie, Papa, and Maman. I pray for your children: Estelle, Paul Jean, and little Jean Charles.

Your loving sister,
Cecile

Charles let the letter drop from his hands. His mouth remained open as he tried to process all that Cecile had disclosed. Marie was poisoning his mother and his sister. He would never tell Comfort these things—hysterical things. Maybe Marc was right. Maybe Cecile was suffering like their mother. He put his head in his hands. What if she were right? He would watch his children suffer in this life. He knew he had to talk with Alexandrine. He would not keep this from the mother of his children. She deserved to know. She was strong and would know what to do. He decided to wait until they had an evening to themselves. Meanwhile, he would read as Cecile had instructed.

He took a small key out of his vest pocket, opened the small drawer under the desktop, and then pulled out his mother's journal and a few letters Cecile had left him. He also got a bottle of brandy. He was sure this was something he should not read without calm nerves. He looked at his mother's initials and ran a finger over them. It made him sad to think about her. He felt sad for Cecile as well. He had always blamed himself for not being able to save their mother. All of these years, Cecile had felt guilty as well. *Everyone knows Father drowned the night he disappeared. Of course Cecile is wrong about that. She has to be.*

He read through several entries that were just about life as she saw it and everyday things that made her happy or sad. He really started to pay more attention when he saw the entry for November 1749:

> The days go by so slowly sometimes, and other days fly like the blackbirds that watch me from the tree outside the window. I wonder what they see. The ghost of a happy, dancing young girl in love that is what they must see. I can almost hear them laughing. I miss Maman and Papa. I miss Paris. I love my children, I know, but I get so tired, and little Charles just cries with me. I do not think he likes his Maman very much. He does not cry with Belle. She has become quite a pretty girl. I hope for her that she finds a good husband like my Philippe and has many children with him. I would be sad to see her go, but she must have a life too, yes?

The next entry he read was about Olivier's death and the devastation his mother felt. She blamed herself for his death. *Is this the curse Cecile was talking about—each generation of Danetrees feeling responsible for the death of someone in the previous generation?* But these things happened in life, and there wasn't always an explanation or an answer. He read further. There were entries about the Ursulines and Monsieur and Madame Veisze in New Orleans. They were very special to her and tied her heart to the city. He read about his christening and his little bald head. These things made him smile—made him feel special. He came to April 1750:

April 12, 1750—I have spent so much time in bed with these head pains. Philippe has hired a new man to take care of the grounds. Philippe is gone quite a bit. He says there may be some new crops coming to our land that are possibly more profitable than indigo, though I cannot imagine what they would be. He does not discuss much business with me, but he does keep me informed as to news and the comings and goings of friends and acquaintances in New Orleans. I have heard him talk to Pierre about another crop he wants to replace the indigo with soon—sugar cane. I suppose it sounds very interesting when you understand the whole thing. I wish he would talk to me more about these things.

Charles is getting so big. Cecile complains about his fussiness, but I suspect she enjoys helping with his feedings and dressing him up. Belle spends so much time with him and Cecile. It is as if she were the mother and not I. Dr. Boudreaux says I need to spend more time outside in the sun or in the garden getting fresh air. He said I am suffering from melancholia and must get more involved with life.

I have employed a portrait artist to come and paint the children's portraits—one for our home, and one to send back to Paris for Maman and Papa. We received a letter yesterday from them. It just takes so long for the correspondence to be delivered. Such a distance it must all travel. Philippe told me we should host a spring ball here at the house. I am afraid I have not been very good company for my poor husband. The closeness we once shared has somewhat become a bit colder. I cannot seem to feel happy anymore. I have everything, but I feel as if it could be taken away at any moment. I must stop now. There is a pain in my head, and I must rest.

Charles began to see a pattern of his mother feeling less and less in control and her perceiving that her role was being taken by Belle. He hadn't thought their marriage had any problems. He'd been too young. He was starting to wish Cecile had never told him a thing, but he had to read on.

> **June 12, 1750**—Today is my Cecile's birthday. She is five years old and so very beautiful. Her grandparents would love her so much if they were here or we were back in Paris. Philippe has mentioned that we may close up the house and go back to France for several months and visit. I think he is worried I am no longer happy with him and our life here. I do not know how to tell him that every day, no matter how hard I try, I cannot find the will to be the young, exuberant girl he married. He has not been a husband to me for a couple of months now. I fear I may be losing him. What is to become of us? Will he just become busier and I more morose? I will get up and fix my hair and put on my best dress for the party today. I will try to have a better day. Cecile and Charles need their mother, and my husband needs his wife.

So she did try to change. Even though she was ill, she tried. Charles was still not seeing anything that would make him think his mother or Belle might have murdered his father, as Cecile inferred in her letter. Most of the entries sounded like a sad young woman trying to reclaim things she felt she had lost. He felt sorry for his mother, and his heart ached for her. There were more entries about family, friends, and her longing for Paris and her parents. Charles read on.

> **Christmas Eve Bonfire 1750**—How do I explain my day? It is another Christmas, another tree, and another

bonfire that I will not attend. Of course there is no need for me when Belle has always done this with Philippe and Cecile. Marie tells me to be careful with Belle—that I should send her away if I am to keep my household safe. She had heard stories from others at the market about the things that destroyed homes and hearts, and that Belle might be someone to watch. I do not know what to think anymore, and Marie has a special tea for everything. Maybe she can make a tea for forgetting. I would gladly drink this one.

January 1751—The head pains are getting worse. I can hardly read for too long anymore. Marie reads to me from her book. She is very good to me. She has become almost as a mother to me. I am grateful. I have been having nightmares. There is always fire. And there is always the shadow of a man and a woman at the fire. Sometimes they look like they are dancing very close, and other times they fall to the ground. The man reminds me very much of Philippe, but I do not think the woman resembles me. It is all very strange. Marie says she'll make my sleeping tea stronger so that I may rest. I cannot get stronger if I cannot sleep.

March 1751—Belle and Daisy are gone from Greyfriars. Marie has told me Belle has gotten married and moved away. I would have liked to attend the ceremony. Her father and Philippe still work together. I suppose one day she will visit with her new family. Cecile and Charles are unhappy without her around, but I suppose they will grow accustomed to her absence, as I will. I have also noticed that Marie and Philippe act strangely around each other. I sometimes feel like a stranger in my own home. I long to wake up in Paris.

Charles took another sip of brandy and looked out of the study window. It was turning dusk outside. He hadn't realized how long he had been in there reading. They weren't many more pages left. And there was a huge gap of time between the entry he had just finished and the one he was about to start. There were quite a few pages torn out. He had to finish the journal. He decided he would read the letters tomorrow.

March 1755—How do I begin to try to explain my days anymore? One day blends into a week, then a month, and then a year. So many things to write about. We have received packages from Maman and Papa in Paris. The cloth is beautiful. There are books for Cecile and Charles, and cognac for Philippe. Florine's broken heart has been renewed by Pierre, and they have married. Comfort is such a joy. She is more like Charles than Cecile is. Florine is teaching them how to make baguettes. It is very sweet. Sometimes I like to sit in the parlor when they have their music lessons. We have hired Monsieur Duncan Mc Martin from Scotland. He is very good with the children, and they seem to enjoy their time with him. Still have the head pains. I fear they will never go away.

April 1757—I must state that things have most definitely grown cold at Greyfriars. I fear that I exist in a large tomb of my own making. Belle surprised us on a rainy night with a visit. She and her son rode through a storm to talk with Philippe. She had no husband with her. Her son looked very much like my Charles. Marie says I should not think on such things and that Belle will not come again. Philippe and I had a terrible fight, and he left in the skiff. I do not remember striking him. The rain was so very cold. I saw the boy's eyes—so green. Skin like his mother's and eyes like Charles's and Philippe's. I suppose it is possible that his father must have these same eyes. Marie tells me this is perfectly natural. She takes very good of me. I do not know what I would do without her. When Philippe comes back, we will start again. I will be better.

July 1757—The world is a darker place now. My Philippe is never coming back, but I will not believe he is dead. He is merely away. I have driven him away with my depression and moods. Monsieur Rieu has been taking care of his affairs. Marie has been acting strangely, and we now know that her tea was bewitched. Monsieur and Dr. Boudreaux have found out her secrets. My heart is broken again. All these years she tricked me and poisoned my mind against innocent people. Poor Comfort. If I could take her, I would. What we do not know is why Marie was extorting money from Philippe. We shall never know. She put a small piece of folded paper in my hand as she was leaving. It read, "The birds in the sky will bathe in our sins, and the dragonflies will keep our souls, until the caramel boy with the eyes of green comes to collect the tolls."

That was the last journal entry. Charles put the journal down. He felt sick. Cecile's letter was starting to make sense now. But he would never believe his mother killed his father. He was starting to remember things—memories surrounding the night his father died that didn't make sense now. He would find Pierre. He would tell him everything. A knock on the door made him feel as if he'd jumped out of this skin. "Yes?" He called out. The door opened. It was Paul Jean. He was seventeen and had become a capable, well-built young man. "Father, Mother says you have been in here for so long that Anne had to set aside a meal and you will have to eat it cold." Charles looked down, gathered the letters and journal, and put them in another drawer. He pushed himself away from the desk and stood up. "Well, your mother is right, Paul. My behavior is an affront to the culinary talents of dear Miss Anne. I shall apologize tomorrow. Now let us go." He smiled and walked past Paul, who rolled his eyes at his father's sarcasm. He closed the door behind them both, and they headed for the kitchen.

Murielle Marie Marleau was born January 2, 1794, to Christophe and
Estelle Marleau, bringing great warmth to a chilly winter day. A month
later, there was a nice feast at Greyfriars to celebrate the christening.
Paul Jean was turning eighteen but expressed little desire to take on the
sugar cane business. Jean Charles was only twelve but loved being out in
the fields with his father and learning the trade.

Charles often thought the boys were quite different, but he loved
them equally. The families at Greyfriars had many blessings to be
grateful for. Sylvie spent more time there as well with Anne to talk to.
Christophe's bakery in Teal Bend was doing quite well, and Comfort had
no time for Charles. Privacy at Comfort's cottage was at a minimum with
a full household. Charles and Alexandrine spent more time together,
playing chess and smoking cigars. She even taught him how to tan the
hide of a deer she had taken down with a bow and arrow—something
that he had simply never had the occasion to do. He watched her in
wonder as she gently ripped the flesh from the hide. "Truly, Alexandrine,
you still manage to amaze me. You have a, shall I say, sturdy fortitude."

She didn't even look up. "Please, Charles. After all these years, do you
think I do not realize manipulation when I hear it? What do you want?"

He shrugged. "Well, I really want you to stop doing this. It's just not
pleasant to me. And it's cold out here. And the smell—how do you stand
it?" He grimaced. She smiled and made the cigar in her mouth go up
and down. When she did this, it all made sense to him. "Of course. My
cigars. You are attempting to cover the odor with the smoke. Silly me.
Well, I give up. I am going to wash up. But I do have something we need
to discuss later if we can find some time together tonight."

She stopped scraping the hide and took the cigar out of her mouth.
"Really, Charles? This gets a rise out of you?" She smiled.

He shook his head. "Oh God no, woman. I didn't mean that. It's
about the boys. Later then?"

She nodded. "Of course, Charles. After supper in the study, right?"

He shrugged. "Thank you, Alexandrine." *She is a strangely exciting
woman,* he thought. If she had been a man, he would have definitely
wanted him on his side. He left her to her tanning. As he walked back
to the house, he glanced over to the birdbath. He spied a small bird in

the water. He shivered. *If I'm cold, how in the hell is that bird faring?* He remembered the words in his mother's journal: "The birds in the sky shall bathe in our sins." He continued into the house. Greyfriars had survived near-bankruptcy, an insect infestation that nearly took their crops, volatile politics, and hostilities. Surely they could survive sin.

Chapter 6

An Angel Gets Her Wings

Thanks to the Boré method of granulating sugar in 1796, Greyfriars was able to capitalize and began to shift from producing sugarloaf to processing granulated sugar. Boré's method of crystallizing molasses into granules gave sugar cane plantations new life and a promising future. Charles was always trying to keep up on the newest methods to keep his plantation solvent, as were other planters. The Treaty of San Ildefonso which came along in October of 1800 and the Treaty of Madrid in March of 1801 saw the territory of Louisiana transferred back to France from Spain, allowing Americans to utilize the Port of New Orleans. Anytime the politics changed, so did the access to the port. Anything affecting the ebb and flow of trade and commerce on the Mississippi River affected everyone doing business at the port and along her banks. The Danetree boys were becoming smart young men and learning to keep in step with the changing times were a prerequisite for opportunity and success.

Charles took Paul and Jean Charles to New Orleans to sit in on some meetings and to enjoy the ever changing city life. He had taken them just a few times before, as Alexandrine was not comfortable with the safety of the boys in the city. Duels to the death were common and often sought by those quick with the tongue and the sword. A careless look or word could be very costly. She told Charles she would relent only if there was a cotillion Paul could attend to get him into the social circles to meet marriageable prospects, but they were not to roam the city aimlessly.

Alexandrine and Charles had changed so much since they were young. Becoming parents and raising two young men made them see things differently, and they now understood some of the reasons why their parents had made the decisions for them when they were that age. Charles promised her he would keep them in at night and told her that since the day was full of meetings they needed to attend with him, they would be fine. She gave her blessing.

Charles understood Alexandrine's concerns; however, he was raising young men, not delicate flowers. He wanted them to understand that life existed and was lived in many different ways by many different peoples and cultures. He wanted them to be educated about the international world and what made it flourish in some places and perish in others. New Orleans was rich with color, language, and cuisine. The boys needed to understand how the decisions made in the big cities, especially port cities, could make or break Greyfriars and plantations like theirs that depended on agreements with agents abroad. He had included them on smaller decisions, but the time would come when he would be leaving the business to them. Well, Jean Charles anyway. He still had not persuaded Paul to become a planter. Paul loved the water and wanted to sail ships. He had heard that the new President Jefferson would possibly be beefing up the American Navy to present a stronger force at sea, and he had thought about going up north and taking his chances training and getting accepted on a frigate. Jean Charles had no desire to leave home and had become quite capable out in the cane fields.

They stayed in a new apartment Charles had purchased, after a terrible fire in the city had destroyed their old one. This one was mostly of brick construction with cypress and shared a lovely courtyard with several other private apartments. The arched courtyard entryway had an ornate black wrought-iron gate that faced the street. There was a large beautiful magnolia tree in the middle of the courtyard and trailing fragrant orange and yellow tropical flowers with their dark, glossy leaves curling around the bannisters. It was a nice respite after a long day of attending meetings and roaming the streets and port area. It was their last night in New Orleans, and they had received a supper invitation from a business associate in their complex. Also invited was a Colonel

Gabriel Acosta and his daughter Miss Genevieve Maria Acosta. They were visiting from Cuba and would be in the city for only another week. A lovely table was set in the host's apartment complete with wine, candles, bread, roast pork, roasted vegetables, a delicious paella, and French wine, of course.

While awaiting the arrival of the Colonel and his daughter, conversations centered on the survival and current status of Greyfriars. Soon a knock on the door stopped everyone and Colonel Acosta and his daughter joined them. The conversations weren't the only things that stopped. Paul and Jean Charles would later declare that their hearts stopped as well when Senorita Genevieve raised a white lace veil that covered her beautiful face. She lifted it up and over an ornate hair comb that secured her black hair into a bun on her head. She wore a white muslin empire-waist gown with light blue trim and long white gloves that reached almost up to the hems of her cap sleeves. She had a shawl that matched her dress with the blue trim and tassels. On her wrist was a small dangling beaded reticule.

She raised her eyes slowly as her father introduced her, her long black lashes making her large grey eyes even more dramatic. She had high cheekbones and a fine, straight nose. Paul leaned over to his brother, whose mouth was still open, and whispered, "She looks like a painting."

Jean Charles nodded.

"Oh, and close your mouth. You look like a dying fish."

Charles looked to his sons to introduce them and recognized the looks in their eyes. This wasn't exactly a cotillion, as Alexandrine would have preferred, but it was a start.

The evening went well, and discussions were kept charming and pleasant out of courtesy for the young lady present. Charles noticed that Paul barely talked or ate, whereas Jean Charles more than made up for his older brother's distance and silence. The fact was that poor Paul was so mesmerized by Genevieve that he was afraid to say anything for fear of saying or doing anything that would make him look or sound like a fool. At evening's close, name cards were exchanged and the Acostas were invited to visit Greyfriars should they be in the territory again. As the parties made their way to the Acosta coach, Paul made his move to assist

Genevieve as she stepped up. "Please, senorita." He turned and looked at her father. "With your permission, sir." Her father nodded and moved aside. Paul stood next to the coach door and held out his arm. She placed her dainty gloved hand in his. He could see her full lips stretch into a smile under her veil, her eyes batting several times. As the coach pulled away, Paul remained in the street and stared. Jean Charles brought him around with a swift kick to the backside. Charles laughed as Paul chased the younger sibling back into the courtyard. He looked at his friend and said, "I believe we just might have to entertain some sort of business venture with the Cubans after all."

His friend handed him a cigar and said, "Better the Cubans than the Americans, I say."

Charles smiled and patted his friend on the back. "Now let us have that smoke."

In the Acosta coach, Genevieve put on her best manipulative manner. "Oh Papa, what a wonderful evening. Please, could we not stay and visit Greyfriars? Would we not be remiss if we did not honor the invitation? After all, who knows when you'll bring me back? You probably already have me married off to some old man that will bore me and mistreat me. Is that what you want?" She worked up a tearful worried look at stared at her father until he turned to face her.

He smiled. "My darling daughter, do you think I do not recognize the same warfare your mother used on me all those years ago? Please do not insult me or the memory of your dear mother. She was a masterful tactician when it came to getting what she wanted. But I must say I am impressed by the tears. They came on so quickly." He began to laugh.

She frowned and smacked his arm lightly with her fan. "Oh Papa, that is not fair. I was simply thinking of you and your duty to see me well married."

He smiled again. "Oh, I see now. So which Danetree do you prefer? With the younger one, you would never want for words. He has plenty. Or would it be the older son, of few words? I do admire his quiet assertiveness, but he seems dark and brooding."

Genevieve rolled her eyes. "Papa, *you* are dark and brooding. That's why Mama chose you. Please, can we stay another week or so and visit Greyfriars? Oh please? I promise I will not bother you to take me shopping for the latest fashions for at least six months. Maybe even a whole year!"

The colonel shrugged. "I will only agree to this if you agree that when we get back home you will consider the dashing young Juan Carlos Santos as a proper suitor."

She looked at him, appearing to be horrified. "Oh, how can you say that? He is not young, Papa. He is fifteen years older than I, balding, and smells of cheap rum and cheaper tobacco. Is that what you want for me, Papa? *Do* you want grandchildren that smell like rum and cheap tobacco? Mama would not have this if she were here."

He rubbed his eyes. "I am tired, little Genny, and bringing up what your mother might have decided will not resolve your case. Enough now. We will speak tomorrow morning, but for now I will agree to two more weeks and *one* brief visit to Greyfriars."

Genevieve kissed her father's cheek and said nothing. Of course she had won this time.

Gabriel Acosta stared out of the coach window and thought of his wife, who was also named Genevieve. Little Genny was a constant reminder of the woman that had captured his young heart. Even ten years after her death, she still held him prisoner. He would never love another and could not entertain the thought of marrying again. It would be unfair to any other woman he would try to share his life with. He loved his daughter very much and wanted to see her happy, but it was hard being a single father, and he prayed every day he was making the right decisions for her. Even with female nurses, governesses, and servants around them constantly, he also worried about her like a mother hen. But he would live his life, do his best, and then wait for the moment he would be reunited with his love.

Charles and the boys stayed in Teal Bend for several days before they traveled back to Greyfriars. They had much to share with their mother. She couldn't hug or kiss their cheeks enough. She was just glad they were home and safe. She was also grateful Charles had respected her wishes and kept them as far away as possible from obvious harm. She shared a message that had come from New Orleans two days prior to their return with an invitation acceptance from the Acostas. She had never seen her boys like this. They were almost giddy but nervous at the same time as they tried to talk over each other. Alexandrine looked from one son to the other. She could make out the words "beautiful," "black hair," porcelain skin," and "orange blossoms." She covered their mouths with her hands. "Boys, boys, please. One at a time. Better yet, I must speak to your father about something." She turned to Charles.

He shrugged. "Can this wait until we've settled in?"

She shook her head. "No Charles, I am afraid it cannot. In the study then?"

The look on her face made him nervous. "Of course," he answered. They left Paul and Jean Charles to take care of the unpacking.

Unfortunately she had news for him that she knew would distress him greatly. She held his hand as they sat side by side on the settee in the study. "Comfort has been ill almost the whole time you have been away. I wanted to send a messenger as soon as I found out, but she forbade me to do so. She said it would pass, Charles. I did send Christophe to fetch the doctor. He said it is something in her stomach. He gave her something to make her throw up, but nothing is coming out of her. She has been in terrible pain. Chamomile teas are not working. I suggested absinthe for her pain. Marc sent a small bottle from Switzerland that we have never used. Estelle has not left her side. Murielle has spent most of her days here with me. You must go to her now."

The pain in Charles's eyes was unbearable. He stood up and embraced Alexandrine, holding her tightly, and began to cry softly.

She held him back. "I know, my darling Charles. I know. I love her too." She pulled away from him. "I will give you a few minutes before you leave. I'll have Emile ready your horse." She headed for the door but then stopped and turned around. "I do not expect you back tonight or any night as long as she is ill. She needs you now."

Charles nodded. "Alexandrine, thank you." She smiled and left, closing the door behind her. When Charles got to Comfort's cottage, he was shocked at the way she looked. They had been around each other during their youthful illnesses, but she looked different now. Her eyes looked dazed and dull, her breathing was shallow, and her stomach was distended. She almost looked pregnant, but he knew she was not. He asked Estelle to leave the bedroom for a few minutes. Christophe had gone to Teal Bend on business. Charles knelt beside the bed. He wondered if she even recognized him. Comfort looked so fragile, and he felt so helpless. He gently sat down next to her on the bed and spoke in a low, soft voice.

With tears in his eyes, he whispered, "My love, I am here." He took her hand in his. It was cold. The once beautiful caramel color of her skin had been changed by whatever had taken over her body. She had no fever.

She turned to his voice. "I am so weak, Charles, so weak. It has happened so fast. The doctor"—she swallowed and tried to get her breath—"he said he would come back tomorrow. I cannot eat, and I barely can drink the tea poor Estelle brings in. I am so tired, Charles. So much pain."

He tried not to cry in front of her, but his eyes were hot with tears. "I know you will be fine, Comfort. We will make you better. I will stay with you until you are better. What do you want me to do?"

She tried to smile. "You are here. Now everything will be perfect. I have loved you my whole life, Charles. I need you to do some things for me."

He kissed her hand. "Anything you want."

Her voice was shallow and breathy. "My drawings of you, remember? I want you to keep them. And the paintings ..." she pulled her hand away from him and placed it on her stomach and moaned. Her eyes grew dark and large as the pain became too much. "The pain, Charles. Make it stop."

He stood up, trying to remain calm. "I'll be right back, darling. I'll make it go away."

He left the room and went to the kitchen area. "Estelle, I need a glass of water, a spoon, and some sugar. She prepared these things for him and watched as he made a greenish concoction with a small dark green bottle he took out of his vest pocket. "What is this?" she asked.

"It is called absinthe," he answered. "Marc sent it to us last year from Switzerland. It is not available here yet, but it has the reputation of making you feel relaxed. Your mother is in a lot of pain, and until the doctor gets back I would like to help her. I need her to live, Estelle. My heart will not be worth very much to me if she does not live. Of course, you know this."

Estelle looked down. "Yes, Father, I know."

He put his hand on hers and then touched her cheek. "I will be staying in her room until she is well. Murielle is doing well with Alexandrine, Sylvie, and Anne."

He went back into the bedroom and put the items on a small table next to the bed. "Comfort, I have something that may help you with some of the pain. It might help your stomach. Do you want to try?" She nodded and watched as he prepared some kind of concoction for her. "It's absinthe. It might help with the pain, Comfort." He gave her half a spoonful. "It's sweet and bitter at the same time. She opened her mouth for another half spoonful. He gently wiped her lips and said, "We will wait and see what this does." He sat there for several minutes, waiting to see whether she would react or not. He did notice she began to shake a little. "Are you cold? Shall I get you another blanket?"

She smiled. "Oh no, Charles. I am not cold, but I do feel shaky. My head is starting to feel a little clearer. May I have some more?" He gave her a full spoon this time. "That is all for now. If you tolerate that well, we will see."

She attempted to sit up but could not. "You must take care of Estelle and Murielle if something happens to me, Charles. I know you will."

He shook his head. "Please don't speak of these things. You are going to be fine. You will recover, Comfort. I need you to believe that."

She smiled. "I am sorry, Charles, but these things must be said. It is normal to discuss these things. I must tell you how wonderful Alexandrine has been also. She is very dear to me. I am glad that she is there for you." He noticed her voice sounding livelier as she continued to speak. "So many things, Charles. What a life and love we have had, yes? We are lucky, you know. We have had so many precious years together in times when so many families have been torn apart. Our love has been a glorious gift. My paintings—I would like you to sign them and sell them in the city. That money will go into Estelle's account. We also need to make sure the house and property are properly recorded in Estelle's name. I know my mother, in spite of her troubles, would want to see this all continue for her line. Do you agree?"

All Charles could do was remember his mother's diary entries and how this had all come about. Comfort had no idea how devious her mother had been. There had been bribes and threats. He would make sure she never knew. He had to protect her. "Yes, she would want that. I am sure," he said. "But I cannot sign your paintings, Comfort. When you are well, we will go to New Orleans and sell them—maybe even arrange a private show at the apartment. Yes. That's what we'll do. I cannot believe we have not done that already."

She managed a smile and nodded. "The years have gone by very fast, haven't they? They seem to go faster as we get older. Another spoonful, please?"

He frowned at her. "One more and that is it until the doctor sees you, my dear."

She asked, "Could you send Estelle in? I need her assistance now for a little while, Charles."

He stood up. "Of course," he said, and he left to get Estelle. When she entered, Comfort patted the bed next to her and Estelle sat down by her mother.

"You know how much I love you, my darling daughter. And how fortunate we are to have this time. You have made me so proud, and Murielle is our littlest angel. I want you to know you will never have worry about the house and property. It is all yours, you know. Your father will draw up the necessary paperwork and have it recorded in the city. Murielle will always have a home. As long as Greyfriars stands, we stand. Never forget that. Who knows—one day that might be yours too. You are a Danetree, with eyes like your daddy's. He loves you too. Things may seem odd to you, but you have always been wanted and loved. I have asked Charles to sell my paintings for your accounts." Comfort grimaced and grabbed her stomach. "Bring me out to the toilet, please."

101

When they came back into the house, Comfort was smiling. She was barely walking, but her eyes looked brighter and shinier than they had when he arrived. Estelle was smiling too. "How did our girl do, Estelle?" Charles asked.

"I must say Mother is doing much better right now. I guess your Swiss medicine helped a great deal," she answered, but he could see in her eyes great sadness. Charles walked up and held Comfort tenderly. Estelle stood back and looked at her parents. She wished they had had a complete lifetime of memories like these—not bits and pieces.

Charles spoke. "I'll take you to your room."

She stopped him. "Actually I would very much like to take a bath. I know that might seem a strange request, but my stomach is feeling better and I just want to feel clean again ... and maybe some broth later Estelle?"

Estelle was happy to hear her mother ask for a meal. "Of course, Mama, anything." Comfort turned to Charles. "I am feeling much better, Charles. Are you sure you can stay tonight?"

He nodded. "Alexandrine said as long as you need me."

She smiled with tears in her eyes. "Then I am afraid she will never get you back."

Estelle spoke up. "I'll get the water warmed for your bath now, and when Father gets you back in the room, he'll get the tub?"

Charles smiled. "Of course I will. But you must both rest well tonight. The absinthe will wear off, but hopefully it has sent you on a better path. The doctor should be here in the morning."

Estelle helped her mother clean up and put a fresh dressing gown on her. Charles changed the bedding and gave her another spoonful of absinthe. He told Estelle he would go and get Anne and Hubert to help around the cottage until Christophe returned. Comfort went right to sleep. Charles brushed her long black hair and fixed it as one long braid, just the way she liked it. He slept next to her and held her all night. Estelle slept in the front room, waking up periodically to keep the fire going.

Charles awoke to the smell of coffee and bread. He yawned and stretched. Comfort was on her side, her back to him. He stroked her head and whispered, "Comfort." She did not stir. It smelled as if she had gotten sick during the night. He pulled her shoulder back to see her face. It was ashen, and her eyes were dull. There was no life in her face. He noticed that the side of her face that rested on the pillow was darker than the other, as though all of her color had slipped into it and pooled there, trapped jut under the skin. He screamed, *"Estelle! Estelle! Quick!"* He jumped out of the bed. Comfort was not breathing. He put his head to her chest and felt her pulse. Everything became a blur. *"You will not die, Comfort! I will save you. I can save you."* He picked her up as if she were a baby and began to rock back and forth, sobbing uncontrollably. First his mother and now his true love. And he could not save them.

Estelle ran into the room. She knew immediately what was happening and fell to the floor at Charles's feet, reaching up to take her mother's dangling hand. She put her face into it, her tears anointing the hand that had disciplined her, taught her to bake, stroked her hair, and soothed her brow.

The days following Comfort's death went slowly, methodically, at the cottage and Greyfriars. It seemed as if they had all died with her. With Estelle's blessing, Charles and Alexandrine had Comfort buried in the Danetree family crypt. It was a beautiful June day. A bright sun bathed the mourners, as if Comfort herself were beaming them from the heavens onto those she loved and cared about. As they walked back to the house for the memorial, Alexandrine put her arm through Charles's. "There is nothing I can say to make things better or to console you, Charles, and I know that. I will be there for you if you ever need a friend. For I am your friend, Charles. I will always be there for you."

He put his hand on her arm. "I know, and I am grateful even though it may seem I am not. You are very dear to me, and you were dear to Comfort as well, you know. She cared deeply for you."

She smiled. "You have a beautiful daughter and granddaughter that need you now. Comfort lives in them both, and her love for you and your memories of her will bring you solace and serenity one day. You will see her again, you know." She could see tears in his eyes. She also noticed Paul and Jean Charles were walking alongside them now. She stopped and said, "I am going to catch up to Estelle, Christophe, and Murielle. I will see you all later." She walked away from them.

Paul spoke up first. "Father?"

"Yes?" Charles answered.

"Jean Charles and I were wondering if we might talk to you later in your study after things have settled down. Is that all right with you?"

Charles could tell Paul was trying to speak softly. He could hear the sympathy in his voice. He smiled and looked at his sons. "Of course. Later it is, then. Now go and help your mother." They left him to his solitary walk. They understood what Comfort was to him and what Estelle and Murielle were to them. They would all need time to grieve together, and alone.

Several days later, special guests arrived at Greyfriars. The black wreath on the front door alerted Colonel Acosta and his party that this household was in mourning. They had waited a week before heading to Greyfriars and making their introductions. A messenger from the Danetrees let them know that their visit would be much appreciated during this dark time for the family, and that they looked forward to their families meeting. As the coaches pulled up, Gabriel gave his daughter a few words: "Now remember the words in your head when you think the words in your heart might speak first. It is but a short visit, and we will be back in Cuba soon. There are to be no promises made, and no rendezvous planned. We made a deal."

Genevieve smiled. "Of course, Papa. It is the wrong time for these matters of the heart. I shall charm no Danetree man today."

He nodded and smiled as he got out of the coach and pulled the door sash. Paul and Jean Charles heard the sound and looked up immediately from where they were. They had been anticipating this very moment since they knew there would be a visit. Paul ran down the stairs, and Jean Charles bolted from the kitchen. Paul got there first, and Jean Charles slid into him, elbowing him in the ribs. Paul opened the door and both boys snapped to attention. "Colonel Acosta—welcome to Greyfriars, Sir." Jean Charles looked around him at the coach. He saw Genevieve being assisted out of the coach by the footman and watched two more young ladies exit from the second coach.

Gabriel smiled. "I hope it is no imposition, but my daughter's handmaids accompany her most everywhere."

Just then Alexandrine came up behind her sons and extended her hand. "You must be Colonel Acosta. Welcome to Greyfriars. Please forgive my sons. They should have alerted me to your arrival. I am afraid living so remotely has made them rough when it concerns social civilities." He took her hand. "Gabriel. Please call me Gabriel Senora Danetree." He bent slightly at the waist and kissed the back of her hand.

She smiled. "And you must call me Alexandrine. This must be your lovely daughter my husband and sons have spoken of." Genevieve had come up next to her father with her maids behind her, carrying boxes.

Gabriel smiled. "I would like to introduce my daughter, Miss Genevieve Maria Bergeron Acosta, and her attendants, Adela and Carmen."

Genevieve curtsied, and the girls followed suit. "I am most pleased to meet you, Senora Danetree. My father and I are very grateful for your hospitality, although our hearts are heavy knowing we arrive at this time of mourning. Please accept our condolences."

Alexandrine's eyes sparkled. She loved her already and was thinking she would make a fine addition to the Danetree family. But which son would she choose?

Gabriel spoke. "We have gifts for your family. Please accept these tokens of goodwill and good wishes from our family to yours." Alexandrine smiled and said, "Please come in, and again, welcome to Greyfriars." Alexandrine stood aside as they entered. Paul and Jean Charles relieved Adela and Carmen of their packages and placed them in the parlor.

Just then Charles appeared at the top of the stairs. "Ah, Gabriel, my friend, you have arrived." He headed down the stairs. He seemed happy to see their visitors, but Alexandrine knew he was suffering terribly from Comfort's passing. She was proud of him for pushing forward and trying to live through it all. Anne worked quickly in the kitchen as the family made their room arrangements and laid out a very nice table in the dining room with fruit, breads and pastries, meats, and refreshments. It was very nice and was enjoyed by all. Adela, Carmen, and the footman ate in the kitchen with Anne, Hubert, and Emile. Later everyone went to the back lawn to sit and talk and watch the bayou. Genevieve spent most of her time with Alexandrine, much to the angst of Paul and Jean Charles. They made frequent visits to their mother to make sure the ladies had all they needed. Sylvie thought it entertaining to watch her grandsons vie for the young ladies' attention. Adela and Carmen sat on a blanket not too far from Genevieve.

The men sat closer to the dock, smoking cigars and talking. Their occasional laughter floated across the lawn.

Genevieve looked at Alexandrine. "I understand from Paul that he plans on becoming a sailor and joining the American Navy. Do you think he will be gone long?"

Alexandrine smiled. *So it is Paul she is interested in.* "He has spoken of that, yes. But it is the hope of his father and me that he take over Greyfriars as the eldest son. If he wants to sail, he can have a boat at the dock." She nodded with her head toward the dock.

Genevieve smiled. "But surely he is spoken for or betrothed?"

"No." Alexandrine answered. "Currently he is not, but we are hopeful to welcome a daughter into our family."

She could see Genevieve's mind working. Being a planner herself, she understood the business end of arrangements and securities. She noticed how the senorita glanced at Paul frequently. She asked, "Surely a young lady with your beauty and grace is spoken for or betrothed, yes?"

Genevieve sighed, shrugged, and said, "Papa means well, but he is somewhat old-fashioned. He and my mother had an arranged marriage, but they fell in love. I am not even in like with the man my father is considering for me. I would rather be captured by pirates and quartered than marry Senor Santos." They all laughed. "You know," she said, "it is so lovely here. I understand the climate is similar to where I am from. And I adore New Orleans. The buildings remind me of home. The parties are quite lovely, and one can always find the latest fashions when the ships arrive from Europe. I am sad we must leave so soon. But I would very much like to visit again."

Alexandrine had an idea. "Then you must come and stay with us when you return. It would be quite lovely to have another woman in the house. Please. You must come back soon. It is lovely in the spring. We could even accommodate your maids as well. Shall I ask your father?"

Genevieve smiled so broadly Alexandrine thought her face would break. This was easier than she had anticipated.

"Oh yes, please, madame. I would be eternally grateful to be here in the spring."

Alexandrine rose and crossed over to the men just as they were getting up.

Gabriel spoke first. "Madame, I want to thank you for your graciousness."

Alexandrine smiled and stood next to Charles. "You are most welcome, Gabriel. I must say your daughter is as pleasant as she is beautiful. She must be such a joy for you. May we talk frankly?"

Charles and Gabriel looked at her strangely. Gabriel shrugged. "But of course, madame. What is it you wish to address?"

Alexandrine glanced over to Genevieve and then back to her father. "I would like to extend an invitation you and your daughter to stay with us in the spring. It would make me happy to have another lady in the house, and I find her absolutely delightful. She has expressed a desire to come back, and I would like her to. On a more serious note, I believe our son Paul has shown an interest in her status. Being that she is not currently engaged, I would like it very much if you considered him as a suitor for Genevieve. One day Greyfriars will be his, and it would be advantageous for both of our families should our children decide to marry and combine our interests. Please forgive me if I have spoken out of turn, Gabriel, but I can see they would make a lovely match."

Charles just smiled as if he were aware of what was going on. Alexandrine had always been quite sensible when it came to these matters. He was the planter, she was the planner. It had worked well for all their time together. He would not start second-guessing her now. Gabriel looked flustered. "Charles, Madame, I do not know what to say. This is so sudden. It is certainly not what I expected this visit to achieve. I am flattered that you would consider my daughter. You have two fine sons that would be most worthy sons for any father-in-law. Genevieve is twenty now, and there is a possible suitor back in Cuba that we must answer to." He hesitated, and Alexandrine tensed up. Charles could feel it by the way she gripped his arm. She had a strong grip, too.

Gabriel looked over to his daughter, smiled, and then laughed heartily. "Yes. I will consider this match. Of course I will. And I accept your invitation for the spring as well. This is all such an important time in our children's lives. Being a single father, I must say, madame, you quite remind me of my dear wife, Genny. She had the same directness as you, and I appreciate that. I think she would approve." He looked at Charles and held out his hand. Charles took it, and they shook. "You are a fortunate man to have such a strong and confident woman by your side. And, if I may be so bold, quite beautiful as well. This has been such a wonderful time with your family, but I am afraid we must be leaving for Teal Bend before the daylight is gone from us."

They walked over as everyone gathered at the back of the house exchanging smiles and handshakes and curtsies. Genevieve did not see Paul until he ran up to the group. Everyone stopped as he handed her a hibiscus bloom from the tree. "Please, Genevieve, accept this flower as a token of your visit to Greyfriars. I am afraid it will perish away from the vine, but it will stay beautiful while you hold it."

Genevieve blushed and took the flower. Her cheeks almost matched the bloom. Charles and Alexandrine looked at their son with astonishment. The awkward silence was soon interrupted as Jean Charles handed her a rolled-up piece of paper with a blue ribbon around it. "It's my favorite piece of music. I understand you play the piano quite well. I hope you like it."

She accepted the scroll. "Why, thank you, Jean Charles. You are a very sweet young man. I look forward to playing it. Thank you."

"Well," Alexandrine said, "let us go inside and get your things then." She and Charles walked with Gabriel and Genevieve. The boys escorted Adela and Carmen inside. When the coach doors were secured, more farewells were exchanged and the Danetrees waved the Acosta party on their journey home. They then turned to their sons. It was almost as if they had grown up in one afternoon. And they were perfect. Alexandrine kissed each of them on the cheek. "Paul, I had absolutely no idea you had become so poetic. And Jean Charles, where did that ribbon come from? What a lovely touch. Has your father been giving you both charm lessons, or did you learn those in the city?" She gave Charles a sly look and went inside. Charles smiled, the boys laughed, and they followed her in. The door closed, and Greyfriars was tucked in as the evening approached. Alexandrine lay in bed thinking about Paul and Ambrose. Paul lay in bed imagining Genevieve lying in bed thinking about him, and Jean Charles was already planning how he would ask the lovely senorita to marry him in the spring.

Charles sat in his study. He had a glass of water and placed a small slotted spoon over the top. He then put a little chunk of sugar on it. He reached into his evening coat pocket, pulled out the small bottle of absinthe, dripped the last of it over the sugar, and watched as the droplets fell down into the water. He replayed the doctor's words over and over in his head: *"Nothing you could have done for Comfort. Nothing you could have done."* They swirled in his brain like the greenish sugary liquid swirling around in the water. He drank the potion and then waited for the green fairy to take him to the cottage—and Comfort's arms.

Chapter 7
The Heart Chooses Love

December 1801

There was no Christmas bonfire for Pere Noel at Greyfriars in 1801. Estelle and Christophe had invited another family to spend Christmas with them as they had several children Murielle's age. Charles was in a depressive state and smiled or made attempts to be happy only when Murielle and Estelle were around him. Comfort remained alive for him when they were near. Hubert, Anne, and Emile built a small pile for the bonfire by their house. Paul and Jean Charles had gone to New Orleans to purchase kettles for the sugarhouse. Alexandrine was not happy about them going without Charles, especially at Christmas, but she didn't want to pressure him into anything. She knew his heart would never heal, but she was hoping his mood would improve in a couple of months with the spring and was willing to grant him that time.

Alexandrine decided to celebrate the season in her own way. She invited her mother and father over for Christmas dinner. She and Anne not only decorated the house with ribbons and evergreen boughs but also prepared mashed turnips, roast rabbit, buttered lima beans, and bread. She even tried her hand at concocting a spiced toddy. There was peach brandy and apple cider as well. After their delicious dinner, everyone except Charles went to the Vicknairs' for the bonfire lighting. Alexandrine kissed Charles on the forehead before she left. There were hugs from her parents and gentle urges for him to join them, but they understood and left him in peace while they took the walk to the bonfire.

In New Orleans, Paul and Jean Charles made their purchases and arranged the shipping of the large sugar kettles to be delivered to Greyfriars. They could be shipped right down the bayou to the property and unloaded at their dock. What they would not tell their mother or father about was the time they spent walking around the city, talking to merchants at the port, and publicly drinking. Two days after Christmas, they planned their return and purchased gifts to bring home. They bought packages of pralines for Mother from the Pralinieres, enterprising ladies that hawked the divine sweets from street carts and baskets. They bought rum and brandy for Father. From other vendors and "interesting characters" at the port, they purchased a book for Murielle, *Adventures of the Pincushion*, since she was learning to sew. There was a new iron pot for Estelle and baking pans for Christophe. They also stopped at the convent and made the yearly donation as Charles had asked. The Sisters were quite pleased and gave them a Bible to take back to their father.

However, the most exciting thing was a post from Cuba that was delivered to the apartment from Colonel Acosta. It had been slid under the front door while they were away. They put their packages down. Paul picked up the envelope and closed the door. It was addressed to their father. Paul looked at Jean Charles. "I'm going to open it. If it's important, maybe we can be of assistance while we are here in the city."

Jean Charles rubbed his chin and looked down. He looked back at Paul. "Well, I suppose you are correct. It might involve Genevieve, and"—he shrugged—"she's probably chosen me as a suitor. I am terribly sorry, Paul. You're a good man, truly, but you are too old for her."

Paul smiled and punched him in the shoulder. Jan Charles grimaced and grabbed his arm. "Not bad for an old man now, am I?" said Paul. "I am going to open this while you finish crying, poor baby. I am quite sure she'd prefer maturity to changing your diapers." Paul pulled the letter out and started to read.

Jean put his hands on his hips. "Out loud please, sir."

"Oh, sorry," Paul answered. He began to read.

December 1801

My dear friend,

It is with the utmost gravity that I impart this message to you. I do hope you and your family are well and in good spirits. Genevieve and I were so looking forward to a spring visit; however, I write to you now and beg you to consider an earlier arrival. As you well know, there have been regular uprisings in and around here for some time now. Genevieve and I barely escaped St. Domingue with our lives when we departed for Cuba at the beginning of the revolution. I understand Napoléon is to send troops soon.

I have been appointed a post at Baracoa on the coast to assist with securities while we await the completion of the fortress at Fuerte Matachin. It is a position that demands my full attention and does not afford me the opportunities necessary to see to Genevieve's safety and well-being. I have secured passage for her and her maid Carmen to New Orleans in early March. I know you to be an honorable man and a respectable parent. Surely you can understand my predicament.

I believe her arrival might very well be an advantageous one for both of our families, as she is considering your son as a suitor. Should this arrangement be successful, I would be very pleased to have your son trusted with the future of my only child.

I await your consideration and response.

Regards,
Col. Gabriel Acosta.

"Your son. Your son?" Jean Charles said quite loud. "Good God, man, which son?"

Paul shook his head. "Of course it's me, Jean. Please. You are too young. She is already two years older than you."

Jean Charles felt his anger rising up in him. He and Paul had never had to seriously deal with the business of being marriageable before. He spoke in an even tone. "She wants a planter, not a plunderer, dear brother. Really, Paul. You've seen her ways as well as I have. She must be kept, not corralled. She's not like our mother, you know. She won't help you tan hides and gut fish. She is all lace and silk and handmaids. Besides, is it not your desire to sail away from Greyfriars? What kind of life is that for her—or any woman, for that matter? You'd be home once a year to produce a child, then back to sea the next day. Do you really think Genevieve would consider that sort of life?" Paul was livid and threw a punch that landed on Jean Charles's right eye. Jean Charles answered, bloodying Paul's nose.

Paul put his hand up. "Parlay, brother, parlay!" Blood began running down onto his shirt. "We are fools."

Jean Charles started laughing. "Look at us. Women are trouble, I tell you. We'd better clean up. Mother will be furious when she sees what we've done to each other. She might gut us both."

Paul stared up at the ceiling, pinching his nose. He began to laugh. "Nice punch. I didn't know you had it in you. Good thing we've no swords here, or we might have run each other through." Paul stuffed a handkerchief up each nostril, and Jean Charles wet a small cloth, placed it over his eye, and then held it on by tying one of his stockings around his head. This made Paul laugh even harder. "You look like you're worthy of the dock life, matey. Sure you won't consider the high seas yourself?" Jean Charles smiled and shook his head. He poured them each a brandy. They held their glasses up. Paul spoke first. "To the lady Genevieve. How I long to be the orange blossom perfume she caresses herself with."

Charles smiled and said, "Good enough, brother. To the lady Genevieve. You may be satisfied as her perfume indeed, but I will do the caressing."

They smiled, clinked glasses, and drank. They would be heading home the next morning, and they had a lot of explaining to do.

Alexandrine watched Charles through the kitchen window as he sat out on the dock, just staring at the water. She grabbed a couple of cigars and headed out there. It was time. He turned slightly when he heard someone approaching. She handed him a lit cigar and then fired up her own. "We need to talk, Charles." He nodded and she continued. "You are holding this family hostage to a loss and to a memory. We do not deserve this. You have two sons, a daughter, and a granddaughter that need you to be alive for, and you behave as if we are dead too. Living your life does not mean you are forgetting Comfort's life. She would not want this for you, and you know it. I loved her too. She was a kind and beautiful woman and was worthy of grieving. But now we must go on." He did not move or respond. She was afraid maybe she had gone too far, but she was also his friend—and a very good friend at that. He looked up at her, his eyes full of tears. He threw the cigar in the bayou and held his arms out to her. She went to him and stood before him. He wrapped his arms around her hips and held her tightly as she cradled his head against her. And then he cried until he had nothing left.

Paul and Jean Charles decided to forgo staying at the Teal Bend apartment and traveled straight home, stopping only to relieve themselves, eat, and take care of the horses. One brother was to keep watch while the other rested. The fog was unpleasant, and the mosquitos bloodthirsty, but they were driven by the desire to share the letter with their parents as soon as possible. When they pulled up in the gate in the carriage, they were tired, sweaty, hungry, and relieved. They were always grateful when they made it home safely—as were their parents. Alexandrine had been on the stairs when she saw the carriage pull up. She smiled and thanked God her boys had returned from yet another long trip away. She always prayed the hardest when they were gone: two rosaries a night—one for Paul and one for Jean Charles. So far she felt her prayers were being heard and answered.

Paul jumped down from the coach and ran to his mother as she opened the door. He hugged her hard and kissed her on the cheek. "Where's Father?" he asked.

She thought his eyes looked different. There was a new life in them. "He is out back. Why don't you …"

Before she could get another word out, he was off and running. She put her hands on her hips and looked at Jean Charles, who was coming up to her with a hug and a kiss. "What kind of greeting was that?" She took a second look. "Oh my goodness, Jean. What happened to your eye?"

He smiled. "Mother, you are going to laugh when I tell you, but I really must unpack." He turned back toward the coach. "Don't worry about Paul either. His nose will heal just fine."

"Father, Father!" Paul yelled. He held up the envelope. "A letter from Colonel Acosta. Genevieve will be here soon!"

Charles could hear the lively spirit in his son's voice. He and Hubert were repairing damage to the henhouse caused by hungry possums. Charles remarked, "You know, we never really had these problems when Willie was here. I think she might have put a spell on them or something, but the possums stayed clear of our chickens most all the time. What is it, Paul?" Charles put his hammer down and walked toward his son.

"Genevieve, Father. She'll be here sooner than the summer. There is trouble with the uprisings in Saint-Domingue, and they are making preparations in Cuba." He handed the letter to his father. "I know we should have waited for you to open it, but …"

Charles smiled and stopped him. "I understand completely, Paul. I remember having that feeling myself when I was young. Let's go inside. Your mother will need to know what preparations are to be made."

They met Alexandrine and Jean Charles in the dining room. Alexandrine was taking a bite out of a praline. "Look, Charles. I am positively enamored of this. What a treat. Jean, get one for your father before I eat them all."

They laughed, and Jean handed Charles a praline and a bottle of brandy. "Paul and I thought you might need another bottle."

Charles took the gifts and looked at Alexandrine as he held the brandy bottle. She smiled and blushed. She knew he was remembering the night they spent with Comfort. "Well," Charles said, "if Jean will get us some glasses, we can read the letter, eat our pralines, and listen to the explanation as to why our sons look like they may have spent some time at the docks." Paul put his hand on his nose as Jean put his on his black-and-blue eye. Some of the swelling had gone down, but he wore the discolored skin like a badge.

The brandy was mellowing, but it did not detract from the seriousness of the request from Gabriel. It was the beginning of January, but March would come soon enough. After the unpacking and cleaning up, the family talked at supper about the upcoming events. Alexandrine was excited to have Genevieve back—especially now, since her intentions regarding a suitor were noted in the letter. Unfortunately that intention was not specific as to which young man she was considering. Although Paul and Jean Charles were laughing and joking about who had bested whom, referring to the black eye and the busted nose, their mother knew what kind of controversies might arise between the brothers when a choice was made.

Through January and February the Danetrees readied the house for Genevieve and Carmen's arrival. Charles had sent his reply to Gabriel, and the Danetrees prayed for his safety in Cuba and his daughter's safety on her journey. Alexandrine decided that Charles and Paul would go to New Orleans to get the ladies, which angered Jean Charles, but he did not go against his mother. Genevieve would have the back bedroom, along with the smaller room next to it for Carmen. To avoid any uncomfortable situations between Paul and Jean Charles, Alexandrine made arrangements for the boys to stay the nights with their Broussard grandparents, Sylvie and Jean.

Genevieve and Carmen arrived safely in New Orleans, but Genevieve was distraught with her father left behind. Charles did everything he could to reassure her that as soon as things calmed down in the islands her father would be joining them at Greyfriars. He could also tell from the way she spoke to Paul that he was the suitor she sought to claim. Jean Charles would just have to understand and wait for the woman that was right for him. It was a rough journey home. They left with two coaches, one of which was just for her trunks and bags. They stayed in Teal Bend for one night to refresh the horses and themselves, and they then headed home. It rained off and on, but the sun was shining when they arrived at Greyfriars.

Once everything was unpacked and everyone was settled in, there was a light supper before Paul and Jean Charles left for the night. Alexandrine watched how Paul doted on Genevieve and how Jean Charles tried to remain cordial. Her heart hurt for her youngest. The lessons of love are sometimes the most ruthless of all in one's life. She and Charles would have to keep him occupied with the plantation while things unfolded with Paul and Genevieve.

Genevieve adjusted quickly to life at Greyfriars. She even got Paul to go to mass every month in Teal Bend at Saint Catherine's. Teal Bend shared Father LeBlanc with several other parishes. Alexandrine and Charles had been less successful in that regard and were happy to see Paul focusing on something other than running off and joining the American Navy. He seemed to know what he wanted, as did Genevieve. Alexandrine and Sylvie made sure to take turns chaperoning their outings. Picnics, walks, dining—everything was covered. Alexandrine felt as if she had a daughter and wanted things to be different for Genevieve rather than her having to live with the decisions and concessions she had made. She didn't blame Charles for anything—just the times. There were moments when she thought she could have been more assertive with the running of the plantation, but something else always came up. She and Charles did love each other in their way and still enjoyed each other's company. She was still besting him at chess, and he didn't complain as much about her cigar breath anymore. And as much as she missed Comfort, she was glad she didn't have to share him any longer.

Genevieve received a letter from her father in August. There was another for Charles as well. She was so happy to know he was still alive. His words to her were loving and careful with a promise that he would be there soon. His words to Charles were realistic and pessimistic, stating he would be there before the fall season. He wanted to know how Genevieve and Paul were getting along and whether there would be something to celebrate soon. He was sending money to support her and another trunk of her items from the house. There were things he shared with Charles that he absolutely did not want his daughter to know. The house was gone. It had been burned down in the night. The culprit was unknown. He had managed to save a small casket of her mother's jewelry. She would find it in the trunk. The fort was almost finished. He was sure he would be relieved of his position there when it was complete. The French were fleeing Saint-Domingue for Cuba, but many more lay dead from the violence of the uprisings. Charles read aloud.

July 1802

Toussaint L'Ouverture has been arrested, and I am sure he will never see his soil again, but I know we will see a new country arise out of the turmoil. I have also heard your Napoléon is quite frustrated and seeking to raise funds to war against England and has not a strong enough navy to secure French interests in the Louisiana Territory. Be wary, my friend. Politics are shifting in all classes, even on these islands. But that is the way of the world, is it not? Though I serve the Spanish crown, live on Cuban land, and secure business with the French and Americans, I must say the causes addressed by the slave revolts must not go unnoticed. Do we not all want freedom? Do we not all search for a better life?

Please forgive my ramblings, Charles. I am weary these days, and I miss my only child. I long to see her smile. She looks so much like her mother. Please give my regards to your family. Your generosity and kindness remain in my heart.

Your friend,
Gabriel

Charles put the letter down on his desk and looked out of the study window. He understood Gabriel's concerns and sympathized with his position on the causes of the revolt, but he owned slaves, as had his father before him. He had also learned from his father to not mistreat anyone regardless of his or her position, but he also knew any plantation could not run without a strong, disciplined workforce. He had never even considered a voluntary workforce for the plantation. Enslaved labor had

119

been the way for so long he just accepted it. He had learned much with the revolts and rulings from New Orleans regarding the rights of slaves, and he now wondered if they were going to face another uprising as a residual effect of what was happening in the islands. He would have to set up more meetings with his overseers and slave representatives to better gauge where Greyfriars stood.

His next concern was Genevieve. Of course he would honor Gabriel's confidence. He understood what it felt like to have to keep things from your children for their own good. He decided to write back right away to let Gabriel know Genevieve was happy with Paul and doing well. He was sure she would have a swift response for her father as well, to be delivered as soon as possible. Charles had a feeling time was of the essence.

August was ending, and the beginning of the burning time was upon the sugar planters. Paul knew Genevieve was no stranger to the process. Her father had dabbled in planting in Cuba, but this would be her first experience in Louisiana, and the smell and smoke of burning cane wasn't the most pleasant thing for everyone—especially for a lady of her sensitivities. His brother had been right about what she expected from those around her. It was apparent she was somewhat spoiled and used to getting her way. But when she smiled and batted her eyes at him, something inside of him changed and he felt blissfully subservient. He looked forward to Senor Acosta's visit so he could ask his permission to make sure she continued to be treated in the manner she was accustomed to. Until then, he would get more involved with the plantation and maybe have another house built close to Greyfriars so that she could have her own home as Mrs. Paul Jean Danetree. When the time was right he would seek her father's blessing.

Baracoa, Cuba, 1802

Gabriel Acosta stood outside by the cannon wall overlooking the bay. It was warm, with a slight breeze. He could see small fires here and there in the distance and hear his own men, not too far away, talking and laughing. He looked up at the moon, which was full and bright, and he smiled to think Genevieve might be doing the same thing. He had received Charles's letter and knew that if anything happened to him, she would be well taken care of and loved. He wrote back, giving his permission for Charles to speak for him should anything prevent him from doing so in person. In another month, he would be sailing to Louisiana and hopefully to a wedding. He was sure of it. In Genevieve's letter, she had received her mother's jewels and ivory mantilla—the one her mother had worn when she married Gabriel. She wrote it would be perfect with the Spanish lace shawl from her *abuela* Victoria Acosta, Gabriel's mother. That was the entire clue he needed. She also asked for another bottle of her favorite orange blossom perfume. He would bring her a case. Her letters felt like a blessing and gave him peace when he needed to look away from the seriousness of the times. He would not miss these tribulations. He smiled once more at the moon, and for a second he thought he saw his wife's face. He walked away and turned in for the night.

Greyfriars, September 1802

It was a warm September day on the bayou. Although the burning of the cane was just over at Greyfriars, the scent of burned sugar was still prevalent. Genevieve complained that she would never get used to the smell, but Paul pacified her repeating it was only for a short time each year. Charles and Alexandrine had asked for Paul and Genevieve in the study. Paul was nervous and wondered if he had done something inappropriate with or around Genevieve. His fears were quickly squelched when Charles read the portion of Gabriel's letter regarding permission to marry. He left out the part "if something should happen to me."

They blushed and smiled. Paul let it be known that he did have intentions to marry her but would prefer to wait until her father was present, and this seemed to make Genevieve extremely happy. She was beaming. Alexandrine could tell the year 1803 was going to be a big year at Greyfriars. There was a wedding to plan. She stood up. "My dear girl." She reached out to Genevieve, who also stood and took her hands,

"It would be a pleasure to call you daughter and have you as a part of this family. In some ways I feel you are already a part of us. I have never seen my son this attentive or this happy. I must say I am wholeheartedly pleased and hope the two of you find much happiness in your plans and decisions." She hugged her. "If there is anything you need, Genevieve, please let me know. I am always there for you, my sweet girl."

Genevieve had tears in her eyes. "Please, Madame, then I would like you to call me Genny, as my father does—and you too Paul."

She looked at him quickly and then glanced back to Alexandrine, who replied, "Genny it is. I am sure your dear mother is smiling from heaven at this time. You will make a lovely bride. And please call me Mother Danetree if you like. I think we are quite past the 'madame' formality now. We can have Father LeBlanc perform the ceremony right here at Greyfriars." She saw an uncomfortable look overtake Genny's eyes. *Ah*, she thought, *I know what she is thinking*. "We will have a proper ceremony at Saint Catherine's in Teal Bend in the spring, and then another here, but I promise it will be done long before the cane burns in the fall." Alexandrine could see the relief on Genny's face. *Mission accomplished*. She hugged her son. "You are a good man, Paul, and will make a wonderful husband and father. I am proud of you."

Charles shook his son's hand and hugged his daughter-in-law to be. Jean Charles had accepted the choices made and wished them every happiness as well. Now they would wait for Gabriel.

Genny loved her new family and felt quite at home at Greyfriars. The only things that bothered her occasionally were how little Murielle was allowed the run of the house, and the familiarity with which Estelle was treated. Although Estelle and Murielle were not part of the household staff at Greyfriars, Genny felt it odd that they were treated as family. Carmen certainly knew her place, and Genny had never had to remind her. When she and Paul were married, and if they were to someday run Greyfriars, things would have to change. She was not ungrateful for the hospitality, she just had a difficult time with the household's relationship dynamics. She had grown up with very clear statuses and boundaries. Things were very different here.

Baracoa, Cuba

Gabriel Acosta boarded the ship that would take him from his past to his future. It was a seasoned barquentine named *El Destino*. He never expected to see Spain again, but he hadn't thought he would ever leave Cuba and his wife's gravesite. He put a red rose on her grave before he left. He knew she was not there in the ground, because he carried her in his heart everywhere he went, but leaving the rose was something physical he could do in her memory. Now he would live in Louisiana, watch his daughter get married, and teach his grandchildren about the things he knew and had done and seen in his life. And he would tell them stories of their beautiful grandmother and how she was with the angels and would always watch over them.

He had wanted to leave in September but did not finish his business until early October. He normally did not like to sail this late in the season, but it could not be helped. He prayed for calm seas and fair winds. The weather started out friendly enough, and the first night he slept very soundly with the rocking of the boat. The next day he spent a bit of time on the deck, courtesy of the captain. The second night produced a different result. He was awakened by someone banging on his door. The boat was rocking violently and he could smell smoke. He had slept in his clothes, so he slipped into his shoes and put his coat on and then opened the door and looked around. He heard more yelling. It seemed to come from everywhere. He ran up top and saw the squall they were surrounded by. He had seen these same skies from the safety of the fort and had known people who perished during storms like this, but he also knew those who had survived. He thought of Genevieve as he rushed around with others, trying to help where he could. He could hear them yelling about the "fire in the galley" and an "oil lamp." Heavy smoke was pouring through every opening in the deck. He didn't know what was worse—the storm that looked like it could tear them apart or the fire that would certainly do the job if it could not be contained. He heard an explosion then felt something heavy hit him from behind knocking him down. He was having a hard time breathing. He saw one of the crew pointing at him, and then another running at him with a bucket. The man slipped just as he got to him when the ship pitched, and he watched him slide and hit the side. He tried to move but could not get back up. Everything was happening so fast. Gabriel started to feel as though he were moving in slow motion as he tried to raise himself up. He felt heat upon him at the back of his head. He tried to reach back and knew something was very wrong.

He could feel his coat was on fire, and now his sleeves were engulfed. He could see the flames. He tried to get the coat off, but the fire was already burning through it and onto his skin. He screamed and tried to roll over onto the wet deck, where water was splashing and spraying from the high waves. He could feel the cold water on his skin and smell the terrible odor of burning flesh. Then he passed out.

When he opened his eyes, he saw his father, Antonio, standing over him next to his mother, who was crying. He reached over to touch his mother's dress. "Please do not cry, Madre. I am fine. Why do you cry?" His parents stood aside, and his angel sat on the bed and stroked his head. He could hear her say, "My darling Gabriel, I will take care of you now." It was his Genevieve. But that was impossible. She was dead. They were all dead.

He could hear men's voices.

"He's in a bad way, sir."

"He won't make the next sunset, Captain. He's burned too badly."

Fire. Fire! It was coming back to him. He started to feel pain—true, deep, excruciating pain—everywhere. He knew he was on his stomach. His wife knelt by the side of the bed until he could see her face. She smiled and kissed his lips, and peace filled him—peace and light. The pain was gone. And so was he.

Chapter 8

To Walk in Another's Shoes

Charles, Paul, Genevieve, and Carmen were settled in New Orleans at the apartment when a messenger arrived to let them know *El Destino* had limped into port. It had been in a storm and had suffered fire damage but had managed to make it through. There was no word as to loss of life or cargo. Paul could see the tears in Genevieve's eyes and put his arms around her. "It is all right, my darling." He kissed her forehead. "I am sure your father is well. Maybe it would be best if Father and I went to get him and bring him here."

She shook her head and took a deep breath. "No. I must go. He has always been strong for me. What kind of daughter would I be if I could not be strong for him. I will go." She turned to Carmen. "You will remain here and ready Father's room."

Carmen smiled and nodded. "*Si*, Miss Genny."

The greeting party left for the port.

When they arrived there, it was alive with the sounds of hawkers wanting to trade or sell anything one could possibly seek from the rest of the known world. The docks bustled with men moving things on and off ships. The sound of water lapping the sides and bottoms of the boats was ever present, as were the cries of sea birds circling for edible gifts from anybody willing to give them up.

A shoeless, skinny, ragged brown boy approached them at their coach. Genevieve stepped closer to Paul and took his arm. The boy looked up at Charles, holding his hand out. "Find your ship, monsieur? Help you find your ship?"

Charles looked down at him and smiled. "I'll tell you what, my good little man. I'll give you a whole doubloon if you find *El Destino* and help us with the trunks."

The boy's eyes grew very wide, as did his smile. "Oh, *oui* and *si*, monsieur. They call me Garcon. I will be your man today, yes?"

"Yes," said Charles. Now run along, Garcon." Garcon nodded and took off.

Paul looked at his father. "Really, Father, a whole doubloon? I could have easily found the ship for nothing."

Charles smiled again. "Do you remember the soft, warm bed you put your shoes under when you were his age?"

Paul looked at Genny and then back to Charles and shrugged. "Of course I do. But what has this to do with …" He stopped and raised his eyebrows. "Ah. I see what you are getting at. I did not think of these things."

"Exactly, my son," Charles said. "This child may have never had a bed or the shoes to put under it. Tonight he shall have both."

Genevieve looked at her future father-in-law. He was certainly a kind and generous man, much like her father. She was sure they would grow to be great friends.

Several minutes had passed when Garcon came running back. He stopped, putting his hands on his knees, trying to catch his breath and slapping a mosquito on his cheek. "Monsieur, the burned ship is third from the last. They are unloading now. Do you want to follow me in your coach?"

Charles went over to the coach and held the door open. "You will ride with us, Garcon."

Garcon looked from the coach to Charles's face. "Oh no, monsieur. That would not be right. I will walk."

"No Garcon, you will ride. Now in with you. We are wasting time."

Garcon jumped up into the carriage. Charles looked at Paul, who offered his arm to Genny to help her up, but she hesitated and whispered something in his ear.

He looked at his father. "Genny would like to walk, Father. We will meet you there."

Charles looked at her. "Are you sure, my dear? These docks and ports can be very rough, you know. They're certainly not the kind of place a proper young lady should be exposed to for too long anyway."

She smiled. "Thank you, but Paul will keep me safe, I know." Charles jumped into the coach and hit the roof twice, and they rode away. Genny held her parasol over her head and yanked on Paul's arm. "Come along, Paul. We've quite the walk ahead."

He shrugged and said, "We could have ridden. Why did you want to walk?" Her face looked as if she were taking her time, trying to calculate what she was going to say. She looked up at him. "How do I say this … I am not accustomed to your familiarities here with servants or those who serve. And the child was so filthy, Paul. I am not unaware of the unfortunate situations that befall the underclass, but to let him ride alongside us in such a state! Please don't think ill of me or judge me harshly. These things will take time, Paul." She smiled and batted her eyes.

"Of course, Genny," he answered. "It will take time. I understand." They continued their walk to the ship, filling in the minutes with civil conversation. Paul was seeing something in her he wasn't quite sure he found acceptable, but that would all change once she became more comfortable in the Danetree world.

When Charles got to the ship, he could clearly see where the fire had done its damage. The crew looked ragged and weary as they unloaded the last of the cargo. Anxious family, friends, and agents were among those milling. He noticed a long, sealed wooden box being carried carefully down the gangplank by four men. He watched as they placed it gently on the dock and saluted it. One stayed behind while the others returned up the plank to the ship. Charles looked around for Gabriel. When he thought he had waited long enough, he approached the young man by the box. He asked, "Could you please tell me if all passengers have left the ship?" The young man nodded. Charles asked, "I am waiting for Colonel Gabriel Acosta of Cuba. Have you knowledge of him?"

The crewman looked as if he wanted to say something but changed his mind. "Monsieur, if you will kindly remain here, I will get the captain to speak with you."

Charles nodded. He stood there with Garcon and slipped a doubloon into his small, rough hand. The crewman returned with the captain. The captain removed his hat and smoothed his hair back. He gave a slight bow to Charles. "Monsieur, I am Captain Alfonso Sandoval. My man tells me you have questions about a passenger?"

Charles nodded. "Yes, captain. My name is Charles Danetree. I am here to meet Colonel Gabriel Acosta. His daughter is also here, but I have not seen him leave the ship yet."

The captain looked down at the box and then at Charles. "Oh, Monsieur Danetree, this is a meeting indeed. We faced a storm soon after leaving Cuba. The winds were terrible, monsieur, and the water rough. We are a seasoned crew, but there are always challenges. You see, there was also a fire. It started in the galley when the ship pitched and a large lamp smashed and spread a fire with the oil. We were unable to stop the fire from reaching through the deck and up the mast. Even with the waves splashing over the sides, the fire was quicker."

Charles put his hand up. "Captain, I am grateful your ship survived this voyage, but please, what has happened to my friend?"

The captain looked at the box. "Colonel Acosta ran out onto the deck just as a burning sail fell from the mast and landed at his back, setting his coat on fire. I think he must have been in shock. One of my men tried to get to him but slipped and fell before he could douse him with water. The colonel was badly burned and in great pain. We kept him on his stomach, but his back was a terrible sight, monsieur. There was nothing we could do but give him rum to keep him calm. At the end he was talking to someone named Genevieve, but there was no one there. He smiled and passed quietly. I am so sorry, monsieur. We have his trunks and property accounted for and ready to claim. He will need to be buried quickly, I am afraid. We placed his body in all the salt we had left and charcoal ash from the burned timber."

Charles was in shock himself upon hearing the terrible news about his friend. He felt sick. He turned just in time to see Paul and Genevieve walking up. She was laughing and smiling. *This is too much*, he thought. *Poor child. She was so devoted to her father, and he to her.*

Genevieve looked at Charles's face, then to the captain, and then to the box. She felt something was not right. Her heart started to beat faster. "Has he come down yet? Where is my father?" When she felt they took too long to answer, she grabbed Charles's arm. "Where is my papa, Monsieur Charles? Where is he?"

Charles could hear the panic in her voice. There was not going to be an easy way to handle this. "My darling girl, your father … There was an accident—a fire …"

Before he could get another word out, she screamed, "No! No! Where is my father? Bring him to me now. Do you hear?" She looked at the captain.

He had seen many terrible things in his line of work, but he also had a daughter, and his heart was breaking for this girl. "Senorita Acosta, I am sorry. He was a good and brave man."

She swung around to face Paul. Her mouth began to move, but nothing was coming out. Paul watched as her eyes rolled back into her head, and he caught her as she fainted.

When Genevieve awoke, Carmen was sitting on the bed, wiping her face with a moist towel. Her eyes grew large, and she shot up in bed screaming. "My father. Where is my father?" She began to cry. Paul moved Carmen from the bed and took her place, holding Genevieve tightly and rocking back and forth.

Charles brought in a glass of rum. "Here, Paul, she needs to drink this."

Paul stopped and took the drink and put the glass up to Genny's mouth. She drank in between sobs. Paul was heartbroken to see her so distraught. "Oh, my Genny. I am so sorry. We will leave for home tomorrow. You will be home soon. Just try to sleep." She nodded and lay back. She turned away from him, and he covered her with the quilt. Charles motioned for Paul to join him outside and told Carmen to stay next to her. Paul got up and followed his father outside of the apartment.

Charles could see the distress in his son's eyes. He put his hand on Paul's shoulder. "There is no easy way for this situation, my son. She will be hysterical for some time. Such a terrible tragedy today. We can only do so much for her. But you have been remarkable with her. I can tell she loves you. Maybe a quicker marriage might be in order. We will discuss this with your mother when we return home, yes?"

Paul tried to smile. "Yes, Father. I feel so helpless. I want to fix all of this."

Charles nodded. "I know exactly how you feel, dear boy. Gabriel is with God—I am sure of it—and his beloved Genevieve. The rest of us are left earthbound to grieve and move on. It can all seem so unfair, I know. Let us sleep well tonight. I must make arrangements for his body to be buried here in New Orleans, hopefully tomorrow. The body will be decomposing fast now. It will not be safe to transport it all the way to Greyfriars. I will go to the Ursulines tomorrow for guidance. Carmen will stay with Genny tonight. We are next door should she need anything."

Charles went back out to find Garcon sitting with his back to the wrought-iron fence. Garcon jumped up and smiled when he saw Charles. "Monsieur, look," he said excitedly as he pointed down to his feet. Charles saw a shiny pair of shoes at the end of two little brown legs.

"Well, well," he said. "You are quite the gentleman now, aren't you? Tell me, Garcon—is that your name? Should you not be home with your mother and father at this time of night?"

Garcon looked down and then back to Charles, smiling. "My mother is sleeping with the angels, but she told me my father was the king of Spain. Her name is Angelina. I do not remember my real name anymore. She said I should not tell anyone, though, because the French king would have my head. I am called Garcon by most everyone when they call for me to help them find their ships, monsieur. You are French, yes?"

"Yes," Charles answered. "Well, French and English."

Garcon looked thoughtful and then asked, "Then why have you been so kind to me? Are you going to take my head now that you know who I am?"

Charles smiled and shook his head. "I will tell you what, boy. From now on, I will call you Gabriel Garcon. It seems a fitting name for someone so honest and hardworking. How old are you?"

He held up both hands, fingers splayed. "Ten years now, I think. I like that name, monsieur, but isn't that the name of the crying lady's father in the box?" He frowned.

Charles opened up the gate to invite him in. They sat at the patio table. Charles lit an oil lamp. "Yes, it is her father's name. He was a great man—a colonel, you know. Many men respected him, and he was beloved by his family. Gabriel is a very honorable name."

The boy nodded and extended his hand. Charles reached out and shook it. "Then I am Gabriel Garcon for always. Are you sure the French king will not find out?"

Charles laughed. "No, my little friend. I will never tell him where you are. In fact, I have a business proposition for you. Do you like searching for ships?"

Gabriel looked down. "Not really, monsieur. It is a hard life. There are other boys working at the same thing, and sometimes there is not enough to eat, so we have fight with the sea birds to steal fish or hide in the alleys waiting for scraps from the rich people that throw away their food. Sometimes the good Sisters feed us. I will have to hide my shoes so the other boys do not steal them. Just last week one boy stabbed another over a coat. He died in the alley and lay there until the soldiers came and took his body. We followed them. They tied rocks to his body and threw him in the water. They did not put him in the ground. He will never find his angels now."

Charles tried to compose himself. His heart was breaking for this boy and others like him. He couldn't help them all, but he could help this one. He would bring him home to Estelle and Christophe. "I know a family, Gabriel, which may need a good helper. I believe you may be just the right gentleman for the job. Do you think you could leave the city? I mean, you would have to sleep in a bed at night, have a good breakfast in the morning, and then work during the day. Is that something you could do?"

Gabriel looked down at his shoes and then to Charles. "Yes, monsieur. I am very good at finding things, and I am a very fast runner, and I do not each much. I would only need a small bed, and I can be very quiet."

Charles shook his little hand again. "Then Gabriel Garcon, you are now in my employment. Leave your shoes here and run to say good-bye to your friends, but do not tell them you have a new position. They might be jealous, you know. Be back here first thing in the morning. Do you understand? We will get you proper clothing and a bath, and then we will travel to your new job."

Gabriel took off his shoes and handed them to Charles and sped out of the gate, and he then stopped and turned around. He ran back to Charles and hugged his arm tightly, then he was gone. Charles took out his handkerchief and dabbed his eyes. He went upstairs and told Paul of his plans for the young man.

The next morning, Gabriel was there at the gate. Charles had sent Paul to get two sets of clothing, complete with stockings, breeches, shirts, coats, and underclothing. He had Carmen draw a bath for Gabriel. He didn't care too much for the soap, but he did as he was told. It took quite some time for Carmen to get the soap out of his coarse matted hair then Charles took him to a barber for a haircut. Although he felt silly and itchy in stockings but said not a word. He was Gabriel Garcon now and a proper young man. He would do whatever Monsieur Danetree would have him do.

A quick funeral and burial were held at St. Louis Cemetery No. 1, with a rosary being carried out at the convent. Genevieve let Paul guide her through everything. She was weak and overcome with grief. She didn't even notice the new passenger in their coach. She barely ate, and she didn't speak until they returned to Greyfriars two days later. Like a fragile porcelain doll, she was treated gingerly and with great tenderness.

Charles introduced Gabriel to the household and then met with Estelle and Christophe. They determined they would put Gabriel up in a small room in the barn where he could learn to look after the horses and assist Christophe at the market. Murielle wasn't sure about him, but having someone her own age at the cottage became a welcome arrangement. Gabriel learned fast and had a very pleasant manner and spirit about him. He even gained weight with regular meals. After talking to Charles, Gabriel was decided he would celebrate his birthday in October because that was when he first met Charles and his young life changed.

After two weeks, Alexandrine noticed Genevieve had not dined with the family once since she had returned, so she decided to talk to her privately. She brought tea to her room and found her in the rocking chair, looking out of the window. "Genny, would you like tea?" she asked softly. "I thought we could talk also." Genevieve nodded. Alexandrine poured her a cup and took the chair next to her. "There is nothing anyone can say or do to bring your father back, my darling. He is your angel now. Please trust what I say. He will watch over you forever. I believe that, and you should too. You know Paul loves you so much. He is hurting with you and wants to take care of you, but he is afraid you are not thinking of him anymore. Please speak to him, Genny. He is there for you, child." Alexandrine put her cup down and put her hand on Genevieve's arm. "Look at me, Genny."

Genevieve turned toward Alexandrine, her eyes full of tears. "What do I do now, Mother Danetree? What kind of wife could I possibly be now? I feel like the whole world has stopped."

Alexandrine pursed her lips. "Your whole world did stop, my dear. It stopped the moment you realized your father was gone. But now a new world is before you, as is a new family. We will always be here for you. You are not alone. Now I will send Carmen in to help you with your clothes and hair. You will join us for dinner, and afterward you and Paul can take a nice walk and maybe talk about your plans, yes?"

Genevieve managed a small smile. "Yes. You are right. I do love Paul, and you all are my new family. I will try. I promise."

Alexandrine kissed her on the cheek and left. Carmen entered, and Genevieve got up and gave her a tight hug. She knew Carmen grieved as well. "Please, Carmen. Help me with my hair and dress."

Carmen smiled. "It will be my pleasure."

Anne had prepared a special midday meal for the family. Genevieve sat next to Paul and even made light conversation. The healing was beginning. Afterward, she and Paul took a nice walk together and talked about moving the wedding up to November instead of the spring. Charles and Alexandrine were overjoyed. It was going to be a busy fall in the

Danetree household. Alexandrine arranged for Estelle and Christophe to provide a splendid buttery wedding cake rich with plump currants and blanched almonds, nutmeg, and brandied lemon and orange peels. Greyfriars was filled with the scents of pine and baked goods and Genevieve's favorite orange blossom scent. She wore her grandmother's Spanish lace shawl and the ivory mantilla to help secure her upswept long black hair. She decided it would be a good omen if they could wear her parents' wedding rings, and Paul agreed. They fit perfectly, and she knew this was meant to be. Instead of taking the front bedroom suite as the newlywed Danetrees had done before, Paul announced that they would stay in the back bedroom until their house was completed. There were tears too. The absence of Gabriel Acosta weighed heavily on Genevieve. It was a bittersweet celebration.

She was soon exhausted and went to sleep quickly. Paul lay next to her for the first time. His desire for her was strong, but he did not have the heart to wake her. She looked like an angel in her sleep. He watched her until he fell asleep himself. Desire would be but a dream tonight.

Two weeks later, Paul was in Charles's study. "Father, I need to talk to you about something, but you cannot talk to Genny about it—*or* Mother."

Charles frowned. "Is something wrong, Paul?"

Paul looked extremely uncomfortable. He fidgeted for a minute before speaking. "When you and Mother got married, how did 'things' go in the beginning?"

At first Charles was unsure about what Paul was asking. Then it sank in. "Oh. Yes … well …" There was no way he could tell his son the truth about their arrangement. "It was very nice. We were nervous, it was awkward of course, but we soon got over that. I know this must be frustrating for you, but give her some time. This has been a traumatic time for her. She will come around. Just give her the Danetree charm you know."

Charles winked, and Paul laughed. "Of course, the charm. Well, this was a good talk, Father. I did promise her we would go to New Orleans in the spring to stay for a while, and she can visit her father's grave then.

She also wants to stop in Teal Bend and have our marriage blessed at St. Catherine's."

"Yes. I remember her talking to Alexandrine about a church wedding." Charles said. "It is thoughtful of you to consider that. That might be the key to her embracing you as her husband in name and spirit. I know we only attend Mass once a month, but that does not mean we do not pray daily, and sometimes hourly, to God and thank him for our blessings. On another note, until then might I suggest you take matters into your own hands?" Charles stared at him.

Paul stared back and then blushed. "Oh. My. I am slow to wit today. I have house plans to look over with Genny. I will see you later." He got up and left.

Charles smiled as the door closed. He wished he could fix things, but the best teachers in these matters were time and patience.

That Christmas the Danetree bonfire blazed with new life. Paul noticed Jean Charles was civil but kept his distance from Genevieve. However, he did disappear every now and then toward the henhouse with Carmen. They were joined by members of the Berwick and O'Brien families and Christophe, Estelle, Murielle, and Gabriel too. Charles could not have been happier. He thought of Marc and Cecile in Paris. He had not heard from them for some time, and the years were going by quicker as they all got older. He decided to write very soon.

In April of 1803, Paul followed through with his promise to Genny with a three-week stay in New Orleans. She was ecstatic until he asked her if it might be just the two of them, with Carmen staying at Greyfriars. She cried and called him cruel. "Who will do my hair and help me dress and carry my purchases when we shop! Oh, Paul!" She flung herself across her bed and cried into her pillow.

He put his hands on his hips and looked at her backside. Normally the sight of her derriere aroused him. At this moment all he wanted to do was apply a sturdy switch to this childish tantrum. But of course he relented. She kept him in a constant state of guessing her moods. They had not even consummated their marriage. She let him kiss her now and then, but the matrimonial bliss he thought he would experience was not there. He was too ashamed to speak to his father again and suffered in silence. Princess Genevieve was proving Jean Charles's preliminary observations correct. Still, he loved her and hoped the church's blessing on their union would lead her to accept him fully as her husband.

On the first leg of their trip, Paul noticed several new clearings for settlements between Petit Coeur and Teal Bend. They had been fairly isolated for so long he was glad to see more families moving in. This would eventually lead to more businesses bringing the outside world closer to Greyfriars. He was not unhappy about that.

They stayed the night in Teal Bend then went to St. Catherine's the next morning. Genevieve had her shawl and mantilla on when Father LeBlanc blessed their marriage in the church. They took the paperwork to record in the city. Paul noticed a very different wife after the ceremony. She clung to him and kissed him on the cheek and lips often. She had not been so affectionate until now. His anticipation of how this might translate to the evening was intense, but he still wanted to play it safe. They arrived in New Orleans later in the day and set up at the apartment. While Genny and Carmen got settled in, Paul went to the bank, stopped by the convent to make a donation, and picked up flowers for Genevieve to bring to her father's grave. He took in the sights and sounds of the port. He could not explain to Genny how his heart felt when he saw the ships and water. The exotic smells of spices and cooked meat filled his nose as they wafted in and around the port. But one also had to accept the other odors, such as mud, garbage, and horse manure. It was so different in the city, but he liked the life. He felt more alive in the city near the water.

After the graveside visit, they decided to take a walk. She held tightly to his arm, a parasol in the other hand. "Paul, how would you feel about living here in New Orleans? I was born here, you know. We moved away when I was quite young, but I have always preferred the city life. We could hire a few more servants to help Carmen. I know you love your home, and I would not ask you to sacrifice them for me, but would you please consider it?"

He was surprised that she would want to live here in New Orleans. She was so finicky. The atmosphere was very fast paced and ever changing. She would not be as protected here as she was at Greyfriars. It seemed that every time she wanted something, she would cling to his arm, soften her voice and dive deep into him with those beautiful grey eyes, and he could not resist. "I suppose we could talk to Father about living here at the apartment while we make a home for ourselves. It may take some time, you know. I do like being close to the open water. But I am sure there will be no relief from the noise, gnats, and mosquitoes. Are you sure you could tolerate the city smells? Burning is once or twice a year, but here it could be somewhat unpleasant every day of the year. Madame Danetree I cannot believe you would choose marsh and manure over burning sugar and bayous."

She made a face at him then stuck her tongue out. They both laughed and walked arm in arm to the apartment. Paul had arranged for Carmen to prepare a light supper for them. He wanted to surprise her. For him this was going to be the honeymoon they should have had in November. They ate lightly and turned in for the evening. Carmen went to a separate one-bedroom apartment Charles had purchased the year before. Paul was very nervous, but brandy with supper helped to take the edge off. They got into bed, and she kissed him. He kissed her back, and all the time he had spent waiting for this moment culminated into a quick shudder and a moan. Genevieve pulled away. "Oh Paul, are you all right, my love? Have I hurt you?"

He was embarrassed and did not know what to tell her, so he told her the truth. She laughed, but he did not find it to be humorous. "It will be all right, darling. Carmen told me about this thing that men sometimes do when they are anxious. I'll turn my head, and you can clean yourself up then get back into bed. Carmen said it does not take long for a man to be ready again. That is, unless he has had too much to drink or the night is too hot, and we have neither of those things to deal with, do we?" She got out of bed and took her nightdress off. She still had her eyes closed, and he had to laugh as she felt around the bed for the quilt.

"Open your eyes, Genny. If you fall and hurt yourself, we may have to wait even longer to consummate our marriage. She opened her eyes and started to laugh too. "I am sorry, Paul, but I am nervous. I laugh when I am nervous. Have I been too cruel a wife to you?"

He got into bed, and she followed suit. He pulled her close, kissed her neck and ears, and then moved down to her breasts. They were soft and warm. *Surely this must be what heaven is like*, he thought. His father had explained a few things to him about pleasing a woman, but he wanted to find out what Genny wanted, so he took his time. He found out pretty quickly, once he was hard again, that rolling on top of her and fumbling to put himself inside of her was not as easy as he had thought it would be. She was breathing heavily, and he watched her chest rise and fall. She was moaning, but he could not manage to position himself just right. He grew more frustrated, and then he felt her hand move toward his member. She drew her knees further up and said, "*Now!*" He plunged forward, it went in, and she cried out. He began to grind into her. When he popped off and she tried to catch her breath, he suddenly realized that this had been worth waiting for. She had been worth waiting for.

He raised himself off of her and held her. "Are you all right, Genny? Was I too rough for you?"

She turned toward him. "I did not think it would hurt as much as it did. I feel so tingly down there, Paul. Do you think everyone feels this way? Should we do it again?"

He smiled and kissed her. "I will make it all better." He had the urge to kiss her down there. He ran his hand over her stomach and lightly over the hair below her navel. She began to moan again as he kissed each breast and kissed down her belly until he reached her nether lips. He wanted to taste her and flicked his tongue over the little fleshy throbbing bud in her hair. It was salty and musky. He felt her hand on his head, pushing him deeper into her. His tongue took over as she moaned louder. He felt her thighs begin to shake, and then she grew rigid. He heard her take a very deep breath, and then there was silence for a second until she let out a sound he had never heard before. He went faster until she slapped his head away and turned away from him, still shaking.

"Genny?" he said softly. "Genny, are you all right?"

He sat there for a minute, wiping his face and mouth with his shirt, waiting for her to answer. He was not prepared for the next sound he heard. She began to snore. She had gone to sleep, just like that. He didn't know if that was a compliment or an insult. He covered her with the quilt and then moved up behind her and held her. This was the best night of his life. They would live here in this city and make love, make children, and make a life for themselves. New Orleans was his miracle city now, and the whole world lay before them.

Chapter 9

When Blood Is Thicker than Water

1803

Alexandrine was not happy that Paul and Genny had decided to live in New Orleans. Greyfriars seemed empty to her without them. She liked having more women in the house too. Now she had lost two, with Carmen gone as well. She had her mother, Sylvie, move in after her father passed in June. Greyfriars grounds man Emile Vicknair moved into Sylvie's old house, leaving his parents, Anne and Hubert, to their house next to Greyfriars. Anne suggested building a summer kitchen off of the main house, as it was so hot cooking in the main house most of the time, to give Alexandrine something to plan for. Jean Charles poured himself into running the plantation. No matter how Alexandrine plotted, she simply had no luck finding a nice girl for her youngest. Charles wanted her to let him make his own choices, but she knew he still carried a torch for Genny, and she wanted him to move on. When Paul and Genny visited in August, she had great news. Genny was with child, and they had found a nice house. Paul had become an agent for Greyfriars, and the arrangement was working out well. Paul flourished in New Orleans, and he was happy to be living near the port.

While Alexandrine and Genny talked about baby names and clothing and furnishings, Paul and Charles went into the study for a brandy. "Father, there is talk that Napoléon has sold out to the Americans. He made some sort of deal with their president, Jefferson. I must say I have noticed more American ships coming into the port, and families as well."

Charles shrugged. "Business as usual, as I see it. We have always been on the fringe of these territorial decisions, and they usually concern only New Orleans. Since Jefferson has labeled the city an enemy, maybe he will be turn his attentions to West Florida and let us be. Maybe we should blame Spain. Although they have most certainly eased trade from the river to the port, their weaknesses are evident in other matters. Do you think the Americans will interfere with our trade? They have had enough experience with port politics to know it will not be tolerated. I cannot imagine Napoléon would consider such a loss. You know, Gabriel spoke of these possibilities in his last letter to me."

Paul shook his head. "It's not just New Orleans and port rights, Father. I believe it is the whole massive territory the Americans are seeking. I have heard of it from more than just dockworkers and sailors. And yes some of the other agents are worried about disruptions at the port. What if the Americans become hostile? They seem to be a riotous lot. I can tell you that from just the few I have had dealings with. They are most certainly a very different breed of businessman."

Charles swirled his brandy in his glass and pursed his lips. "If this is true, then they will have power over all of us and control the port completely. When you return home, I want you to make it a point to get to know some of them. I will travel to the city soon. We can set up a few meals with those you choose and get a feel for their sentiments." He looked at his son with great pride. Paul had made the right decisions with his life, and things were going well. "Look at you. An excellent son, husband, and now a father. You have persevered and done well, my boy." He held out his glass, and they toasted. "By the way," Charles asked, "have you received any post from Marc or Cecile? I sometimes wonder if they are still even alive. It is not like Marc to let this much time pass without a word."

Paul shook his head. "I have heard nothing. If you have another letter to post, I can send it when I return home."

Charles smiled. "Then I will write tonight. Now let us join the ladies. This gives them less time to talk about us behind our backs."

Jean Charles spent just enough time around the house to make an appearance and give his congratulations to his brother and sister-in-law. When he looked into Genevieve's eyes, his heart flipped while externally his hand was steady and his manner compliant and calm. He wanted no one to think he still coveted his brother's wife. He wished them well but secretly hoped that one day she would belong to him. Until that day, he would remain a servant to Greyfriars and to his hidden desires. And he would dream of Genevieve and her beautiful grey eyes.

In March of 1804, Paul and Genevieve Danetree became the proud parents of a healthy baby girl. They named her Victoria Cecile Alexandrine Danetree. Genevieve spent the last few weeks of her pregnancy at the convent, and her baby was delivered there. Charles and Alexandrine left Greyfriars as soon as word reached them. Alexandrine helped Carmen take care of Genny and the baby while Charles and Paul scouted American agents for possible business liaisons with the North and the East Coast of their new country. Gabriel and Paul had been right. Charles was not surprised when he arrived, as he had decided to go with a fresh mind. The world did not belong to his generation anymore. New blood and new relationships would need to be forged to keep the Greyfriars name on the tongues of these young, fast Americans.

The next few years would find the old families of the territory at odds with the new government and new laws reviewing the titles and claims to land already established. New roads and settlements were being established far into the territory on both sides of the Mississippi. Charles saw all of this as a positive for Greyfriars, but the O'Briens had not fared so well. They had lost almost their entire plantation on Tiger Island in land grant disputes. The Danetrees and Berwicks managed to hold on to quite a bit of their property, but their comfort levels had become concerns. Now it was a constant thought that anything could change, and they had to be able to adapt quickly.

Little Victoria grew fast and toddled her way into everyone's hearts. She was a gentle and clever little girl who carried a doll with her everywhere. Alexandrine and Charles spoiled her mercilessly, and she loved her uncle Jean Charles. When she visited Greyfriars, she loved being able to run around the property and lie in the grass, just looking at the sky. She liked to stand by the hibiscus tree and babble to the dragonflies.

On her third birthday, they had a picnic out back. One moment Carmen and Victoria were next to a tree, and the next the child was screaming for her grandmother as she ran toward Alexandrine, now Grandma Alex, grasping a flower. She held her tiny hand out with a hibiscus in it. "From Ambrose, Grandma Alex. He said it is pretty like you. He said do not forget him."

Alexandrine's jaw dropped. She took the flower. "Who is Ambrose, darling?" she asked in a quiet voice.

Victoria turned and pointed to the hibiscus tree. He's a dragonfly, but he used to be like Papa. He said you liked the color red. He said—"

Alexandrine picked her up before she could finish her sentence. "Well, this is a lovely flower, my sweet girl. Now what do you say we go inside and you can help Grandma Alex read a book." Victoria nodded and smiled.

A chill went up Alexandrine's spine. Too many memories flooded her mind. *There is no way the child could know that name.* She had to keep her wits about her. If Victoria repeated this to anyone, she could cover it by saying the child obviously meant "a rose" instead of "Ambrose." She hoped Victoria would not repeat the story to Charles. If she did, well, maybe Charles would not remember. She went on for the rest of the day, distracting her granddaughter with anything she could. That night she said two rosaries—one for her and one for Paul. She could not pray enough.

When Paul and family headed back for New Orleans, Christophe joined them and left Gabriel to be the man of the house at Comfort's cottage. He thought Gabriel was turning into quite a fine young man, and if he and Estelle had had a son, he would have wanted him to be just like Gabriel. Maybe one day the young man would join him in the bakery business. With the influx of Americans and Haitians fleeing civil unrest into the territory, he saw great opportunities and sought to reopen a bakery in the city. It was quite a venture, but he felt maybe it was time to get back into a major market. He was to meet a man about a building near the docks. He too was benefiting from the growth Louisiana was experiencing, but he also had more competition now, and he needed to expand his business in order to stay successful.

Traveling went smoothly and upon arrival he and Paul dropped Genny, Carmen, and Victoria at the house and then headed for the location where he was to meet an American named Mr. Ballinger. He was grateful for Paul's company, seeking his advice and discussing possibilities. It was getting dark, and Paul disliked New Orleans at night, but Christophe promised they would not be long. They rode to the corner of Port and Decatur. There was a brick building there and just enough daylight to look through the glass and see what was inside. On the streets, people were walking from everywhere, going anywhere. Buskers and hawkers tried to outshout each other before packing up their goods for the evening and heading home.

Another carriage stopped just behind theirs, and a man stepped out and walked toward them. He tipped his hat at them and held his hand out, speaking first. "Mr. Marleau?" He looked at Paul and then Christophe.

Christophe put his hand out. "Yes. Mr. Ballinger?"

They shook, and the American answered. "Yes." He then looked back to Paul. "And you are?"

Paul put his hand out to shake hands. "Paul Danetree of Greyfriars Plantation in Petit Coeur." Paul could tell Mr. Ballinger was an American, but he had a definite Irish accent.

Ballinger looked at them both and said, "There is very little light left. Shall we go inside, gentlemen?" They stood aside as Mr. Ballinger put a key in the lock and opened the door. Paul waited at the door while the two men looked around and talked business. When they got back to him, Mr. Ballinger shook Paul's hand again and got into his carriage.

Christophe looked at Paul. "I do not mean to be so abrupt, my friend, and I do appreciate the company, but I will be going with Mr. Ballinger now. We are going to meet the other owners, and I know you must be very tired. Besides, I will be fine, and I do not want Genevieve angry at either one of us. I am going straight to the apartment after the meeting and will be fine."

Paul raised his eyebrows. "Are you sure, Christophe? I sure do not want Estelle angry at me either."

Christophe smiled. "I am very sure, Paul. Come by the apartment tomorrow, and I will have good news for you."

Paul smiled. "Good night, my sister's husband. Be careful or you'll have Father to answer to." He shook Christophe's hand and left in his carriage. Christophe entered the Ballinger coach and rode off into the night.

The next day, Paul kissed his wife and child and then headed for the apartment. He knocked on the door. "Open up, old man, before I use my key." He knocked again but heard no response. "Christophe, are you still drunk?" He decided to open the door with his key. He was not comfortable with what he saw. The bed had either not been slept in or Christophe had never made it back. Paul had a very bad feeling and decided to head toward the docks. He went from ship to ship, asking about Christophe, until he found a fellow that remembered a man that looked like Christophe. He told Paul that two men were obviously drunk and having an argument about a building when the tall man slapped the shorter man across the face and challenged him to meet him under the oaks at the park. Paul put his hand to his head. His sense of dread made him feel queasy. *I should never have let him go off with that stranger.* He assumed the other man had to be Ballinger. "Did you know the other gentleman, the American, who made the challenge? Did you hear the name 'Ballinger'?" Paul asked.

The man shrugged. "No, monsieur. But the tall man spoke only in English with an accent. These Americans, you know, they all look alike to me."

Paul thanked him and turned away. *This cannot be good.* He got on his horse and rode toward the morgue. It was more than just a guess. There was usually only one place to look for someone after a duel. He hoped he was wrong.

When he got there, the smell was quite off-putting. Monsieur Camille was the proprietor there. Paul asked him if any bodies had been brought to him from The Oaks. The man wiped his hands on his filthy apron and took him to an area behind a curtain while swatting flies away from his face. He looked at Paul and then swept his arm through the air. "Go on, monsieur. Pick one. Take two. There were only five brought in between last night and this morning. Your friend—what was he wearing?" Paul knew about The Oaks, but he had not even considered this part of the process. He tried to steer clear of situations that might put him in places like this.

"He wore dark blue breeches and a matching coat. He was light skinned with black hair and …"

Monsieur Camille put his hand up and said, "Say no more." The man walked over to a table and pulled the sheet back. Paul gasped. It was Christophe. His flesh was ashen, and his eyes frozen and glazed in a death stare. His coat was missing and his shirt was stained in various shades of red. The smell of blood was dizzying. "Looks like he took a ball to the heart, monsieur. Are you here to claim the body?"

Paul's voice became very soft. "Yes, monsieur. How much?"

The man cocked his eyebrow. "You are paying in gold or notes then?"

"Yes, gold. Have you his coat as well?" Paul asked.

"He was found as you see him now, monsieur. If you are traveling, I can prepare the body for extra."

Paul nodded. "Fine then. I will be around later to get the body. My name is Paul Danetree. Do you know who brought the body here? Do you have knowledge of an American named Ballinger around here?"

The man shook his head. "No. The body was at the door when I opened up this morning. Well, I will get to work then. Would you like to pay now, monsieur?"

Paul reached into his vest pocket and pulled out a gold coin and handed it to the man. "There'll be more when I pick him up. We've a two-day ride. Make sure he is prepared well." The man nodded, and Paul left. What was supposed to be a good productive trip was now a slow death ride back home. How could he face Estelle and Murielle—or anyone, for that matter? He should never have left him. He decided not to report the incident to the authorities. Although Christophe was a freeman of color and held a fine reputation in the city among the other businessmen, Paul wanted to find this Ballinger himself. A duel was a duel, an agreement between gentlemen, and any deaths that resulted were not necessarily considered murder in the eyes of the law. He would search for this Ballinger himself.

When Paul informed Genny of what had happened to Christophe, she was horrified and then relieved. "Do you realize that could have been you too? My heart breaks for Estelle and Murielle, of course, but Paul, this was not your doing. This was Christophe's decision—not yours." He would not look at her. She took his face in her hands. "Look at me, Paul." He did. "This was not your fault, my love. And I do not want you to travel alone. Do you hear me? What about your associate Mr. Prejean? Go and get him. Do you want me to go with you?"

He put his finger to her lips. "Please, Genny. I know you are right, but everything is happening so fast." His eyes were full of tears.

Her heart was breaking for him. "Oh, my darling." She kissed him and wiped his eyes with her sleeve. "Go now and find Monsieur Prejean. I will prepare a bag for you."

He nodded and headed out of the house. Genevieve prayed for Christophe's soul and thanked God her husband had not been there. She got his bag ready for the long and solemn trip back home.

Christophe was buried near the cottage next to Marie's grave. The rain fell, muddying the gravesite and beating down on the flowers as though the whole world were crying along with Estelle and Murielle. Gabriel tried to remain strong. He would have to take care of them now. And he would not let them down. He would cry later, privately, in his room, for the man that had treated him like a son.

1804 - 1808

The passing years would see more tragedies and challenges for the Danetrees. Genevieve miscarried almost bleeding to death and Alexandrine's mother Sylvie passed away in her sleep, followed by her beloved Jean two weeks later. There was a fire at Greyfriars that threatened to burn the house down, and then the rain miraculously let loose from the skies and saved them all from burning to death. It would take almost six months to repair the damage.

Jean Charles and Paul worked hard together to keep the plantation up to date, Paul from his city office and Jean Charles in the fields. As long as they produced between seventeen and twenty tons of cane per acre, they would be doing very well. Charles tried to remain active, but Paul and Jean Charles noticed him slowing down. It was not easy watching their parents getting older. Every now and then they discussed how they would proceed when the time came to take over the running of the plantation entirely.

Murielle was becoming quite the businesswoman at fourteen. Gabriel noticed she was a beautiful one as well. Her mother, Estelle, changed after Christophe died. She became more withdrawn and let Murielle and Gabriel run the business in Teal Bend. Murielle thought maybe they should carry on Christophe's dream of opening a bakery in New Orleans, but Estelle would go into fits whenever Murielle mentioned moving to New Orleans, so they stayed in Petit Coeur and opened up a bakery there too.

Estelle saw the way Gabriel looked at Murielle. She remembered how Charles had looked at Comfort in the same way, and also how Christophe had once looked at her. She talked to Charles about her thoughts when he visited one day while the young ones were at market. They sat in the front room of the cottage by the fireplace. Charles looked at his daughter. *So beautiful*, he thought. She had his green eyes and her mother's grace, gentleness and long thick black hair. He noticed she had placed a picture Comfort had painted on the mantel above the fireplace. It was a portrait of Comfort's mother, Marie, smiling with her red turban on and her eyes with a fire in them that seemed to stare straight through him. He smiled. "You know I bought those paints for your mother when we were teenagers. She had such talent, you know. But she refused my offer to show her art in a gallery in New Orleans."

Estelle smiled. "You two loved each other very much, didn't you, Father?"

Charles nodded. "One day we will be together again. I believe you know that." He stared off into the fire.

Estelle looked at her father. At sixty-one, he still had that twinkle in his eyes, but his black hair had grown silver and grey and his shoulders drooped slightly. She knew he loved her and had always provided for them. She looked up at the portrait. "What was my grandmother Marie like? Mother would not speak of her much. Was she a free woman?"

Charles had to be careful with his answer. After reading his mother's diary and Marie's attempts to destroy the Danetree family, he did not want to poison Estelle's mind with Marie's evil. He looked at her. "She was a very determined woman. A strong-willed woman. I do not know of her life in the years before she knew us. She was just an unfortunate young girl with responsibilities. She did not come to us as a slave, but as a hired person for my mother, from the convent in New Orleans. I think I remember she spoke French and Spanish though. She watched Cecile and me when we were little, you know. She was my wet nurse too." That disclosure made Charles shudder inside. "She loved your mother and tried to do everything she could to secure a good future for Comfort."

Estelle nodded and looked at the portrait. "I wish I had her strength now. Some days I just don't want to get up, Father."

Charles reached over and held her hand. "You have turned into a fine woman, Estelle. Never feel you are not strong enough. It is just that you have a broken heart. These things may heal, but there will always be a scar to remind you of what you have lost. You loved Christophe very much, and no one can take that away from you." He squeezed her hand and let go. She fidgeted for a second and then asked, "Mother said Marie only spoke of her family once to her—of her brothers Narcisse and Victor. And she said that her mother was from Spain, or some islands near Spain, and Marie's father was a Spaniard and French too. Did you know them? Did my mother know her own father?"

He shook his head. "I was too young. Marie came to us from the Ursulines, where she had your mother. She never mentioned Comfort's father around us or Comfort, I believe. She would have said something about that, I am sure."

Estelle stood up. "Would you like more coffee?" He handed her his cup. "You know what I think about every now and then, Father? I know you love me, and I know Paul and Jean Charles love me too, but how come you and Mother never married?"

Charles felt his heart grow heavy. "My mother approved of us growing up together, but she never approved of us progressing beyond that. She was very French and traditional. Comfort was too brown for her and of Spanish blood. I should marry a good French girl, she said. Comfort and I talked about running away, but we were too young, with nowhere to go and no money of our own. In many ways you are very fortunate, my child. My mother never knew you were mine. Alexandrine saved us both. We staged our marriage so that Comfort and I could stay together and I could be around you. I know this might be terrible for you and hurtful to hear, but we did the best we could for everyone involved. And now we will love and spoil Murielle as we did with you."

Estelle returned with their cups hot and full. "Alexandrine? What do you mean?" She saw a thoughtful look cross over Charles's face.

"Alexandrine was in love with someone else, as was I, but our parents pushed us together. She saw a way to keep us all happy, and we all agreed. Unfortunately her lover, Ambrose, left her. Comfort and I were very sad for her, but Alexandrine did not complain that we stayed together."

Estelle got up again and said, "There is something I want to show you, Father." She left the room and then came back with a box. She handed it to Charles. "Open it." She said. He did. She watched his face as tears came to his eyes.

He pulled out and unfolded an old yellowed piece of paper with a drawing on it—one dark hand and one light hand. He smiled. "I found this in her room when she lived at Greyfriars. She was so angry with me for prying. That's when I knew I loved her and she loved me. And you, my darling, are our gift to the world. Would you mind if I kept this?"

Estelle had tears in her eyes too. "Of course not, Father. I am sure she would have wanted you to have it." Charles folded it and slid it into his vest. "I must be getting back now, Estelle." He hugged her. "I love you, my darling. Please come by the house more often. You really cannot stay trapped here. And I know Alexandrine would love to see you."

She kissed him on the cheek. "I love you too, Father. And I promise I will come by." He pulled away from her and smiled. She smiled back and saw him to the door.

Two years passed, and although Louisiana was not yet a state, New Orleans was growing by leaps and bounds. It was still mainly a French-speaking city but was becoming more Americanized. Paul and Jean Charles were now running Greyfriars Plantation, with Charles and Alexandrine spending their days visiting others or hosting picnic lunches, playing chess, smoking cigars, and fishing off their dock. At night they would sit in the study and read or sit in the back gallery, just rocking and talking. They had been invited to spend the Fourth of July week in New Orleans with Paul and Genny. Box seat tickets at the Theatre St. Philippe for a celebration gave Genevieve, Victoria, Alexandrine, and Murielle a chance to wear ball gowns and have their hair done. Estelle, Jean Charles, and Gabriel decided to stay home.

It was a lovely evening with hundreds in attendance. The attendees wore beautiful gowns and fancy formal wear. The smell of spices, sweet perfumes, and powders swirled in the heavy air. Alexandrine watched as Victoria and Murielle marveled at the sights and sounds, but something about Genny bothered her. She noticed Genny seemed to act standoffish around Murielle, and it really bothered her. She knew that Genny understood the Danetree family dynamics. Genny had even tried to make separate sleeping arrangements for Murielle upon their arrival, even though Victoria was excited about sharing her room with Murielle, whom she considered a cousin. Paul did not share Genny's notions, and Victoria got her wish. Genny seemed to not want to be in the same coach or arrive at the theatre with Murielle, so they went in separate coaches. Paul thought nothing of this, as their dresses took quite a bit of room and two coaches seemed normal. It became painfully obvious to Alexandrine that she would have to have a talk with Paul about Genny's behavior. Murielle was Charles's granddaughter and Victoria's cousin. Alexandrine would not see her treated in this way. They enjoyed the lovely evening and the remaining visit. Too soon it was time to leave.

The journey back to Greyfriars was an interesting one. Murielle went on nonstop about her adventure and loved staying up late with Victoria, telling her stories and reading to her. She had brought the pincushion book her uncles had purchased for her years before, and she gave it to Victoria.

Alexandrine was surprised. "But why would you give it away, my sweet?" Murielle looked pensive, as if she were trying to find the right words. Alexandrine reached over and touched her cheek. "Please, Murielle. Is there something wrong? I promise you this will remain between you and me."

Murielle smiled and nodded. "Victoria said her mother took all of her books away except for her lesson books, which she can look at only when her tutor is there. So I gave her my book. She is going to keep it hidden from her mother so she can read it when she is alone. Besides"— Murielle looked down and smoothed out her skirt—"I am sixteen now. That book is for a younger girl."

Alexandrine frowned. "She took her books away? How could she do such a thing as that?"

Murielle shrugged. "Victoria said it was because she told her mother her friend Ambrose read with her at night. She told her mother he doesn't have a human mouth, because he's a dragonfly, but she can hear his words—like he is talking to her with his eyes. He talks about you too. She said he has a beautiful red flower for you—like the ones by the bayou on that that old tree. He watches over Paul too. I think Miss Genny is scared and doesn't understand. And I do not think she likes me very much."

Alexandrine's blood froze in her body. *Think fast. Think fast,* she kept saying to herself. She tried to breathe normally. "Well, it sounds like Victoria is a lonely child with no brothers and sisters."

Murielle nodded. "That's what I think as well. I can certainly understand that feeling. I wish she lived closer to all of us. And Genny is somewhat distant from all of us, I think."

"It is not you, my beautiful Murielle." She reached over and patted Murielle's gloved hand. Her mind was going round and round with memories. The smells of gunpowder and blood, As well as the deep stain of betrayal, were on her conscience. She looked down at her hands. The look on Ambrose's face after she shot him always fresh in her mind. There wasn't a day that went by when she didn't see those damned flowers and watch those cursed dragonflies darting everywhere. She smiled at Murielle. "I'll tell you what we'll do, and it will be our secret.

You and I will collect books for her—secret books. And we won't tell a soul. We must never mention Ambrose. Do you understand?"

Murielle smiled. "Oh yes." She seemed excited at the prospect of performing a covert task and keeping a secret. She would do anything for Alexandrine and Victoria as well.

When they arrived at Greyfriars, the first thing Alexandrine wanted to do was take a machete and cut that damn hibiscus tree down, but she knew Charles would kill her if she did that. And part of her was terrified. She had absolutely no belief that Ambrose was a ghost in a dragonfly body. That meant someone must have seen what she did and was torturing her after all these years, trying to drive her crazy. But who? Nothing made sense anymore. The children could not know. No one here knew him or his name, except Charles. But Charles had never met him. He just knew his name. Anne helped her unpack her bags and then left with a torn stocking to mend and a couple of petticoats to wash.

Alexandrine went to find Charles. She opened the study door and saw him slam a piece of paper down on the desk as he jumped. "Good Lord, woman, are you trying to scare me to death?"

She smiled. "I thought I did that the day we got married. I'll take that remark as a compliment that I have not lost my touch." She walked over and kissed him on the cheek and then sat down across from him. He was still handsome even with his grey hair. She reached over to get the paper, but he cut her off with his hand and grabbed it first. She looked surprised. "Charles, what are you reading? Surely we have no secrets between us."

He raised an eyebrow at her. "Another letter from Marc. Cecile is not well. They have sold the family home and purchased an apartment in Montmartre. They have sent a few things on for us, which should be here in a month's time—some things that belonged to our grandparents. That is all."

She looked at him and cocked her head. "That is not all, is it, Charles? What else is there? Please, Charles."

He slid a page to her. It was a separate letter from Cecile to him. She glanced over it and asked, "May I read it aloud? I will read it silently if you prefer. I do not want to upset you."

He shook his head. "I have already read it. Maybe it is time I share these things with you, although I will understand if you find her words a result of her illness." Alexandrine began to read.

April 1810

Dearest darling brother,

These words will be my last to you. My words may sound feverish to you, but my mind is clear. You must cut down that tree, Charles. It is evil. I had another dream, Charles. Marie was standing by the hibiscus, laughing. She spoke to me. She said our children would suffer, and their children, until we were no more. There were dragonflies all around Greyfriars. Like little devils they were, trying to pierce our souls. And the screams—it was as if they were screaming and crying at us, beckoning us to come closer. That tree was at first a symbol of what our mother and father should have had. Everything beautiful. Growing year after year. Getting stronger. But we know what really happened, Charles. They will trap your souls, Charles. You must cut it down. Please, for God's sake. I say a rosary every day for us, brother. My eternal love to you and yours. We will see each other again.

Your loving sister,
Cecile

Alexandrine could not believe her good fortune. Here it was: proof that the tree must go. It was a sign from God himself that she should cut it down. She looked up at Charles. "Charles, this is horrible. What evil does she speak of? And the dragonflies? What are you going to do? What are we going to do? Something must have happened for her to make these statements. Her soul is tortured by this."

Charles spoke softly. "She is not mad, you know. We saw things when we were young. She more than I. There are letters and a diary too.

Bad things have happened here. But I always thought we would be safe. Maybe I was wrong. Why are we to pay for the sins of our parents?" He put his head in his hands.

"You have known about this before now?" Alexandrine asked. He nodded. Her brow furrowed. "Why would you not share this with me, Charles? At least for our children's sake. We also are not without sin. We answer for our own, but not for the sins of others. Still, if Cecile felt this strongly, then we must cut it down. I'll have Hubert do this immediately, for our own peace of mind. You said there is more to read. May I read the others also?"

He looked at her. She noticed his eyes had changed. They looked as if they held more sadness. He reached under the desk. She could hear a drawer sliding as his hand moved. He produced a small journal and a small stack of letters. He pushed them toward her and then rose from his chair. "You can read them tomorrow. And don't bother poor Hubert with the tree. We'll take care of it before the cane is harvested and burn the damned thing with the trash. Hopefully it won't curse the crops. It is getting late. Let's go to bed now, please."

She left the bundle on the desk and took his hand. "Of course, darling. We are both tired now." They headed up the stairs as Anne and Hubert snuffed out the remaining lamps in the house and then headed for their own home.

Alexandrine spent most of the next day in the study, reading the letters and diary entries of Hyacinthe. It was late afternoon. Jean Charles was in Teal Bend and would not be home for several days, and Charles stayed away from the study while she was in there reading. She found that some of the letters were not Hyacinthe's. She noticed two were from Philippe, to someone named Francois Fleur and someone named Belle. They had been written but never delivered or opened. There was a knock on the door, startling her. "Come in," she said without looking up.

It was Anne. She carried a tray holding coffee, cake, and figs. "Please, have some to eat," Anne implored her. "You missed the midmorning meal, and I know there is only brandy in here." She cocked an eyebrow, and Alexandrine had to smile.

"Thank you, Anne." She cleared a space on the desk for the tray. "Surely we do not want the others thinking I survive solely on good French brandy and cigars. You will be happy to know I am still thinking on that summer kitchen idea of yours. Charles has even weighed in positively on it as well. We absolutely do not know why it wasn't planned and built sooner. What would I do without you?"

Anne nodded and turned to leave.

"Oh, Anne, could you please ask Charles to see me here as soon as possible?"

"Of course, ma'am." Anne smiled and left, closing the door behind her.

Alexandrine cared for Anne and Hubert very much. Their families had survived the great expulsion from Acadie when so many others had not. And that tie was unbreakable in her mind and heart. She would always make sure they were taken care of.

When Charles got to the study, the desk was covered in pages and envelopes. Alexandrine had bags under her eyes, and strands of hair were sticking out of a hasty bun atop her head. He sat down across from her. "I figured you would be here early. I did not feel you get up."

She smiled. "You were sleeping quite soundly, my dear. I rose gently. After reading the things I have read in these documents, I don't know if any of us should want to wake up at all if these things are true. Who is Tomas, Charles?"

Charles folded his hands, looked down, and took a breath. "I will tell you he is a product of my father's indiscretions and a girl that worked for us—Belle Fleur. She was like a nurse and guardian to Cecile and me before Marie came. She helped my mother for quite some time while she was ill. Belle apparently helped my father in other ways." Charles shifted in his chair. Alexandrine noticed his eyes seemed to water a bit. She waited for him to speak. He looked at her. "Is it too early for a brandy?"

She smiled back and patted his hand. "I think it is the perfect time for a brandy." She poured while he continued.

"We were too young to understand, really. Well, I was. I think Cecile gave the whole situation more thought than I. But she was more affected by what happened than I was. Our mother was ill often, so Belle and her sister Daisy were also our playmates when we weren't at lessons. That is, until Marie came. But then everything changed with Marie. She took over caring for Mother, so Belle spent more time with us, mostly Cecile. And then I remember her being gone. Daisy was gone too. There was another couple that was hired, but they disappeared as well. Then Marie brought Comfort with her, and we were together all time: Cecile, Comfort, and I. We ate together, had lessons together ... Well, you know the rest."

Alexandrine picked up the journal and turned to a page. "Here it is. A sweet memory for you. Not everything in all of this is wicked," she said. "May I read it to you?"

Charles nodded.

> December 20, 1749—Father Warren christened our
> darling today. Charles Philippe Olivier Danetree. That
> is a fine name, I think. It was a very nice day. Florine
> made baguettes the way Olivier used to make them, and
> there was butter and jam, bouillabaisse with local fish,
> and wine and cheese. It was all so very special. Amelia,
> Florine, and Willie made sure our dining table was
> beautiful with fresh flowers from the garden and candles,
> with Maman's lace tablecloth underneath. Cecile was
> running around with Daisy chasing after her. Belle took
> care of Charles while Philippe and I entertained Father
> LeBlanc and the good sister. She is so kind to have stayed
> this long. In the spring, I must visit the convent. Philippe
> has told me there are improvements being made to the
> Ursuline buildings. It would be very nice to see the city
> again. Maybe we could call on Monsieur and Madame
> Veisze if they are still living there."

Charles smiled.

"You see?" Alexandrine said softly.

Charles put his head in his hands. "But none of that changes the damage, yes? What if there really is something to Marie witching Greyfriars and the Danetree family for generations to come ... if you believe that sort of thing. I do swear that a great part of me rebukes the notions that Marie wielded something evil upon my family, but another part of me wonders how much power one can bestow in hatred. Why would she hate us so? We gave her a home, land, and a future. We can only pray that the saints will preserve us."

Alexandrine's eyes drooped. She felt Charles was a good man. He had not sinned like she had. He had not murdered like she had. The only thing reserved for her was judgment and fire. She did not look forward to dying, but she was beginning to understand she would not be the only Danetree on the wanting side of Saint Peter's gate.

"I am going to meet Jean Charles in Teal Bend today," Charles said. "Will you be all right?"

She raised an eyebrow. "Well, honestly, Charles, what will I do without a man here to protect me?" She smiled.

Charles smiled back. "I would worry more about the fate of any man trying to accost you. You have always been a better shot than I."

This time she smiled only on the outside. She knew Charles had no idea about Ambrose's fate, but any innocent mention of things close to that subject made it fresh for her. On the upside, she would take this opportunity to rid Greyfriars of that tree. She would face whatever scrutiny Charles showed when he returned. Again, this would be another sign from God. "Shall I have Anne prepare anything for your journey?" she asked.

He rose and headed for the study door. "Yes. I think something light for the road would be very nice."

Alexandrine stood at the pillars and waved as Charles headed off down the road to Teal Bend. When she could no longer see him, she headed to Hubert's shed at the back of the property to fetch an axe. She felt empowered and resolved. When the tree could no longer be seen, it could have no power over them anymore. She would save the family from itself.

It was a beautiful morning. Mockingbirds were singing, and there was a light breeze and full sun, with no one else around. Even as she approached the hibiscus, she felt sad to see such a lovely thing imprisoned by the evil of humans. It wasn't the tree's fault. Those beautiful blooms were eyes to everything around them. And then there were the dragonflies. She had never liked them. Little devil's darts they were. She stood close to the base of the tree and raised the axe. The dragonflies stopped buzzing and flying. It was a checkmate, and she was the queen. She had them now. "Looks like you will have to find another home, you little bastards." She swung down at the bark. At the same time, a dragonfly flew off of a branch right at her face. She closed her eyes and took a step back. It all happened so fast. The axe shifted when her stance did and came down on her right leg, wedging itself into her dress and petticoat, and finding her shin bone. She heard a cracking sound, felt something painful and jarring, and then she felt the ground. One odd, loud scream and she was out.

When she came to, Anne and Hubert were standing over her. Anne was crying. Hubert looked horrified and kept repeating "What have you done? What have you done?"

The second time she woke up, she was in her own bed. Charles was sitting beside her. He was wiping her head with a cool cloth. He spoke softly. "You are one very lucky woman, you know. I was not far down the way when Hubert caught up to me."

She moaned. It was hard to speak through the excruciating pain. "Charles … I … I wanted to …" She took a breath.

"Shhh," he said. "Let me tell you what you were trying to do. You never listen and decided to take matters into your own stubborn mind and chop that damn tree down to free the terrible Danetrees from the family curse. But you are a woman and got distracted by something shiny in the water and almost chopped your leg off." One corner of her mouth went up as she tried to smile. He brushed her cheek lightly with his hand. Her mind was spinning, and thoughts scattered like leaves in a wind. "Hubert has gone to fetch the doctor, Anne is in shock, and you have pissed off every dragonfly on the property. We have fashioned a splint on your broken shin until the doctor treats you. You have lost a good deal of blood, with most of it soaking your clothing. Good thing it hit your clothing first. I have just enough brandy left to keep you drunk until he gets here, but that will only dull things a little. Just nod if you understand me."

She looked at him. There were tears in her eyes as she placed her hand on his arm and nodded.

Charles reached over and kissed her lightly on the lips. "If you wanted my attention, all you had to do was let me win at chess or smoke my last cigar. I suggest you try not to move at all. I will have Anne come in here now. I'll go and get another bottle of brandy." He left, and Anne came in. Her eyes were swollen from crying. She also chastised Alexandrine for her rash behavior. Alexandrine didn't care as long as the brandy kept flowing and her periodic losses of consciousness sedated her.

The doctor's report was not good news. "I am sorry, madame and monsieur." The doctor looked from Charles to Alexandrine. "The bone is shattered, and I cannot save her lower leg. If we amputate, it will be unpleasant, but hopefully there is no infection and we can prevent any further damage. Of course there are no guarantees that this operation will not have other results. I am sorry. Are you agreeable we must not wait any longer?"

Charles held Alexandrine's hand while she cried. "Take it! Take the damn thing then!" she screamed. Charles nodded.

The procedure was performed. Alexandrine lost more blood but seemed to be sleeping as peacefully as possible considering the pain and shock. Jean Charles had come back from Teal Bend with more brandy. Anne made poultices for the wound and did her best to make sure everything was comfortable. She, Estelle, and Murielle took turns seeing to Alexandrine's every need. News had reached Paul and Genny, and they planned their trip to Greyfriars. They would be there in a couple of weeks with Victoria to help with whatever tasks and chores were necessary. They were also bringing medicine from New Orleans. Paul had seen what the restorative powers of laudanum could do, and it pained him to think of his mother in that kind of distress. He was confident the drug would help.

Alexandrine was happy to have Greyfriars full of family again, but not for this reason. It was almost as if God were giving her time to resolve any issues that she may not have addressed when she had the chance. She was humbled. She was also grateful for the laudanum. It took the edge off of the residual pain and made it easier for her to sleep and adjust to her physical status. Hubert had carved a prosthetic leg for her. "Out of good Louisiana cypress," he said. "That way the termites won't gnaw on it."

She was grateful and promised to try it soon but laughed when he mentioned the termites. She hadn't laughed like that in a long time. It felt good to see the humor in all of the mess she had created. But the hibiscus tree still stood, a constant reminder. She and Charles now both believed it possessed something they could not understand. Charles did not want to touch it.

Several months went by, and it came time to burn the cane. Charles and Jean Charles went to the fields. Paul returned to New Orleans, but not before Alexandrine had a chance to talk to him about Genny's treatment of Murielle. He said he would have a talk with her. Victoria was growing fast and was so smart. He told his mother about Genny being afraid Victoria was under some kind of possession because of her imaginary friend Ambrose. She was spending more time at the convent, making sure Victoria was surrounded by the Ursulines for protection. Alexandrine dismissed it as Genny being a doting, devoted mother. She claimed it would pass when another child came along. Paul wanted to believe his mother was right.

Alexandrine had moved downstairs into the front parlor so she could move about more easily. The stairs were too much for her, and she wanted to feel like part of the family again. Anne noticed Alexandrine had begun to lose weight and chose laudanum over meals sometimes. She was worried, and she shared this with Charles. He agreed but felt he could do little. If the medicine worked, then he would not deny her. He couldn't bear the thought of another trauma like Comfort's death.

The summer of 1811 began well enough. Everyone was relatively healthy and happy until Paul visited one day with disturbing news. He and Charles went into the study. "Father, I was wondering if it would be all right if I brought Genny and Victoria to stay here for a while. I just feel it would be safer here. There is an undercurrent in the city I am not comfortable with. There is also talk of an American war against the

British, and I fear New Orleans will not be safe for most anyone if this happens."

Charles looked surprised. "Of course you can all come home. So messy, this port business. Again trade will suffer. No telling who will control us if this war happens. Who will save us? These Americans are wildly aggressive. What are your thoughts, Paul?"

Paul looked down and shook his head. "I don't know, Father. Maybe next week our port will be full of warships instead of trade ships. The news changes as fast as the cargo and crews coming and going from the boats. I just know I must keep my family as safe as I can."

Charles agreed, and accommodations were made.

Paul had the situation right. He had moved the family back to Greyfriars just as things worsened in the northern territories, with the South supporting the war as well. He closed up the New Orleans house, staying there himself only when necessary.

Alexandrine seemed to be healing slowly. If she was in much pain, she hid it well. Every now and then, she tried out her cypress leg. Victoria held Alexandrine's hand when she tried to keep her balance while walking, fetching a shawl when she had the chills. The child was very nurturing and said her prayers every night. Jean Charles rarely came by, knowing Genny was there. He kept himself extra busy and called on his mother only on random Sundays while Paul, Genny, and Victoria were at mass in Teal Bend. Christmas came, and Victoria helped decorate the house. She followed her cousin Murielle everywhere, carrying magnolia branches secured with red velvet ribbons for the fireplace mantels, tying gold ribbons around candlesticks, and watching Murielle make breads and cakes in the kitchen.

One evening, Genny went to the kitchen looking for her daughter. When she saw her sitting next to Murielle while Murielle read a book to her, she grew angry and grabbed Victoria's arm. "Come with me now, Victoria. You are distracting Murielle while she is working. The kitchen is for the help." Murielle's eyes welled up with tears, but she tried to control herself in front of Victoria.

"Ouch, Mother, that hurts," Victoria cried out as she slid off of the stool and yanked her arm away. She stood there and looked up with angry little eyes at her mother. "Murielle is teaching me how to read recipes."

Genny raised her hand as if to slap the child just as Paul walked in. He grabbed Genny's arm and saw Victoria's angry face. Genny spun around. Paul let go. "What in the world is going on here?" he asked.

Victoria spoke. "Mother hates Murielle. Every time Murielle tries to teach me something, Mother comes in and gets angry and I have to leave. She hurt my arm right here." She showed her arm to Paul.

Paul looked at Murielle's face. He saw the sadness in her eyes. His mother had been right. Genny said nothing. Paul asked, "Murielle, if you don't mind, could you please take Victoria and ready her for bed? I would greatly appreciate it. I will be up in a minute." Murielle nodded and took Victoria's hand, guiding her out of the room.

Genny was livid. She almost hissed as she spoke. "How dare you, Paul. How is the child to learn how to behave in society if she is not taught at home?" Paul felt as if he were looking into the eyes of a stranger. Then he slapped her across her face. They were both in shock. He had never done or said anything out of violence until now. He was furious. Genny's mouth hung open as her hand went to her cheek. She moved to leave. He grabbed her arm and stared deeply into her eyes. His voice was calm, but there was no mistaking the seriousness in his tone. "Don't you ever talk to or about Murielle like this again! I will not tolerate you treating my family so poorly. Do you understand me?"

She began to cry. "She is not family to me, Paul. How can you call her family? She is not one of us."

Now he had tears in his eyes. "She is my cousin and Victoria's cousin, and her mother is my sister. Not one of us? She is forever a Danetree by blood. You will *always* be a Danetree only by marriage. Do not get me wrong, Genevieve. I love you. But I will *not* stand idly by as you disseminate judgment in my family's home—a home, I will remind you, that we opened up to you as we accepted you into our family. Now go upstairs. It is time for bed." She jerked her arm away and rushed past him. He just stood there looking at the floor. His whole world had just changed. A happy union had been shattered by anger and violence in a matter of minutes. He would have to talk to his parents and seek their guidance. And now he had to convince the woman he loved that civility was the only way they would all survive together at Greyfriars.

Although Alexandrine, Charles, and Paul tried their best to be merry and keep things light for the holidays, Genny stayed reserved and kept mostly to herself. She was especially cold at night when Paul lay next to her. She was incensed that he had not supported her, and worse, destroyed because he had struck her. No one had ever treated her like that before. She literally had nowhere to go. She knew her father had had family back in Cadiz, Spain, but she had never met them. Her mother was the last in her own family. She was going to have to survive here. She still loved Paul, but she could not forgive his violence. She was not ready to give herself to him either. They remained civil in front of the rest of the family, but it was obvious things were different.

Attention to Paul and Genny's issues quickly became secondary when Alexandrine began to feel ill. She was still taking laudanum and was drinking more than usual. She started getting regular fevers, and then chills, when it was hot to everyone else. There was a redness developing near the base of her stump, with a thin red streak as long as her thigh coming from it. Charles was angry when she finally showed it to him. "You know this is like a poison. You *know* this. Why did you not say anything when it first started?"

She could tell he was really angry with her. "Charles, I swear I did not feel it for the longest. Please don't be angry. You know I suffer." She could say no more.

"Where is the laudanum, Alexandrine?"

She opened a drawer by her bedside. He grabbed the bottle. She looked scared. "What are you doing, Charles? I need that!" Her eyes were wide. She held out her hand.

"This is what's wrong," he said, holding the bottle up in the air. "No wonder you cannot feel anything anymore. I was mistaken to let you go on like this. I am going for the doctor. Stay in this bed! I warn you now. I will not lose you too." He stormed out of the room.

The next thing she knew, Anne was in her room to stay with her as Hubert and Charles rode off for the doctor.

When they returned, she was very feverish and sweating profusely. Anne was very upset. Charles took her out of the room as the doctor performed his examination. When he left the room, he closed the door behind him. He looked at Charles. "It doesn't look good, Charles. I would say maybe we should have taken more of the leg the first time. You never know in these cases. I believe I did all I could. I've been on the battlefields and have seen much worse, but an infection has been growing in her for some time now. Why did you not contact me sooner?"

Charles shook his head. "She did not tell me what was happening. I should have noticed she was drinking more and taking too much laudanum. But I thought she was getting better. She seemed better. I failed her, didn't I?"

The doctor put his hand on Charles's shoulder. "I think maybe you should continue with the laudanum then. Just make her comfortable. I cannot tell you how much time she has, but she is in her final stages from the blood infection. It is too late to think about cutting anymore. I am sorry, Charles. Truly I am. Do you want me to stay?"

Charles looked like a lost man. "No thank you. We'll be fine. I do appreciate your time and honesty. The whole family is close. We will see to her now." Charles called for Hubert. "Please escort the doctor back to Teal Bend, Hubert." Anne began to cry. Charles gave her a hug. "She will need us every minute she has left now, Anne." He gave her the laudanum. "I'll get another bottle of brandy."

A week went by with Alexandrine fading in and out of consciousness. Charles and Anne both stayed by her side. Charles made sure everyone got a chance to talk to her. Paul explained to Victoria about grandma going to sleep with the angels. She wanted to pick a pretty flower from the hibiscus tree for her. When she, Paul, and Genny sat next to Alexandrine, Victoria put the flower in Alexandrine's hand as she lay there barely moving. She kissed her grandma on the forehead and then said, "Ambrose is sorry you are hurt, Grandma. He is coming to get you. He said he's your angel."

Alexandrine's eyes opened widely then closed. Genny gasped and put her hand to her mouth. Paul just looked at his daughter and then his mother. He nudged Genny toward the door. "Victoria, go with Mommy now. Daddy would like to talk to Grandma, all right?"

The child smiled, smoothed her grandmother's wet brow one last time, and left.

Paul didn't know what to think. Was Genny right in her concern about Victoria's imaginary friend? Why would she say such a thing to her grandmother at this time? He didn't know what to think about a lot of things lately. He sat on the bed next to his mother and held her hand. "I love you, Mother. Can you hear me?"

She was very feverish, and her pillow was soaked with sweat. The smell of sickness filled the room. She opened her eyes again, looked at him, and reached up with one shaky hand to touch his face. "Ambrose, my darling. I am so sorry. Please forgive me. I had to do it. Don't you see? I did love you so very much. I could not tell Charles. Paul looks so much like you sometimes ... He is so much like you, I thought ... I thought ..." Her eyes moved away from his face to the ceiling, and her hand dropped from his face. Her chest heaved as she drew a few rapid breaths and one last dry, raspy exhale.

Paul just stared at her. He felt paralyzed by both what she had said and her dying in front of him as he watched in horror. He could not even cry. It was too much to take all at once. It was as if her words had reached into him and smothered everything he knew about his life. It was unreal. He stood up and looked at the woman he had loved his whole life, and he saw a stranger. This was more than delirium. Victoria had been right. There really was an Ambrose. *My father?* He thought.

A knock on the door was like a jolt to Paul's system, and he turned around. Charles had entered. He looked into the eyes of the man he had always known as his father and mentor. He did not believe Charles ever even knew of any deception. He would not believe it. At that moment he decided that Charles would always be his father and that whatever his mother had done would not come between them. "She's gone, Father. She's gone."

Charles came up to him and put his hands on Paul's shoulders then hugged him. Finally Paul felt he could cry. He cried for his mother, for himself, and for the man that held him first as a baby, and now as an adult.

After two days, they laid Alexandrine to rest following a quick family viewing. When his mother's service was over, Paul walked back to the house with Genny. There were so many things he wanted to tell her but couldn't, so he said what he thought he should. "I want you to know that I do not believe there is anything wrong with our daughter. She is a child and will believe and say childish things. You must try to understand her instead of fighting with her over everything. She is willful, but she is strong, and she loves you, Genny. And I love you. I need to know if you still love me too."

Genny let go of his arm and touched his face. She was crying. "I do love you, Paul. I do."

He kissed her, and she kissed him back. He believed her, but he still felt lost. *Sometimes secrets should stay secrets*, he thought. He just wanted to leave for a while to be alone and to give himself some time to come to terms with his new reality. Genny and Victoria would be safe at Greyfriars. He would wait until the cane burning was over in October, and then he would go and check on the house in New Orleans and stay awhile in the city.

Chapter 10
No Calm in the Storm

Jean Charles Danetree had spent many a night trying to be strong after his mother died. The plantation did keep him busy most of the time, but having the woman he still carried a torch for living in his family home made things very complicated. His father would come out to the fields every now and then or visit him in his cottage, but Jean Charles resented the fact that he could not visit Greyfriars whenever he wanted. When he learned that Paul would be staying in New Orleans, part of him was tempted to visit Greyfriars and run into Genny "accidentally." But he loved his brother too much to insult him so. He would go to the city to see Paul when he had the chance.

Paul did come home later in the year for birthdays and Christmas, but as the new year came and went, he maintained it was still necessary to watch over the house and family apartment no matter the danger. This time when he left Greyfriars, Genny decided to assert herself carefully as queen bee. Charles appreciated her doting on him. Even when Estelle, Murielle, and Gabriel visited for dinner or spent the day with Charles and Victoria, Genny was polite and gracious, even though she still seethed under her skin. She never wanted to rile Paul's anger against her again, but now she had to calculate her behavior around her own child for fear that Victoria might turn on her as she had before. She felt herself withdrawing emotionally and donning a tougher exterior. She felt abandoned by her husband and despised by her daughter. The hardest thing she had to do was tuck away her privileged, spoiled mentality and adapt to her role as the Greyfriars matron, dutiful wife, careful mother, and tolerant hostess. The latter would be the bitterest pill of all.

Paul came back for several weeks in May of 1812. Louisiana had officially become a state. There was much celebration in the city, but he wanted no part of the excitement, so he headed back to the bayou. It was awkward between him and Genny at first, but after several days, their bond was back. Victoria was overjoyed to have her daddy back, and Charles was happy to have someone to talk to and share brandy and cigars with. He did address his concern about Paul being gone from his family for so long and suggested that he need not spend so much time away.

Paul could not explain that he was a different man now. His mother had ripped his heart out, and he was devastated by her death. His wife's insensitivities and moods tore at him. He felt like a coward for running away instead of facing his reality and being the son, husband, and father he knew he should be. Instead he smiled and made up stories about how his presence at the port was doing Greyfriars a great service and keeping their reputation strong in the face of the new American businessmen that would surely overrun the city. Now was a time to be vigilant and on top of things. Greyfriars had many years of production ahead, and he wanted to make sure the future was secure for his family and those who depended on the plantation for a living. Charles smiled and nodded. He was proud of Paul but did not let up on the need for his hand at home.

Two weeks passed. Paul managed to visit most everyone in the area but spent serious time contemplating a way to let Genny know he was going back to New Orleans. There was really no good time, so he waited until they were in bed after making love. He thought she would be too content and sleepy to confront him then. He was very wrong. She jumped out of bed and turned to face him. She kept her voice low, but her words were loud and clear. "If you leave, Paul, I will consider myself a widow. You treat me like some dog you can leave when you care to and then throw a couple of scraps to buy the love again. Go, Paul. Stay in the city then." She put her nightdress and robe on. "I do not know you anymore, and I am aware you no longer care to know me. My father had such regard for you. Damn you. I will remain in the guest room until you leave." She stopped at the bedroom door for one last remark. "I should have married your brother!" The door shut, and the light from the full moon outside the window was not enough to illuminate the darkness that now enveloped him.

He was not sure he would see Genny the next morning, but he did hear Victoria running down the stairs when Anne called that porridge was ready. He decided he would have breakfast with her and then take her for a walk outside and let her know he would be leaving. After Genny's revelation the night before, he felt almost prepared for anything Victoria might express to him. He did not want to break her heart, but he had to go. He did not expect her to understand.

She held his hand as they strolled outside down to the bayou side. It was very nice outside. She talked and talked. He loved her smile. She let go of his hand and ran to the hibiscus tree. She picked a flower, turned around, and ran back to him. He sat down on the grass, and she next to him. He looked at her. "Victoria, you know that I love you so very much, don't you?"

She nodded. "Oh yes, Papa. And I love you too. I am glad you are home now. Can we go fishing? Grandpa Charles takes me fishing sometimes."

Paul smiled, remembering his fishing trips with his grandfather Jean. "That is a very special thing. I need to talk to you about something. I know that it is harder living here than in the city."

She shook her head and raised her eyebrows. "Oh no. I have a lot of fun here, and I can run everywhere. There are so many places to hide and explore. Don't tell Miss Anne, but sometimes I chase the chickens around the yard." They both laughed.

Paul's heart was heavy having to leave his daughter again. "My darling, I must go back to the city today. I will only be there for a little while this time. Then I will be back forever."

Her eyes filled up with tears. "No, Daddy. You cannot leave me again. I need you here!"

She stood up and started crying. His heart was breaking. "Victoria, please don't cry. It makes me sad to see you cry. I will be back soon." This time he stood up. He went to hold her, but she drew back.

171

She looked up at him, her eyes angry. "You are a liar!" she screamed up at him. She crushed the flower in her hand and threw it up at his face and ran. "I hate you. I hope a hurricane gets you!"

He knew he had let her down. He didn't have to go. She was right. He was a liar. And he knew she would never trust him again. He packed his things, saddled his horse, said good-bye to his father, and rode away from everything he really loved. And he couldn't explain why.

August in New Orleans was never truly pleasant, even near the port. The flies, gnats, and mosquitoes loved the port too and fought for space alongside the people. It was a strange relationship, but then all living things looking for places to live had to try to survive wherever they could. The morgue had more than its share of winged voyeurs looking for a free meal—preferably one that didn't try to swat and smash them. At the city morgue, Monsieur Camille wiped his brow and then wiped his hands on his stained, smelly apron. The constant hum of insects had become a sort of strange symphony. He preferred the winters in New Orleans but was not unappreciative of the year-round business so courteously arranged by fatal tempers, unfortunate illnesses, and heartless tragedies. He did the best he could. There weren't as many ships in port because of the British blockade so some of the supplies he had been waiting for were not arriving. "Damn bloody war," he muttered. Dead soldiers were not the business he wanted though. He had lost his own father in the Battle of Havana when he was just a young boy of ten. His mother and sister died not too long after from yellow fever. He was put on a ship out of Havana as a cabin boy and wound up in New Orleans making his reputation as a mortician's assistant, then took over the business when his benefactor passed away. He shook his head as if trying to shake the memories out and looked around at his patients. At one time he wanted very much to be a doctor like his father had been during the war, but this was as close as he could get to that dream. He wiped a tear away from his eye and looked out of the front window. It was a particularly muggy day but he noticed the wind was picking up. He took off his apron and walked outside to smoke a cigar and breathe something other than blood and decay. It was another day in the city.

Paul walked out onto the porch of his New Orleans home and looked at the sky. It was cloud-heavy and dark. He liked rain, but it looked like New Orleans was in for one hell of a storm. He rubbed his shoulder. It always hurt when rain was coming. He decided to ride to the apartment and wait out the storm there. He locked up the house and left. The rain started as he mounted his horse. The drops were huge, and their intensity stung his face as he rode. The wind had picked up also. It was different this time—not just a normal storm. It was happening very fast. He put his horse in the livery and then walked a block to the apartment. Once inside, he lit candles and opened a good bottle of brandy. He removed his boots, pants, and coat and then lay on the bed, hoping sleep would soon take him away. How easy would it be to just forget his name, forget his family. He could just walk up to any ship in the port and sign on if they'd have him. There was a war going on. Of course they would take him. His thoughts then turned to Greyfriars once more, and the storm brewing there as well. He felt sure he could survive the rain here, but he was not so sure he could survive the flood of tears back home. He felt lost with no goal in sight and he didn't know how to make things better.

Monsieur Camille went back inside as soon as the rain and wind got too bad to stay outside. He could see the smaller boats beginning to rock in the water. At least the rain would help keep the dust and gnats down for a while even though the sweltering mugginess would follow the storm. He made his rounds in each room, making sure the windows and shutters were closed, bade adieu to his silent tenants, and then proceeded to head upstairs to his apartment. He cleaned up, had a shot of whiskey, and then went to bed for a long sleep.

Paul woke up to the sound of shutters rattling and the wind howling fiercely outside. Then he heard shouting and banging. Someone banged on his door. He put on his pants quickly. "I'm coming. Hold on!" he yelled. When he opened the door, the wind almost blew him down. Gabriel stood there soaking wet and shivering. Paul grabbed his arm and dragged him in. "My God, Gabriel, what are you doing here? You are drenched man. Have a drink. Here. Let me get you a blanket. I have extra clothes too."

Gabriel took off his cloak and put it on the floor. "Paul," Gabriel said. He put his hand up, trying to catch his breath. "Paul, I want to tell you something, okay?"

Paul handed him a drink. Gabriel sounded troubled, and his eyes were wide and strange. "Of course. What is wrong? Is something wrong? Did something happen at home, Gabriel?"

Gabriel shook his head. "No, brother. But something is happening here. I went to your home first. When you weren't there, I hoped you would be here. Remember when your father first brought me here, Paul? Remember?"

Paul smiled. "Sure I remember. Like it was yesterday. Why do you speak this way, Gabriel?"

Gabriel took a drink of brandy and smiled. "You know, before your father took me in, I had never had good brandy—only the rot I could find in the garbage or whatever the sailors would throw at us. Once I even waited until a drunk man had fallen asleep. He lay against a building, the bottle still in his hand. There was one drink left, and I took it. You know, I still feel guilty, Paul. That old man needed it more than I, and I took his last drop." There was a loud thud as something large slammed against the ceiling, door, and window, and then a crash sounded as glass flew into the room. A large, thick tree branch protruded into the room like a giant hand reaching in to snatch them both. They could see the ceiling was coming down. They covered their faces as the wind blew anything it could through the broken wall and window, leaving openings big enough to let the rain in, pelting them with heavy, stinging drops.

Paul took Gabriel's arm, and they headed into a corner of the room, crouching. "What the hell! That's the tree from the courtyard!" Paul yelled.

Gabriel looked at him. "It is our time, Paul. Our time to walk with the angels. I saw them, Paul, out in the street and out by the port. The boats cannot even get away. It is a hurricane—a bad wind—the worst I have seen. And now it has seen us. Angels, Paul." Gabriel's mouth went slack, and his head rolled back.

Paul could feel Gabriel's body settle then go limp. "Gabriel, what is wrong?" He shook him. Gabriel's head went forward, and Paul could see blood on his neck. A large piece of thick glass had lodged there. Paul jumped up and walked toward the huge branch, using it to maneuver his way closer to the opening. He did not feel the glass cutting his feet as he climbed out past the branch. He did not even recognize where he was. It looked and felt like the end of the world had come to New Orleans. He had never experienced anything like this, and he was trapped.

He went back to the corner where Gabriel lay slumped over. One of his shoes had come off. Paul grabbed it and put it back on Gabriel's foot. Suddenly the day he met Gabriel flashed upon him and he remembered his father's words about walking in the shoes of another. He passed his hand over Gabriel's eyes to close them and said, "If you are going to walk with the angels, you'd better have a good pair of shoes on, my brother." Just as he sat down next to Gabriel's body, there was a crack and shudder above him. He looked up just as the remainder of the ceiling came down, crushing them. Gabriel would not be walking alone on this journey.

At Greyfriars everyone was housebound as the storm trapped them all in the house together. They lit candles and played cards. Jean Charles, Murielle, and Estelle were there and kept Victoria occupied while Genny paced by the parlor window, hoping Paul was okay in the city. She would apologize when he returned—if he did. She felt truly bad for the way they had parted. She said a rosary after he left, trying to atone for her harsh words to him, hoping one day he could forgive her. The windows rattled and the house trembled a little, but they felt they would all be fine. Anne, Emile, and Hubert had put the animals away just as the raindrops started, then they left to shelter in their homes. Charles and Jean Charles talked about how the storm might affect the harvest, and Murielle worried about Gabriel, hoping he was safe in the city and that he was not out in this weather. And she had exciting news for him. She knew he was going to be an excellent father.

August 19, 1812, was a terrible, dark day for New Orleans and the surrounding areas. The monster hurricane that hit tore through the city's heart and soul, leaving behind death and destruction from deadly winds and flooding. Everything that could be uprooted and tossed had been. The loss of life and property was tremendous. Word had not been received at Greyfriars for several days, as roads had been washed out.

Jean Charles was returning from the fields, checking for any damage to the crops and machinery, when he approached the house and saw someone talking to his father. Something made him walk a little faster. He got to them just as Charles fell. Jean Charles caught him and walked him into the study, where he seated him in a chair. He then returned to the door. The messenger spoke. "Is Mr. Danetree going to be all right? I am very sorry, Sir. These messages are never pleasant. My sympathies to you and your family." He handed Jean Charles a letter. "I must go now, sir. I have to make it back to Teal Bend by nightfall." He tipped his hat.

"Of course, you must stay safe. I understand," Jean answered. He gave the man several coins and watched him walk away. When he returned to the study, he found his father sobbing. "Father? Father, are you all right?"

Charles could not look up. "Have you read the post, son?" he asked through his tears. "Paul is gone. Gabriel is gone. What are we to do? How can we tell the ladies? Poor Victoria. My heart is broken, Jean. Broken. I hardly know what to feel right now except extreme sadness. I need you to call everyone into the parlor please."

Jean read the post as his father spoke. He slowly put the letter on the desk. He felt numb. It was all so surreal. He walked over to his father and kissed him on the head softly, saying, "Yes, Father." And he left.

With all gathered in the parlor, Charles made his entrance. He could see the apprehension and worry on their faces. They had never really been summoned to a family meeting before, except for will readings. As he looked over them, he thought he saw Paul and Gabriel sitting in the back of the room. They were smiling. They looked at him, nodded, and disappeared. Charles frowned and looked bewildered. Jean spoke up. "Father, do you want me to read the post?" Charles nodded and sat down. As Jean read the letter, there were gasps and screams, and then wailing. Murielle fainted and fell to the floor.

As Estelle cried and rocked her daughter, she looked at Charles. "Father, Murielle is with child. She was going to surprise Gabriel when he returned."

Victoria ran to Charles, crying, "I killed him. I killed Daddy. I told him I wished a hurricane would take him. I am sorry, Paw Paw. I am sorry." Victoria sobbed uncontrollably in Charles's arms as he smoothed her hair.

"My sweet child," Charles said, "your words were spoken in anger. You did not really mean them. None of this is your fault. Don't you ever blame yourself, you hear?"

Victoria nodded, but she knew the truth. She had done it, and she was going to hell, and she was scared.

Genny sat there in shock. She had tuned out the moans and sobs of the others. All she could hear were her last words to her husband: "*I should have married your brother.*" Carmen leaned over to put her arm around Genny. Jean Charles thought she had gone into shock. He knelt in front of her and took her hands. "Genny? Genny, what can I do? I am so sorry. He loved you so much, Genny." He had tears in his eyes, but Genny's were dry.

She looked at him as she drew her hands away. "No, Jean. There is nothing anyone can do now. I must go upstairs now and lie down." She turned to Carmen and then stood up. Hubert and Emile walked over to talk to Charles and express their sympathies. Jean stepped back from Genny. Just as she turned to face Carmen, she collapsed into Jean Charles's arms. He carried her upstairs to her room and then left. Carmen would take care of her. He returned to the parlor to see to his father. He loved his brother, and Gabriel was a fine man. This loss of life would be a terrible scar on the heart of the family. First his mother, and then his brother. He was beginning to feel the weight of responsibility now squarely on his shoulders. He would not let his family down.

1813

A year later, black veils had been taken off of the mirrors, the black wreath off of the door, and Genny put on a simple, unadorned baby-blue dress. She packed her mourning colors away and took a long look at herself in her mirror. The face that looked back at her was still full of youth, the grey eyes lively and welcoming, but she felt old inside—old, angry, resentful, sad, unfulfilled, and trapped. She wished she were more like Carmen, who always seemed calm and had her wits about her. Maybe she would talk to her later. She had no one else.

Jean had been sitting in the study, going over the accounts, when Charles walked in. "You really need to have a break from the books, son. May I ask you a favor?"

Jean looked up and smiled. "Of course, Father. Anything for you."

Charles walked over to a book on a shelf. He pulled it out and removed an odd page from its leaves. He then handed it to Jean. "Your grandmother Hyacinthe began the first sketches. I think Father put it aside. I believe he meant to have this built for her.

Jean looked up. "A chapel, Father?"

Charles nodded. "It is small but would be situated next to the family crypt."

Jean could see his father's eyes getting misty. "Her drawing is quite lovely. Was she a secret artist?" he asked.

Charles shook his head. "No, she was not. Comfort actually finished the drawing as Mother described it to her. Comfort was the artist."

Jean smiled. "I see," he answered. He poured two glasses of brandy and handed one to his father. "Of course I will do this. We can build it out of cypress. I can have a friend in New Orleans inquire about the glass for the small rose window. It may take some time. I'll go to the city after the burning's done."

Charles smiled. "Thank you, Jean. My love and confidence in your abilities is unwavering. Now a toast to Greyfriars Chapel on the Teche."

The summer after Paul's passing, Genny sent Victoria back to the Ursulines in New Orleans. Too many times she heard Victoria reading with her ghost friend Ambrose and watching her daughter talking to the dragonflies on the hibiscus. Paul had died after Victoria wished him to die in a hurricane. She was sure the child was touched and must be suffering from demons and guilt. She was also sure the good Sisters would cure her. She would get angry remembering how Paul dismissed her concerns when the problem started those years ago. And she was almost sure Murielle had something to do with it. That's why she had fought so hard to keep them apart.

Murielle's father was from the islands, and her great-grandmother Marie was a witch. Charles let that information slip one night just months after Paul was buried, when he was quite drunk and she went to check on him. It seemed Charles had not left the study for days. He was in a stupor and quite disheveled. He grabbed her hand. "Marie should have killed us all. Curse *all* the Danetrees. Then we would be spared this horrid grief." He started crying as she yanked her hand away and left him there. He made no sense to her. God would protect her and save her child, but she could not be sure about Murielle's baby, Marguerite.

1816

Victoria liked spending the summers at the convent. She had done so for four summers now. She felt peaceful there. She missed her father terribly but felt closer to him when she prayed with the sisters. She made herself very useful and was especially good at comforting the distraught and terminally ill. She began to see a place for herself there and spoke to the Reverend Mother about joining the Order. She did not, however, tell her mother. She had forgiven her many things and prayed for her soul, but the mother–daughter bond she had seen in other families was not present in hers. The best thing her mother had done for her was send her to the Ursulines. It would be her gift and her calling.

Jean Charles had spent the last four years being present for Genny. He made sure to include her in building the chapel and even in redecorating the house. He remembered his uncle Marc had sent some of the draperies, rugs, and paintings from Paris when he and Cecile sold the Drouin house. Charles had them put in the attic and never opened them when they arrived. He felt that would keep Genny busy and maybe brighten her spirits.

There was something else he wanted to occupy her with as well. They had become close in the last four years. He made her laugh, and she made him smile. He took her to the city every now and then, and she took his arm as they strolled the streets and parks.

When he thought the time was right for his proposal, he planned a special dinner at Greyfriars with music, a full house, and a special ring that had belonged to his great-grandmother, Cecile Drouin. Everyone was there, including Father LeBlanc. It was October, so Victoria was home from the convent. Jean had confided in her, and she had given him her blessing. It was a lovely evening, and Genny looked radiant. Jean could tell she was happy. He took her out back to the birdbath. She was smiling. "Oh Jean, everything is wonderful. The house is alive again."

He smiled back. "Well, it wouldn't be so beautiful if you had not worked so hard. Everything looks so fresh and new with the draperies and rugs changed out." He folded his arms, and she put her hands on them. "Everything is new, isn't it, Jean? I know the cold weather will be upon us soon, but I feel warm inside, and content. And it is your doing. Don't think for a minute I didn't know you were keeping me busy. You cannot hide everything from me that easily."

He dropped his arms. "You are too smart for me, Genny. You are right. It is good to see you happy. Genny, I would like us to talk about something."

He noticed her eyes take on a more thoughtful look. She raised an eyebrow. "Oh, please don't tell me you are going away or something is wrong. I could not bear it," she said.

He shook his head. "No … no, it is nothing like that. I think we have established a good relationship. It has been long enough, Genny. I am not lonely with you. I am happy when we are together, and I hope you are too." He looked away and then back at her.

She took his face in her hands and smiled. "Yes, Jean. I will marry you. I would marry you right now, right here, if I could."

He was stunned. He had not expected the swiftness of her answer. "I … I … well, I guess this is the right time." He pulled the ring out of his vest pocket and slipped it on her finger. It fit perfectly, of course. "I love you, Genny."

"I love you too," she answered. He took her hand. "I have an idea. Let's go back inside." They found everyone in the front parlor, laughing and talking. Murielle and Victoria were playing with Marguerite, whom they had nicknamed "Gabby" after her father, Gabriel. Although it still unnerved Genny to see Murielle near her daughter, and now Marguerite, it made her feel better if she thought maybe Victoria was guiding them more toward God with her devotion to serve.

Jean said loudly, "May I have your attention, please, everyone? Genny and I have something to share." Everyone stopped and turned to them. "Genny and I have decided that we would like very much to be married."

Mouths fell open. Charles spoke first. He stood up and walked over to the couple. "Oh, my son, I am so happy for both of you." He looked at Genny. "Genny, I know that you loved Paul very much, but I am once again a most happy father with my son Jean's choice of wife. I believe this is the right time for us all. We dearly need a joyous occasion around here to celebrate." He kissed her on the cheek. "And Jean Charles never was a satisfactory bachelor."

All laughed and then rushed the couple with hugs and kisses. Genny even hugged Murielle and Estelle. Maybe it was time for renewal and resolve. She would make Jean happy, and she understood that meant accepting *all* of the family. It would take work on her part, but she wanted things to be better. At that moment, she chose family. Now she would have to be patient and hope they would accept her.

"Father LeBlanc," Jean asked, "I know this is most informal, but may we get married right here and now?"

Father LeBlanc raised his eyebrows. "You are both christened and confirmed Catholic?"

"We are," they answered together.

The priest then stated, "You have never been married, and she is widowed. I see no reason why Greyfriars should be denied this, as your father said, most joyous occasion. I believe this family could use more hearts and voices to fill these rooms." He got his Bible from his leather bag and had them place their hands on it. "Charles, do you give your blessing on this young couple?"

"I do," Charles said.

"Victoria, do you give your blessing for your mother to marry Jean Charles Danetree?"

She beamed. "Oh yes, Father, I certainly do."

He looked around at everyone. "It is a great thing when people have family to surround them in joy and support them in sorrow, for the first is never far from the latter, and we must be ever constant in prayer and ever mindful of the power of God in our trials and tribulations on this earth." He looked at Genny and Jean. "Do you promise to love each other and be true to each other till death do you part?"

"We do," they answered.

"Then in front of God and these witnesses, I pronounce you both man and wife." Father LeBlanc made the sign of the cross over their hands and then again in front of them. "I believe you know the rest." He smiled and walked over to Charles and shook his hand while everyone else fawned over the new couple. "A bit informal, but I see nothing amiss here in the Church's eyes. They can register in Teal Bend next Sunday when you all come to Mass." He continued to smile and shake Charles's hand until Charles answered.

"Of course, Father, and please let me know if there is anything Greyfriars might contribute to St. Mary's for the good of the parish."

They both smiled. The year 1816 would end well for Greyfriars. The happiness was much needed.

Jean Baptiste Danetree was born to Jean Charles and Genevieve Danetree on June 17, 1820. Mother and son were both healthy, and the new poppa Jean was extremely happy. His life was complete now. He had the woman he loved and a son he adored, and Greyfriars was alive with the sounds of life and love. Victoria visited to see her new brother. She cried as she held him. He was so small and angelic. "You are happy now, Mother?" she asked.

Genny felt as if she could say either too much or not enough to her daughter. There was no way she could apologize for all the years of coldness she had given to Victoria out of fear and uncertainty. She decided to play it safe. "Yes, Victoria. I am happy. Are you happy?"

She looked at her mother and smiled. "I am most happy. I have been accepted as a Novitiate with the Ursulines, Mother. I believe it is right for me. Sending me away for all of these years has given me a chance to observe and decide what I want my life to be like. I wish to serve God and am looking forward to the tasks I will be assigned. I want you to think well of me, Mother."

Genny began to cry. "Oh, I do think well of you, Victoria. I am sorry I have not let you know that before now. We have grown apart, I know, but I have always loved you and tried to make the best decisions for you. Please believe that."

Now Victoria was crying. "I have prayed many nights and rosaries to hear you say you love me, Mother. I love you too. Maybe you and Uncle Jean can visit me at the convent every now and then. That will be nice. I will write to you. I will not be able to come back to live here as I have anymore. Yes, visits would be nice. Today I must go to Teal Bend, and then I go back to the city tomorrow. I will miss all of you very much."

There was a knock at the door, and Jean stepped in. "I am sorry, but we must go, Victoria." She smiled and nodded, handing baby Jean Baptiste back to their mother. She kissed her mother on the forehead and left.

Two years later, Victoria had completed her two-year novitiate, entered her Juniorate period, and taken the name Sister Mary Grace. She was able to visit Greyfriars once before she would return to the convent. She had undergone a remarkable transformation. Her serenity and peace were gifts to all those around her. She made time to spend with Murielle and Gabby too, the latter being now nine years old and showing early signs of becoming quite the artist. Gabby had the most beautiful green-and-brown eyes and cinnamon skin. Her long dark brown hair braided atop her head looked like a crown. Murielle spoke of spending more time at Greyfriars since Anne was having a harder time getting about after taking a fall in the kitchen. She walked with a limp now, so Murielle helped when she could. She mentioned that Genny had warmed up to her somewhat, but Murielle refused to call her "Miss Genny," so they remained polite. Estelle actually spent more time around Genny, and they often went to the family chapel together to pray. Sister Mary Grace felt a warmth go through her when Murielle mentioned this. There were hugs and kisses, and back to the city she went.

Sometimes when things were going particularly well, Charles would grow apprehensive. He was seventy-one years old now, having outlived his parents, his sister, a wife, a true love, a son, Christophe, Gabriel, and family friends. He had questions that remained unanswered, memories that remained painful, and lungs that seemed to be failing him, though he refused to give up his cigars. But he also had hope. Every time he saw his grandson Jean Baptiste—who had been nicknamed T-Jean by Gabby—or heard from or about Victoria, he knew that no matter what he had been through and whatever price he would pay for his sins, it was worth it seeing his flesh and blood live on. And they were happy and healthy. He had it all.

Then, on a beautiful sunny day, Murielle opened the study door, announcing several visitors for him and stating how uncanny it was that the older gentleman looked quite like him. At first he was confused by her statement, and then somewhere deep inside of him, an old memory crawled up out of the darkness. He felt a small headache coming on and put his hand to his head. "Grandfather, shall I let them in?" she asked.

He rubbed his eyes. "I am sorry, Murielle. Please do."

He sat down as she guided the two men into the study. When he saw their faces, he asked them to sit down and asked Murielle to close the door behind her.

An awkward silence followed as Charles stared at the man he had not seen since the night his father—better yet, *their* father—disappeared. The older man began to introduce himself, but Charles interrupted him.

"Yes. I know who you are, Tomas, but the better question is, *why* are you here?"

Tomas Philippe Fleur shifted uneasily in his chair. "Please, Charles, we will not be here long. I, we—you and I—are much older men now. I thought with so much time having passed that maybe you would want to know me before we are no longer here. I also wanted you to meet your nephew. He is aware of the past and of our father. He is Philippe Antoine Fleur. His mother, Mathilde, was taken by the yellow fever some years ago. I also have something for you." Tomas pulled an envelope out of his vest and handed it Charles.

Charles hesitated before he took the envelope. "Is this some kind of legal matter I will now be forced into, Tomas? I can assure you there were no provisions to be found regarding any illegitimate children of my father's." Charles knew he had made a grave mistake the second the words came out of his mouth. He could detect sadness in Tomas's eyes and anger in Philippe's green eyes.

Tomas rose, as did Philippe. "This is not about money or inheritances, Charles. I am sorry you are offended by our arrival. I remember as a young boy, when I first saw you, I was afraid and confused, as you are now. I was hoping that we could be civil and maybe ... well ... we are brothers, Charles. Whatever else you may think of me, first we are brothers. And Philippe is your blood too. Danetree blood. You cannot deny us. I wanted to tell you my mother Belle has passed. Before she died, she said things. I wrote them down and made a copy for you. It is all in the envelope. Please read these things. We are in Teal Bend for the next three days if you chose to contact me. If not, then I am sorry for you, Charles. We will see ourselves out. Good day to you."

As the sounds of their galloping horses grew fainter and fainter, Charles's headache became more pronounced. He began to open the envelope, but his left hand suddenly felt as if it were losing power. His mind was racing with Tomas's words swirling around in his head, but nothing was making sense. He called out for help. Even the sound of his own voice sounded strange—almost slurred. Genny was coming down the stairs when she heard a loud, garbled human voice coming from the study. She was horrified when she saw her father-in-law. The left side of his face seemed slack, as if a heavy weight were dragging it down. His distress was terrible. She screamed for Murielle and Anne. Jean was out in the fields. By the time Hubert reached Jean by horseback and brought him back to Greyfriars, Charles had recovered slightly and was capable of somewhat altered speech. His headache had lessened, although his hand and arm still tingled. Jean rushed into the study. "My God, Father, are you all right?"

Charles smiled faintly. "I believe I will be all right after I rest a bit. I feel tired. I am sorry to have caused such a fright, but I believe I'll be okay now. Ladies, thank you for your kindness. And Hubert, you are always appreciated. Jean, would you bring me to my room?" There was much tension in the air as Jean escorted his father up the stairs to this room.

Jean sat next to Charles's bed while his father began to talk. He laid his hand lightly on Jean's arm. "There is a key, Jean. In the breast pocket of my vest over there. Please get it." Jean retrieved the key. "It is for the desk."

Jean looked confused. "But Father, I have never seen this key."

Charles sighed. "There are things, Jean that I suppose you must know. This key is for another drawer in my desk that one cannot see. There is a false bottom in the top drawer, and a lock. There are things in there I think you should read. Make of them what you will. I know only that your aunt Cecile, at the end, raved about unpleasant things and our family. Dark things, Jean. The mad part, I believe, is how that damn hibiscus tree seems to figure into so many things. It drove your mother to hysterics, you know. She wanted to chop it down until a dragonfly flew at her and she lost her balance. Your niece Victoria spent much time there talking to them. I cannot explain everything to you, and you must never repeat anything I tell you to anyone, but you must read. I am sorry, but this you must bear alone."

He rubbed his eyes and continued. "There is a story that Murielle's great-grandmother Marie cursed our family. She seemed very protective of my mother once. Then something changed. There were two men that came to see me before I became ill today. I let them know they are not welcome here. They rode back to Teal Bend. I will not allow anyone to hurt my family or what we have built here. One is Tomas Philippe Fleur, and the other his son, Philippe Antoine Fleur."

Jean nodded. "But Father, what have they to do with Greyfriars? Are they old employees I have not heard of?"

Charles shook his head. "No, my son." Tears formed in his eyes. "Tomas's mother was a young woman named Belle. She worked for our family at the same time as Marie. Tomas's father ..." Charles swallowed hard and frowned. He put a hand to his head. "Tomas's father was my father as well. He gave me a letter. It is on the desk." Charles turned away from Jean. He did not want to see the disappointment on his son's face.

Jean read the letter to himself. His brow furrowing deeper with each sentence. He looked at Charles. "Father, look at me. I said look at me!" He raised his voice. Charles turned to him. "He is your brother, and Philippe is your nephew, and you sent them away? Why would you do that? Are they not our family, like Murielle, Marguerite, and Estelle? I understand that not all personal matters of the heart are easily explained away, but how could you not embrace them? If what you say is true, then they are entitled to some part of Greyfriars. I felt so alone when Paul died, but now I must say I am intrigued. Did Mother know?"

Charles nodded. "She read the letters and diary as well. She thought that if we cut down the tree and burned the pages, we might be free of what Marie sought to do. Marie wanted everything, Jean. She wanted Greyfriars, and when she was found out, Mother cast her out. After Father disappeared, Marie tried to control her. She found later that Marie had tried to poison her. Comfort never knew. I could not tell her."

Jean noticed Charles's face turning very red. His eyes glazed and fixed as he tried to speak. "You ... must ... protect ... Greyfriars ... I ... am ... sorry ... I ... love ... you." His body went rigid.

"Father? *Father?*" Jean jumped up and shook his father, trying to bring him around. But there was nothing he could do. There was froth at Charles's mouth, and he gave a loud moan. He exhaled and was gone. Jean laid his head on his father's chest and cried. If he had felt lonely before, this was true solitude. He was the man of the house now. He loved his father so much and counted on him being alive and there every day. Now he was lost. His heart was broken. His mind was flashing on everything he had just heard.

Charles's funeral was a very solemn one. Father LeBlanc's sadness was very evident during the service. Every time a parishioner passed, it was like losing another family member. He had known the Danetrees for so very long. A rosary, led by Sister Mary Grace (Victoria), was held in the Greyfriars chapel next to the family crypt, and small meals were served at the main house. Charles was placed in the crypt between Comfort and Alexandrine. No one said a word about that. Many people came to pay their respects. Some of the older Berwicks and O'Briens

187

who had known Charles and had conducted business with him were there with their families.

Jean was happy to see the respect his father had garnered over the years. The whole plantation seemed to take it very hard, and even those enslaved had their own ceremony to mourn Charles. Jean met with the group leaders and reassured them that he had no plans to alter the path of Greyfriars. He knew of their meetings, worship, and secret schooling, as had his father. As long as the work got done and there was no violence, it would be business as usual.

Tomas Fleur heard about Charles passing away. He felt sad that his only brother would not acknowledge him. He prayed for Charles's soul and his spirit to be at rest. But in his heart, he knew none of them would rest until the curse was broken. And he didn't know what to do. He didn't even know how to explain to his own son what a dark cloud they lived under. He tried to have faith that curses were just words conjured up in anger, jealousy, and hate. But the look in his mother's, Belle's, eyes and her words at her death still haunted him. You can take back words or give them less power, but you can't take back memories. She sounded as if she still had tremendous fear. "The dragonfly saw me do it. I swear he looked right into my eyes. Like he knew me. The dark and the rain and the blood—he saw it all. He'll come for you, too. Come for your head. Just like she did—that witch Marie. She'll get us all." And then her heart stopped.

He was grateful he had Mathilde and Philippe at that time; otherwise, he might have wanted to die with his mother. All of this mess now wasn't fair to Philippe, but he wanted his son to know his family before he died. He thought it was important. Maybe one day Philippe would be accepted as Danetree blood, live at the big house, and enjoy the fine things there. Time would tell, and time was all they had.

Every day after his father's death, Jean Charles would pull the key out of his armoire, look at it, turn it round and round in his hand, and then put it back. Every time he held his son Jean Baptiste, he held him close. He loved him so much. He couldn't bear to think that anything horrible would happen to him because of an old family superstition. He would have the house, chapel, and crypt blessed by Father LeBlanc—*and that* damned tree. Even the letter Tomas had brought his father caused him to be cautious. Belle's words and warnings were ungodly. He would have to be stronger—a better and more faithful servant. He would do it to protect his family. If only the slivers of uncertainty that lay hidden in a secret desk drawer beckoning to him did not exist. He would burn them, and the fear would be gone. Yes. A good burning and a curse would go up in smoke forever.

Chapter 11

And the River Rolls On

1828

In the ten years that passed after Charles's death, changes came thick and fast to Greyfriars and its families. They received word that Marc had died in Paris. He had been ill for some time and, according to the nuns, had passed quietly in his sleep at Hotel Dieu. Then, in 1832, beloved Victoria, Sister Mary Grace, took ill while caring for patients during the yellow fever and cholera outbreak in New Orleans. Thousands of lives were lost. Pain, suffering, and profound sadness enveloped the city and surrounding areas. Fear of he "yellow jack" was not unknown, but the devastation and misery were fresh each time. Estelle succumbed as well, but Murielle and Marguerite survived. Murielle had her mother laid to rest next to Marie and Gabriel, near the cottage. Victoria was buried in the Danetree crypt under the name Sister Mary Grace. Genny had her father exhumed from the graveyard in New Orleans, and his remains were interred next to her granddaughter's. Somehow it comforted her to have them nearer to her, even after death.

She was very despondent at that time and spent most of her time at the little chapel, sometimes crying, sometimes praying. She began to watch over Jean Baptiste like a hawk. This included keeping him away as much as possible from the hibiscus tree and the little devils that guarded it. She had eavesdropped at the bedroom door when her father-in-law Charles spoke to Jean about Alexandrine's accident when attempting

191

to cut the tree. She still believed that Victoria had joined the Ursulines to stay safe from the demons that possessed her from that tree and its blood red flowers. She hated it. Paul never understood her fears, and she was pretty sure Jean wouldn't either, so she said nothing to him. She did love him. He was a good man—tenderhearted and kind—but was also hardheaded and did not accept her believing in curses. She would have to be the one to warn T-Jean when it was time. He was thirteen now. It would be some time before she would have that talk with him. She did not think Jean Charles would pass on to his son the dark things about his bloodline. And she didn't want to lose another child.

Jean Charles had tried for years to find Tomas and Philippe Fleur, with no success. It was as if they had disappeared. He had opened that secret drawer in his father's desk. He read the letters, the diary, and the letter that Tomas had given Charles. He didn't want to believe any of it, but these weren't just simple ravings. All of them contained references to the same things: the hibiscus tree, the evil dragonflies, poisoning, and a curse on all Danetrees. But what puzzled him was the poem written by Tomas's mother, Belle, upon her deathbed:

> I saw it flit and flutter by
> Over and over again
> A vibrant orange-red dragonfly
> I saw it sweep and spin
> Then land atop a fragrant bloom
> On the old hibiscus tree
> At once I knew what the dragonfly saw
> As I laid the body deep
> Water water sink it slow
> From bone to mud and brine
> And cover well my scars and sin
> From that ole dragonfly
> —Belle Fleur
> June 18, 1822

He wondered what body she was referring to, and what sin. Maybe the sin was her child with his grandfather Philippe. *Did she bury something or someone?* It was all too much. It just didn't make sense to him. There were logical explanations for the things that had occurred before. He needed to believe that.

He put everything back into the drawer. He had a plantation to run. He had a wife that needed him, and a son that would someday take over. T-Jean was old enough to learn the business now. Genny had become too coddling, and the boy needed to know what it meant to be a man in a man's world. It was time to take him out to the fields and to the city, just as his father had done for him.

He took him to New Orleans and introduced him around at New Citizen's Bank of Louisiana, where Jean had moved his accounts. They stayed at the reconstructed family apartment where Paul and Gabriel had lost their lives. Jean Charles always made sure to do a rosary for every night they stayed in the apartment. Marguerite had sketched pictures of Gabriel and Paul, which had been framed and hung on the wall. T-Jean (Jean Baptiste), enjoyed the trip very much and tried to look interested for his father but felt somewhat disinterested in anything to do with the fieldwork and the cane business. This did not go unnoticed by his father. The boy was young, Jean thought, and he remembered his own resistance to the family business until the one day it just all made sense. He had been running a successful plantation for decades now. As would his son. It would just take time.

1833

At Comfort's cottage, Murielle did her best to make her life meaningful and productive. She did her baking and catering for special events, kept house, kept a watchful eye on her Marguerite, and maintained the flowers on Gabriel's and Estelle's gravesites. She was frustrated because she could not find anything that would grow on Marie's. Everything died there except poison ivy. The vines never ventured off of Marie's grave. She didn't think this was normal, but it became too much trouble to deal with, so she let it grow there. As long as it didn't spread, she wasn't going to mess with it. Her daughter, Marguerite Gabrielle, had turned twenty and was quite lovely with her green-and-brown hazel eyes and full, curly black hair. Most of the time she kept it up in braids, as that was easy for her, especially with the humidity. There was a warm caramel tone to her skin that darkened on the exposed parts if she spent any time in the sun. Murielle thought her sweet Gabby, who now preferred to be called by her first name, Marguerite, was the most beautiful thing on Earth and adored her.

Marguerite liked to help her mother with the baking but felt teaching was her calling. She chose to teach reading, writing, and sewing at the plantation school with Jean's blessing. But she had to be careful, as these practices were not widely accepted. She knew Greyfriars, the slaves, and the community itself could suffer greatly if it was found out. She, Murielle, and Jean came up with a plan. Murielle, a free woman of color, would claim to work at Greyfriars, a place she was known to visit and stay at occasionally. Her daughter Marguerite was also "hired" to help there and at the school. The fact that they were not slaves or of Danetree blood might never be revealed, as outsiders wouldn't have a clue and locals simply would not bring it up. It was a chance they were willing to take. Jean agreed but said that if at any time he thought it was no longer safe, he would have to step in.

This seemed to work until one of the male overseers showed an aggressive interest in the young Marguerite, making her feel threatened and interfering with her teaching. When she told Jean, he made arrangements for a travel pass and traded the man to the O'Brien plantation for an unmarried house girl named Kaila Green. She had been born and raised there, and it was hard for her at first, but working at Greyfriars with Murielle and Anne made the transition easier. Anne was grateful, as it was getting harder for her to handle the big pots and pans and the cleaning as she aged. Jean even finally had a summer kitchen built just off the main house with a small furnished room so Anne could live closer to the house. Although Anne scolded him for not having built it years earlier, she was happy for the convenience and for a younger person to help her and Murielle with the big chores. But not everyone was happy with Kaila.

Genny reacted to her as expected, seeming cold and somewhat aloof. She reminded Kaila of her place in the household with harsh glances and orders. Murielle didn't like it but had to be careful when picking her battles with Genny. Although they had maintained an understanding and were somewhat friendly when Genny was happy, other times were not so pleasant, and Genny's resentment was an old scar with a constant scab. It just never seemed to want to heal. She always had to be wary of what mask Genny wore on any given day and plan accordingly. She would try to remain hopeful that the passing years would soften Genny's heart.

1835

Mardi Gras in New Orleans was in full swing and drew many families from the outskirts into the city. Gaslight torches lit the streets while Krewes made sure the night was full of merriment, masques, and tableaux cars with decorations straight from Paris. No expense was spared, and the wealthier residents made sure the very best was on parade. The Danetree, O'Brien, and Berwick families formed a wagon train and headed to the festivities. They would be able to watch the revelry from the apartment balcony. They shared hot spiced cider and warm brandy while watching the crowds of people dressed in various stages of absurdity dance and celebrate the abandon of cares, woes, and discretion.

Jean Baptiste thought it looked like a lot of fun but was unhappy his parents refused to allow him to attend the masques. Genny did not want their son to be a part of the "debauchery and degenerative behavior" she had heard about during these events. She had remained at Greyfriars and expected Jean Charles to uphold her instructions regarding their young son's soul and reputation. She believed Mardi Gras to be a heathen celebration and said she would remain in the Greyfriars chapel, praying for their souls. She was furious at Jean and T-Jean for going, and the brunt of that fell on Kaila and Anne, who spent most of their time trying to stay clear of her.

Jean was happy to see T-Jean making friends his own age and socializing. Sometimes the plantation was no place to learn the social graces, as they had so few gatherings there anymore. They had been invited several times before to other homes, but planting could be very time consuming, and Jean didn't have as many overseers as the others. He preferred to spend his time in the fields and at the helm. He wanted to know what worked and what didn't and make the necessary adjustments himself. It was easier to secure the accounts and control the expenditures that way.

This trip gave him the opportunity to talk with the others about their methods. There was also talk of some invention meant to ease the refinement of sugar in the development stage. One of the Berwicks had met a man named Norbert Rillieux, who was looking to change the way sugar was processed, making it safer for the workers and more productive for the planters. It had been attempted before. They would wait and see what the others were investing before taking the plunge, not wanting to volunteer their plantations on such a risky venture, as new machinery and procedures would be expensive. Jean Charles was happy to be around the young people. He noticed the Berwick and O'Brien families had their share and more of children. He felt a pang of jealousy. He had always wanted a big family, but the Danetrees never quite managed that one. Sometimes he wished he and Genny had had more children, preferably sons, to help. He was not ungrateful for what he did have. He just wanted more of it.

What was noticeable to him was a particular young lady he observed his son fawning over. He asked and found out it was Clarisse Isabelle Berwick, an American Berwick cousin visiting from Vermont, far up north. She was a pretty, slender girl with brunette hair and large brown eyes. The look on T-Jean's face reminded him of when he first laid eyes on Genny. He smiled. This was going to be a very productive trip after all. He would try to make sure the young couple stayed in touch. Maybe Genny would forgive their Mardi Gras transgressions if the trip produced a possible match for their son.

Just after a few days in the city, the families left the festivities together, with the Danetree men separating from the rest of the party to stop in Teal Bend. Just before they parted, Jean Charles watched as Miss Clarisse Berwick slipped what looked like a small pink handkerchief into T-Jean's hand as they said their good-byes. He saw his son blush and smile, and then bend to kiss her hand. *Well, well,* he thought, *some social graces just come naturally.* He thought maybe Genny had given the boy pointers on how to treat young ladies, but she had been so angry when they left he knew it couldn't have been her. It made him proud to see his son make the effort. Now if he could just get and keep him interested in becoming a planter. With no other heirs, Jean Charles's concern for the future of Greyfriars was growing with each planting season.

Jean Charles was right about Genny's mood upon their return and also about her interest in Clarisse. "Of course," she said as they lay in bed talking one night, "it will be some time now, as they are still quite young. She lives too far away. And she is an American. Surely our son would not leave us for Vermont. Why can she not move here? If it is just her parents there, would she not be better off surrounded by family?"

Jean smiled. "They are a huge family. My God, it would be a huge feast." He kissed her quickly.

She smiled and said, "If you wish me to be quiet, I think the method has not changed." She closed her eyes as Jean disappeared under the quilt. He had such gifts.

Genny made sure to plan more outings with the Berwicks over the next couple of years. She wanted to get to know the family that her son might be marrying into and what their stability might provide for Greyfriars. This turn of events made her more pleasant to be around. She wasn't as moody and at times seemed to be truly happy. She even invited some of the Berwick ladies over to the chapel when they were in the area. They would pray together, talk, laugh, walk, and enjoy simple meals outside, weather permitting. When Genny was happy, everyone benefitted. Kaila even started to sing in the kitchen as she cooked and cleaned—something that had not been permitted prior to the possibility of a daughter-in-law and grandchildren.

T-Jean and Clarisse corresponded by post over the two years after they were first introduced. Her father, Eustace Berwick, made a comfortable living pasturing sheep, and the fishing and hunting were plentiful. She wrote of beautiful mountains, streams, and green valleys in summer. T-Jean wrote her back about the sugar crops, various planting practices, how the crops were suffering from the previous year's weather, the latest international news being passed around from New Orleans, and how he looked forward to one day seeing her again. After all, he wanted to make sure he returned her handkerchief in good condition to show he was responsible. He dreamed of visiting her there and seeing these things.

When he brought the subject up to his mother, Genny remained calm on the outside but was completely gutted on the inside. She had been anticipating obstacles but had remained unscathed until now. And this was a big one. She had to speak to Jean as soon as possible. He was in the city and would not be back for another week. T-Jean was all her hope for the future. She would not let him desert her. She determined to come up with a plan to keep her baby boy close, and execute it in a timely fashion.

Jean returned home to a distressed wife and a son that now wanted to move to Vermont. He had been gone for only two weeks and almost saddled up again to get away. He understood Genny's fears and managed to soothe her temporarily. But he could not do the same for T-Jean. Time would tell. Jean had been in New Orleans with Clarisse's uncle Nathaniel Berwick. Nathaniel told him that it looked like his brother Eustace would be relocating his family to the South to join the rest of them. They were unsure whether it would be with the Texas Berwicks or the Louisiana family, but they would head down the Mississippi by steamboat out of Pittsburg the following spring. The Vermont winters were becoming too harsh for Clarisse's mother, Mary, whose health seemed to suffer more with each snowfall. Eustace was dedicated to Mary's well-being and decided a move was in order. He, like Genny, was anxious for his daughter to marry well, and he was aware of her letters to the young mister Danetree. He had received good word of the worthiness of the young man and thought maybe it was the right time for Clarisse to accept a respectable suitor.

When T-Jean found out, he was elated that soon he and Clarisse would meet again but disappointed that he would not see the mountains of Vermont. Genny was beside herself with glee and pretended to be sad when Jean expressed his dismay that he would never get to travel to the North to see life there. Genny got him involved in planning future outings and visits with the Berwicks. She told him they had been invited to Houston and Galveston with the O'Briens and Berwicks. That seemed to give his adventurous heart a little lift.

The fall and winter of 1839 passed, and T-Jean's anticipation grew as he waited for Clarisse. He spent more time grooming himself and seemed to become less interested in the fields, so Jean put him to the books, inventory, and ordering. With competent field hands and overseers, Jean felt at ease with his son not being at his side. Sometimes love had to come first. And he hoped his son had found his.

Spring, 1840

In Vermont with the sheep and farm sold, Eustace, Mary, and Clarisse headed overland to Pittsburgh to catch a steamboat. They knew it would be a long journey with its own challenges, but they were up for it. Mary's spirits were up, and Clarisse looked forward to what Louisiana held for her. She was a strong-willed girl with a head of her own, but she had a feeling that T-Jean Danetree would help get her settled in her new world. They boarded the side-wheel steamer *Magnolia Pearl* at Pittsburgh. This would carry them to St. Louis, Missouri, and then on to New Orleans.

They shared a small room on the upper deck, but Clarisse spent as much time as possible on deck. She met the pilot's mulatto cabin girl, Jessie Jewell Beaufort, and the two struck up an easy rapport. She was relieved to have another girl to talk to, as was Jessie. She thought Jessie to be quite bold and worldly for her young age of sixteen. And she wore pants, like a man. Clarisse also found out that the pilot—Jessie called him "Butz" Beaufort—was often sleeping or drinking and that Jessie herself was piloting when Butz was sleeping it off. Jessie said she called him Butz because she had to clean the cigar butt stains from his clothes and mend the burn holes when he fell asleep with lit cigars. It drove her crazy. She said she knew every sandbar and bend from Pittsburgh to

New Orleans, and that Butz was not her husband or her father but the man that saved her from the whip of a master that almost killed her. She showed Clarisse the thick scars on her legs and back. She would say no more about that. Clarisse cried that night. She knew of no families in her area of Vermont that had slaves, but she knew that her southern cousin's plantations thrived with the practice of slavery as did some of the northern states. Her excitement was now fraught with doubt and uncertainty that she could be happy, wondering how many people were treated this way. Seeing Jessie's scars made the horrors of slavery all too real for her and she wondered how Jean felt about that kind of life.

St. Louis seemed kind of like New Orleans to her—lots of noise, people, and boats. She was relieved when they set off again. It would be another two weeks to New Orleans, provided there were no hazards in their path. Once there, they would be guests of the Danetrees at the city apartment to get acclimated and rest in comfortable surroundings.

The Jeans, younger and elder, left for the city to make sure the apartment was clean and ready for their guests' arrival. They stayed at a hotel nearby with some of the Berwick clan to greet Eustace, Mary, and Clarisse. On board the *Magnolia Pearl*, Clarisse felt melancholy about Jessie and the prospect of never seeing her again. There were things she wanted to say to her, but she didn't know if she should. She would give her uncle Nathan's address where they would be staying. That way they could write. No one had to know. Jessie laughed and agreed to write when she learned how. Clarisse didn't laugh until Jessie did. "All I seen about words, they nothing but get a person in trouble. And if they on paper too, then the trouble's double. I learned enough river-speak to make it out here with the best of 'em."

Clarisse grabbed her, hugged her, and kissed her on both cheeks. She took a silver hair comb out of her hair and put it in Jessie's reddish-brown braids. "So you don't forget me."

Jessie smiled, nodded, and winked like she always did to people. "Shoot, Clarisse, I'm gonna live on the Mississippi so long they gonna have to rename it after me. The Jessissippi River—yes ma'am. You gonna have to pass this way again someday any ole way."

Clarisse heard her father calling. "Good-bye Jessie," she said, and then she turned and left.

Jessie pulled the silver comb from her braids and stuck it in her pocket. She rubbed her fingers over it and smiled. There was an engraving on it in the shape of a tiny dragonfly. It was so pretty. She knew that if the folks saw it, they would think she stole it or something. This was a forever treasure she did not want taken away from her.

As tired as the travelers were, they were happy to see family and friends in New Orleans to greet them. T-Jean held back from the group, thinking it would be more appropriate for the family to be the first to welcome them. He didn't have to wait long. Clarisse sought him out. It was a sweet and tender moment witnessed by all. He held out his hand, and in it was a pink-and-gold satin ladies' handkerchief. Clarisse took one end of it, and he held the other. When they looked up, everyone was smiling and quiet. Eustace walked over to him and shook his hand while Mary embraced him. There was more blushing for the two young people, and then everyone went their ways so the family could rest for the night. It would be a long ride back to the bayou.

It was not long after that when the first gathering at Greyfriars was arranged for the Danetrees and new Berwick family to get acquainted. Genny had Kaila, Anne, and Hubert running ragged about the house and grounds, decorating, polishing, dusting, and beating rugs. She even pitched in. And the roof did not collapse in on them as Kaila had told Anne it would.

Jean and Eustace went to the study after dinner for a cigar and brandy. Mary and Genny sat in the parlor with Clarisse and T-Jean. Young awkward moments with the parents quickly melted away, and Clarisse and T-Jean went on as though they were still writing letters to each other. Mary and Genny looked on approvingly as they watched the two laugh and talk about most everything. Although Genny was a bit older than Mary, she felt twenty years younger on this night, with the prospect of wedding planning and grandchildren possibly on the horizon.

Over the next two years, it became clear that a proposal was on the way, but not fast enough for the mothers of the prospective couple. T-Jean and Clarisse were in no rush to get married or even engaged and managed to keep things on their own timeline in spite of the parental pressure.

In August of 1842, Marguerite got married at Greyfriars, just as her grandmother Estelle had. Her chosen was Antoine Manier, an overseer at Greyfriars who taught at the plantation school with her. He was a free man of mixed race. His father was Scottish and his mother African and Cherokee. Between the two of them, they hoped their children would represent the whole world and conquer the hateful divisions that plagued human existence. Murielle thought they were dreamers and said so, but she admired their devotion to each other and their beliefs—no matter what dangers that belief system might incur. Thinking back on her own wedding, she recalled how she and Gabriel had jumped the broom in a small ceremony, as Gabriel had wanted, instead of something like this at Greyfriars. They had been married for only a number of months when he was taken by the hurricane. That pain was always fresh in her heart. Marguerite knew her mother was very happy for her, but she also felt her mother's sadness. She had always hoped her mother would find love again, but she understood why she never remarried. She waited to be with Gabriel again in heaven.

Three more years of marriages in the larger Berwick and O'Brien families did nothing to soothe the Danetree quest for heirs. The lengthy courting, all of the time spent on the dock at Greyfriars holding hands, the suggestive parties and teas, and, finally, the begging still had not moved Clarisse and T-Jean to wed. It was not until Jean senior got very ill that they realized maybe it was time to marry while their parents were alive to witness the ceremony. They had been very much in love for a long time. They were happy just to be around each other when they had the chance. Now that they were a little older, it was time to start their new journey as husband and wife. T-Jean proposed to Clarisse by the hibiscus tree on June 17, 1845, and they were married July 21. Jean senior was too weak to stand at the ceremony, so Eustace fashioned a special lounging chair with wheels so he could be maneuvered easily around the festivities. Genny held his hand and never left his side.

Genny liked Clarisse very much. She thought she was strong-minded and driven—strong where T-Jean was not. They would be a good match.

She looked forward to grandchildren, but that excitement was tempered with Jean Sr.'s failing health. She hoped he would live long enough to see his bloodline carry on. In some ways she blamed her son for not being more aggressive in pursuing an earlier marriage with Clarisse. She felt she had paid enough in her life with loss: a father she adored, a husband, and her sweet daughter Victoria. Now Jean Charles was leaving her as well. As much as she wanted grandchildren, she did so with caution. Preparing for misfortune and loss was overtaking any joy she could muster for the future, and she couldn't find a middle ground in her own heart for the joy and the sorrow.

Chapter 12

Sins in the Flesh

It was a sultry summer night in August 1849. Genny lay next to Jean Charles, watching him breathe. His face was mostly frozen with what she could describe only as a vacant stare. No one had expected him to last this long. The doctor thought it to be some kind of intermittent stupor. There was no paralysis of the face, as he had seen in others, and Jean managed to swallow small amounts of water and soft food when he was coherent. As long as he was taking nourishment, there had to be hope.

Sleep became a memory for Genny. Sometimes she lay awake praying that she and Jean would go together. *One last breath together.* She did not want to dress in black again—the horrid shrouds of loss and pain. She was remembering the feeling of her mourning dress, which had been like a cloth coffin to her, all trussed up and snug. She did not understand how wearing black and being uncomfortable for a year was to somehow show respect for the departed. She wore black on the inside all of the time. She wanted the outside of her to show the joy in remembering the love and life of the people she mourned for. Not the flesh-cloaked wretched abyss that held her organs until her own expiration. She kissed his forehead, stroked his cheek, and whispered in his ear. "Whether you wake up or join the others, I shall wear yellow, Jean. Warm and bright like you, my darling." She laid her head on his chest and went to sleep.

She dreamed she was young again. She could smell her own orange blossom scent that she always wore. And her father was alive. It was their first meal with the Danetrees: Charles, Paul, and Jean Charles. There was laughter and food and wine and candlelight. Then there was a knock at the door. Her father got up to answer it. She thought it strange he should answer, as it was not his apartment. He came back to the table and said there was a strange woman at the door for Monsieur Charles. She was wearing a red scarf around the lower part of her face and held a baby in her arms. Genny looked around the table. No one was saying a thing. Charles got up and left the room. He did not return. Another knock and her father again answered. She tried to ask Paul and Jean Charles to please go, but instead but they sat there staring toward the front room. When her father came back, his eyes were fixed as he approached the table. She wanted to jump up and grab him, but she could not move. He nodded toward Paul and said there was a man named Ambrose at the door for him. He was wet, cold, and bleeding. Paul looked at her and then Jean. He stood up and left. He did not return. Genny was terrified.

Still paralyzed, and unable to speak, she tried with her eyes and tears to plead for someone to say anything. Another knock came, and she felt a scream rise up in her. She knew that she was screaming, but it was as if no one could hear her. They all looked at each other but were under some kind of spell. Again her father answered the door. This time he just looked at her and smiled. Suddenly his eyes burned bright like fire, and smoke appeared to be coming from behind him. He crumbled to ashes in front of her and Jean Charles.

She wanted to faint but could not. Jean Charles got up. He looked at her sadly and left the room. He did not return. She looked across the table at their host. He had become skeletal with papery gray skin flaking from his bones, then his remains crumbled in the chair and onto the floor. She was now alone at the table. When she looked at the food it was all in various states of decay and rot. There were maggots and moths all over everything. The flames on the candles and in the oil lams were rising higher and higher. She was afraid she would burn to death like her father. When the last knock came, she felt her body release, as if something were letting her go. She ran from the room to the door. A woman stood there—a strange masked woman. She held a bundled baby forward. Genny took it and watched as the woman slowly undid the scarf around her mouth. The woman's eyes were dark and large.

She could see something writhing under the scarf. When the scarf fell away, Genny was horrified to see the skeleton of a large snakelike beast hanging from the woman's face. Just as she screamed, the woman came at her and then vanished. Genny turned as if to protect the baby, and the blanket fell open. All she saw was wings—small orange wings. It seemed like hundreds of them were flying at her face and around her body. She screamed again, ripped a bone comb out of her hair, and stabbed and swatted at the creatures. Plunging the comb wildly through the air around as the humming of the wings seemed to get louder and louder. She kept screaming and slashing.

Jean Baptiste heard screams and headed for his parents' bedroom. Genny was still screaming and swatting when he ran in. "Mother, Mother!" he cried. He grabbed her hands and held them. She looked up at him as if she did not recognize him. Her long grey hair was matted to her face, which was dripping with sweat. Blood spattered her face, hands, nightdress and quilt. He was horrified. "Mother, it is me, your son. What is wrong?" He looked over at his father. "Oh my God, no." He let go of her hands and ran to Jean's side of the bed. His eyes were wide and his mouth agape. His face, scalp, and throat were dotted with blood. Even his eyes were pooled with blood. His mother's comb was still lodged in his father's throat. He was not breathing. Clarisse had come into the room and gasped when she saw the scene. Genny sat on the edge of the bed, weakly stabbing the air as if she were still in her dream. It was clear she was not in her right mind but in some form of trance. Clarisse stood close to her and held her mother-in-law's head against her nightgown and stroked her hair. This seemed to calm her down, though she remained seemingly oblivious of her surroundings.

Clarisse took Genny to their room, where she cleaned her up, putting her in a clean dressing gown, and then settled her in their bed. Jean checked for any breath or feeling left in his father's body. Finding none, he cleaned his father up and pulled the quilt over his face. He did not want anyone to see what had really happened. He prayed that his father had not been alert during the assault, but the look on his face mirrored what looked to T-Jean like some kind of pain and awareness. Jean and Clarisse held vigil in their bedroom next to Genny to make sure there would be no more violent incidences. The only person sleeping in Greyfriars that night would be Genny.

The next morning, Anne, Hubert, and Kaila arrived for their daily work and were heartbroken to find Mr. Jean had passed in the night. They offered anything to make things easier for Genny. She seemed dazed. Of course she was traumatized and out of her mind, the poor dear. She had doted on him throughout his illness, and their sympathy was all hers. Hubert rode off to get the doctor. While Anne and Kaila took care of the house, Clarisse and Jean Baptiste stayed close to Genny, speaking only in low tones, not letting her out of their sight. They held each other's hands. They too were in shock and exhausted, as if some terrible nightmare had left them all in a perpetual dream state with no rational explanation of events to help them separate the nightmare from the dream.

Jean asked, "What will we tell the doctor? How do we put this into words, Clarisse? What has just happened in this house? How are we going to live with this?" His eyes searched the room. She took her husband's chin in a gentle grip. "Jean, look at me." She stared until she was sure he was focusing on her. "Your mother is not herself, Jean. She is not the same person who kissed your cheek good night last night. Do you understand?" He nodded. She was going to have to be his strength. She would find time later to cry and try to make sense of the situation, if any could be made.

"When the doctor comes," Clarisse said, "you and he will go into the room, and you will explain to him what you know. There is no need to alarm the rest of the family. I will stay with your mother. We will speak to him of arrangements and her possibly staying at the convent in New Orleans if the Sisters will have her. T-Jean, I am so very sorry, my darling. You are too gentle hearted for this shock. But I do believe that your father felt nothing and that he was already gone. And that is what we will believe. I fear we may have to leave with Mother Genny very soon. If she comes around—"

Just as those words were being spoken, Genny sat up straight in bed as if lifted upright from behind. She looked at both of them with such a cold stare that Jean squeezed Clarisse's hand tightly. She spoke. Her voice calm. "She's coming for us all, you know. She's gonna take the children. Turn them into flying things. Evil things. It's all in the wall. All in the wall. When the wall comes down, they will show themselves. Always a price. One for the sin and another for the sinner." She lay back down, closed her eyes, and went to sleep. Jean and Clarisse held hands even tighter and began to pray out loud together. The Lord's Prayer was the first thing out of their mouths.

When the doctor saw the markings on Jean's face and throat and then observed Genny's mental state, he was in quite a state of shock himself. Some of the teeth in Genny's comb had broken off in Jean Charles's throat. He removed the broken comb and wrapped a cloth around it. "I would suggest a quick burial. People will understand, you know. Even if it is a Danetree. I can tell you I must record a death, but I will do so as a natural death with extenuating circumstances. I am quite sure your father would approve. I have known your family for generations, as has the whole of this southern state. We need go no further. However, I cannot counsel you on your mother, although firstly I must suggest a temporary commitment for the safety of all. Charity Hospital in the city is the closest for those afflicted with violent tendencies and such behavior if you are willing to make the journey. Further out is the new hospital in Jackson if you wish to consider more anonymity. I believe the burden of caring for your father these last years has taken its toll. I can only hope she will recover and forgive us for these actions. I cannot recommend the Ursulines. They have their hands quite full with the poor, indigent, and feverish at the convent. We can have her at Charity within the week. I do not suggest she attend the funeral or even interact with family and guests. She will need to be watched, Jean. No one can be certain she will not act out again."

Jean was relieved the doctor wanted to put the family at ease regarding any scandal or speculation among the community, although he knew eventually things would get around. Jackson sounded like a good choice, but it was so very far away and more expensive. He would spare no expense for his mother, but Charity was closer to home and they could visit with ease. He considered that if they checked her in at night under her maiden name, it might go unnoticed. There might be suspicion but at least it would not be on the front page of the *Teal Bend Gazette* or in the New Orleans papers. It could be disastrous in French and English for the family. There were so many decisions to make in a short period of time. Jean did not want to think his mother had murdered his father. She'd had a night terror. It was an accident. Yes. An accident.

He shook the doctor's hand. "I cannot thank you enough for all you have done for us. Truly I am thankful you are here. I must confess I am at a loss at this time. My father is gone, my mother is to leave, and with no children as of yet, this house will seem quite empty, you know. Even with father in his states of varying consciousness, it was a comfort to see him and talk to him even when he couldn't always acknowledge or recognize me. I felt as if he were listening and knew of my presence. If it is possible, could you stay through the night? If we could give Mother something to help her stay comfortable and sleep through as much as possible until we take her away, and we could arrange for a quick service and burial for Father. In New Orleans I can post his obituary in the paper and use the telegraph there and then stop in Teal Bend at the *Gazette* on the way home. I know everyone will understand Mother not being here. I will express her regrets to those that inquire."

The doctor nodded and looked down. "You are a good son, T-Jean, and these are heartbreaking decisions. I know your parents would be proud of you. Of course I will stay. It would be my privilege and my honor to help you all through this time. I will stay, and we can escort your mother to the hospital. It will take some time to get there comfortably. I will do what I can to make sure she sleeps as much as possible through the travels. She will also need a nurse to assist her with her needs. Will Clarisse join us?"

Jean shrugged. "I will go and discuss these things with her. Meanwhile I'll have a room prepared for you. Please join me in the study for a brandy first. I really need to have a brandy right now. I imagine Clarisse does too."

The doctor smiled. "I can manage my way to the study. You go and get Clarisse and meet me there. Have Kaila sit with Genny while we talk, but make sure there is nothing in the room Genny can use as a weapon. Kaila will be stronger than Anne in case Genny has an episode."

Jean nodded. "Yes. Of course you are right. Meet you downstairs."

Kaila was called in to sit with Genny while Anne prepared a room for the doctor. Hubert and Emile were given the solemn task of preparing a coffin for Jean Charles. In the study, Clarisse poured brandy for the three of them. "Our staff can surely handle the house while we are gone, but if it will be more than a week, I can have my parents come to stay here in case there are issues in the fields, Jean."

Jean nodded and answered, "My man Antoine is very capable of handling anything that might arise in the fields. We should be back for burning time though. I am sure things will be well during our absence with your parents here. You know Kaila is strong enough to handle Mother if you feel the need to stay, Clarisse."

She put her hand on his. "Kaila can stay. We will go together. Doctor, you will accompany us, won't you?"

He nodded. "Yes. Jean has agreed that we will take her to Charity Hospital in New Orleans. I will vouch for her quarters with the staff. I also know for a fact that they are seeking funds at this time, as they are overcome with expenses. The Danetrees have always been generous with the good Sisters at the convent. It may be time to also provide a goodly sum to the hospital to secure Genny a good safe place there regardless of the expenditures. The situation is always sad indeed. I must warn you that these types of places are not like home, and I wouldn't want Clarisse's sensitivities to be overcome at the sight of the unfortunate creatures that must survive there en masse. We can only pray that this is a temporary dementia brought on by great duress. I want to personally make sure you are at ease with these arrangements. If you are not, then I can only suggest the hospital in Jackson. It is a new facility but quite far away. In that case, we could catch a riverboat in the city up to Bayou Sara and then travel overland a distance. Whatever the choice, it needs to be done soon. We now know the aftermath of what inaction might be."

Jean smiled and looked over at Clarisse. "Doctor, my wife's character and resolve are sometimes stronger than my own. I am sure her reactions will be those of a healer and mother to any that might cast an eye her way."

211

They all jumped as a woman's shriek rang out through the house. They ran out into the hallway, where the doctor grabbed his bag. Another scream sent them up to the bedroom Genny was in. Kaila had Genny pinned to the bed. Blood and scratch marks were obvious on her arms, and she had tears in her eyes.

"I don't know what happened," Kaila cried. She relaxed her grip and moved away as Jean Baptiste and the doctor held Genny down. "She asked me to open the window in such a sweet voice. But she wasn't asking me. She called me Marie. After I opened the window, she asked for her special tea. Said I should make her some—the kind that helps her sleep. But I know Miss Genny don't care for tea too much, so I said, "Are you sure you don't want coffee, Miss Genny, with fresh cream?" Then she slapped me hard and screamed. She jumped up and ran toward the window. I ran after her and caught her arms. That's when she dug her nails into my skin. It was awful painful, Miss Clarisse. But I held her and dragged her back to the bed. She screamed for me to get my damn brown hands off her body. Called me a heathen!"

Genny screamed again. It was unintelligible. The doctor looked over to Clarisse. "Take Kaila downstairs. I'll see to her wounds in a minute after I calm Genny down." He gave Genny a shot of something while Jean pinned her to the bed. Clarisse put her arm around Kaila's shoulders and gingerly led her out of the room.

After several hours, Hubert and Emile came in and said they were finished with the box for the elder Mr. Jean and again stated how sorry they were about his passing. Jean Baptiste went back out with them. His heart felt as if it were breaking when he saw the coffin, knowing they could not have a proper blessing and burial. "My mother is too ill and distraught to deal with all of this. We will be taking her to a hospital for care tomorrow morning. The doctor has given her something to make her sleep. We will be burying my father this afternoon in a makeshift grave and then having a proper service and burial in the crypt when I return." He saw the looks on their faces. "I understand what you may think, but if we don't get my mother to a hospital quickly, I may lose her too. It is the right thing to do, and his body will not stay in this heat." They shook their heads and looked down.

Hubert spoke up. "Monsieur Jean, please let us know what you need from us, and we will help."

With tears in his eyes he said, "Emile, I will need your help bringing his body down, and then we will have a procession to the chapel. Hubert, take the carriage to Murielle's and ask everyone to come as soon as possible. We need to do this before nightfall."

Murielle and Marguerite rode back with Hubert. They were in tears. Antoine was not back from the fields yet, so they left him a note on the cottage door. Clarisse was with Kaila and Anne in the kitchen when they arrived. Jean Baptiste, Emile, and Doc had put the body in the coffin, wrapped in the quilt that had covered the bed he and Genny had shared for many years. Marguerite picked a flower off of the hibiscus tree and placed it on the quilt. The rest placed roses, magnolias, and other flowers from the garden, and then Emile hammered the lid on. Each time the hammer hit a nail, the sound exploded in Jean's head. They then placed the coffin on a flat cart and hitched it to the carriage.

Clarisse drove the carriage while Jean walked with everyone else to the chapel to apprise them of the situation. The doctor stayed behind and watched over Genny. Antoine had gotten the note from the cottage door, and he arrived at the chapel on horseback just as they began prayer. They placed Jean Sr.'s coffin in the ground and headed back to the house. Emile rode to the Berwick plantation with a letter to Clarisse's parents.

When evening came, Jean and Clarisse were exhausted. The good doctor kept Genny sedated. They moved a chaise lounge into their room for her. Clarisse saw to her needs, and then they secured her to the lounge for her protection and theirs at the doctor's suggestion. Clarisse then gathered some basic things for their journey and readied their luggage. She wanted everything to be as organized as possible so that the morning preparation would be smooth. Instructions were given as to the running of Greyfriars in their absence. Murielle and the Vicknairs agreed to watch over Greyfriars until Clarisse's parents arrived.

It was a long, anxious journey to Charity Hospital. One got somewhat used to the gnats, mosquitoes, and mud, but the possibility of being accosted and the brevity of what they were about to do weighed heavily on Jean and Clarisse both. Genny slept most of the way, with Clarisse waking her up only for the necessities. Every now and then Genny woke to call for her husband. At one point she seemed to be having another episode, twitching and swatting at things that weren't there. Clarisse held her arms until she calmed down. Jean looked across the carriage at his mother, only he felt like he was looking at a stranger in a familiar body. He didn't understand this person his mother had become in so quick a moment. His heart was in turmoil. Was he making the right decision about committing her? If she healed, would she forgive them? Could he forgive her for taking his father away from the family? He did not want to think she had murdered him. It was clear she was demented, but the contorted look on his father's face was now chiseled into his memory to haunt him forever.

He watched as his mother opened her eyes, smiled, raised a hand, and slowly, gently leaned across to touch his hand. Part of him wanted to pull away, but he loved her and desperately wanted to remember the mother he knew just two days before. He smiled back. "Yes, Mother?" he asked. He could see tears gathering in her eyes.

In a whisper of a voice, she said, "When your father wakes, tell him to stay away from the flowers and the little flying devils. Promise me, T-Jean. When the wall comes down, get the box and destroy it. Don't tell her I told you. She showed me the box. Says, there's another one with an unfaithful heart in it. It will be our secret. Must protect your children. I must sleep now. I love you, my son." She nodded, leaned back, and closed her eyes. The doctor shook his head sadly. Jean looked at Clarisse, who shrugged and kept hold of Genny's other hand. There was nothing anyone could say.

The bumps and jolts along the route did not help with the general mood of the occupants. Clarisse did her best to take care of Genny, but at times it was cumbersome in the heat and humidity. Jean remained somewhat removed, and the doctor helped Clarisse when assistance was required. They stopped briefly in Teal Bend for fresh horses and then continued on. They arrived at Charity in the late evening hours, after most of the patients had fallen asleep. They were met by two Sisters of Charity that escorted them to an admissions office after speaking briefly to the doctor. He left with the Sisters for a few moments.

Genny was groggy and subdued. She was seated between Clarisse and Jean on a comfortable green velvet sofa while they waited for the doctor. They spent such anxious moments as they sat there taking in the sights, sounds, and smells. Jean spoke. "Well, it seems to be run well. Not like a prison, as I had thought it might be. I must admit I feel somewhat comforted that the nuns are in charge."

Clarisse nodded. "I agree, Jean. They will be a comforting sight for her. Maybe she won't be here long. Maybe she's just exhausted and they might be able to treat her. She'll be home with us again soon. We must believe that." She tried to smile, but she was so tired, as they all were. The past few days had run them ragged—especially Clarisse, who took care of Genny more so than the men.

Jean looked at the floor. "Clarisse, may I ask you something?"

"Yes," she said. He took a breath as if hesitating before speaking. "Do you ... do you regret that we did not have children before these things happened? They will never know my father, and if Mother never recovers, they will not know her either." His voice seemed so sad.

"Oh my darling Jean. You are suffering terribly, and I am sorry. I believe that your father will be a guardian angel for our children when they come, and that Mother Genny will be well and with us when that time comes."

He admired her strength and the way she could make him believe in good things and positive thoughts. Hopeful—that was it. She made him feel hopeful.

He smiled. "I do love you so, Clarisse Isabelle Danetree."

She smiled back. "And I you, Jean Baptiste—with all my heart."

They heard voices and looked up to see the doctor returning with the Sisters. One of them had a wheeled chair. The other held a lamp. She smiled and motioned for them to stand.

"Bless you, children," she said. "And may God grant your dear friend peace in our care. Please follow us. We have a suitable room ready for Mrs. Acosta."

They got up, holding Genny and guiding her gently into the chair. Her lids were heavy, and her breathing slow. She remained peaceful throughout the process. Jean picked up her bag and followed them to a small room down several long halls. The light from the lamps bounced off of the pale yellow walls making them seem an odd golden color. They passed so many doors with very small barred windows. They could hear crying in some of the rooms they passed, senseless talk in others. There was a scream at one point, but it seemed to be far away. The lantern sister explained a few things as they went regarding responsibilities of the patient's family and friends and how important regular visits were to the mentally deranged. Those words felt like a knife in the heart to Jean, but Clarisse squeezed his hand and eased his worry a bit.

Her room was sparse but comfortable. The Sisters retained her bag and belongings to be kept in storage for when needed. Jean and Clarisse kissed Genny on the forehead before leaving the room. The doctor had given her something to help her through the night. In the lobby, he looked at Jean. "I will stay the night with your mother. It is not permitted for nonmedical personnel or family to stay here, as it could be most disruptive to other patients and staff as well. You and Genny go to the apartment. I will be fine." He put his hand on Jean's shoulder and then shook his hand. "Just come back by in the morning to discuss the finances at the administrative office before you head back."

They left him there and went the city apartment and prayed that they may have a good night's sleep.

In the months that followed, Jean made it a point to visit his mother as often as possible. Clarisse worried every time he left the house for any extended period of time, but in these cases he could become very melancholy after seeing her, although the reports he came back with were promising. She seemed not to be acting out like she had at home. She spoke of a Sister Marie that would often sit with her and tell her stories and bring her tea. It was an odd coincidence after what Kaila had told them during Genny's derangement, but they did not give it another thought, knowing Genny was safe in a hospital. Jean and Clarisse made sure that generous donations were made to Charity for Genny's care and the Sisters kindness. Jean did not feel the need to transfer her to Jackson. Charity had its issues, but she seemed happy and calm there with very few night terrors. But it became a much longer process than they had expected.

1855

Genny was transferred to the Touro Infirmary, not far from the hospital for rehabilitation. Although she had grown thin, Genny had survived the yellow fever epidemic of '53 and cholera outbreaks that had taken so many other patients. Her move was actually suggested to Jean Baptiste by the Sisters, as she had shown improvement under their care. He was grateful to them for showing her such kindness, so he kept the donations going for Charity after she was relocated. He had never lost hope that one day she would return home.

At Greyfriars things had changed little, but this was not so for Marguerite, Murielle, and Antoine. Jean had been approached by another plantation owner from a distance away who told him there was talk among his slaves that Greyfriars slaves enjoyed an illegal school above and beyond that of acceptable learning, and that one of Jean's overseers and another slave were running the school with Jean's knowledge. Jean had to look perturbed that such a rumor was being spread about Greyfriars, and he said he would put an end to it quickly. This seemed to satisfy his peer, but now he was going to have to shut down Marguerite's school.

Jean understood exactly what was being inferred. He did not want to break Marguerite's heart, but the consequences of not seeing this through would be the ruin of his plantation and possibly jail or worse for Murielle, Marguerite, and Antoine. He knew Clarisse would be angry, as she had never been comfortable with the use of slave labor and did everything she could to help Marguerite at her school. Clarisse loved being around the children. She and Jean were still childless, but it wasn't for lack of trying. There were a few times she was sure she was pregnant, but it was not to be, so she busied herself with the school, the house, and sewing and mending. Since Jean spent so much time in the fields, there was plenty of mending to do.

Jean met with Antoine and Marguerite, then a "mysterious fire" destroyed the makeshift schoolhouse. It was heartbreaking. When word got around the outer communities about the fire, the rumors seemed to die down, and Greyfriars was soon out of the spotlight. Jean allowed the worship to continue, but schooling had to be kept very quiet and not as frequent. One night after a late supper, Clarisse showed Jean a book that a cousin from Maryland had given to her, titled *Uncle Tom's Cabin*. "Things are changing, Jean. I know the Danetrees and Berwicks have long enjoyed the benefits of slave labor, but my cousin has recently come from Maryland, and she says things are changing quickly, Jean." She cast her eyes down. "I know I cannot speak to this much, as I have also benefitted from this way of life, but I have never stopped feeling guilty for this way of life, Jean. What if we could have a life free of this cruel system? Surely there are other forms of business that we can invest ourselves in to support ourselves and still provide equal employment for those who choose to work for us and are not forced to do so. My father did it. We had a simple life, but it was a goodly one. I know it would be a lot to give up. I mean, what kind of life do we want for our child, Jean?"

Jean's voice was tempered with thought. He had never dismissed Clarisse's thoughts or words as anything less than his. "Clarisse, I understand what you are trying to say, but what venture would you have us follow? And what of Mother's care? You know we could not have her receiving the care she has benefitted from … Did you say 'our child'?"

Clarisse started crying. "Yes, Jean. Our child."

Jean got up and dropped to his knees in front of her and laid his head on her belly. "Oh my good God, I swear I thought this might never happen. I would have spent the rest of our days just happy you loved me, but now we will see that love in our child's face." He stood up and took her face in his hands, his eyes full of tears. He kissed her tenderly. "Are you well? Is there something you require of me?"

She smiled. "If my calculations are correct, we will have our baby in late spring. But I would like to wait to share this news until another month has passed. You understand, Jean?" He nodded. "Of course. Anything for you."

The months couldn't go by quickly enough for Jean or Clarisse. She was grateful to carry her pregnancy through the winter, as the summer months could be tortuous with the trappings of being a woman. The happiness at Greyfriars was doubled when Marguerite announced that she too was with child, but due in the fall. She and Antoine had experienced several miscarriages over the years, which had made Marguerite reluctant to get pregnant again. Besides, she'd had hundreds of children as students over the years and loved all of them as though they were her own. Now with the school only part time, she took this baby as a sign and blessing from God that it was her time. She had Antoine's 'amen' on that. An extra room was built onto the cottage for the baby, per Murielle's request. She also had Antoine build a new lavatory room out of brick with a seat made out of cypress for the ladies, like the ones at Greyfriars, although Antoine chose the tried-and-true outhouse and was glad to have it to himself.

Clarisse wanted changes at Greyfriars as well. She wanted to change the old, dark wallpaper and lighten up the house. The large back gallery windows provided beautiful light that shone through the house on sunny days, and she wanted to walk into each room and feel light and bright— except for Jean's study. She was not allowed to touch that. She was almost grateful he refused her suggestions for his study, as making even small changes in a house that size could be very involved. And he was relieved she did not try to strongly impress her décor ideas on his only room of respite. He didn't mind what the women decided for the rest of the house, but he would not, could not, let them touch his study.

Marcel Philippe Danetree was born in May of 1857. He came into the world kicking and screaming—until he was fed. He was a constantly hungry baby, which kept Clarisse very occupied. Jean was so proud that they had a male child to carry on the Danetree line. Like him and the Danetree men before him, Marcel would carry on the blood and the estate. Clarisse, for the time being, had not spoken of their conversations about changing the Greyfriars lifestyle and economics. He also hoped that maybe Clarisse would agree to more children, since it looked as if they were to be blessed late in life with a family.

Marcel was a happy baby and active toddler. Marguerite would visit with her twins, Antoine and Antoinette, who were just four months younger than Marcel. She and Clarisse would sit and sew together while the cousins played. They often talked about abolition and how it was spreading and shifting people and ideas. They were concerned about family dynamics and how the changing times might affect their family situation—especially their children. Regardless of how they got there, Marguerite's twins were Danetrees as well, but the concern was of skin color. Antoine Jr. was darker than Antoinette, and Marcel was fair. They knew the twins would have to be protected through it all. One day Marcel would have to understand his role in their protection.

Clarisse spoke to Jean again about the changes she had heard about. These things were probably being discussed very differently between the planters than they were with those enslaved. She thought it might be time to revisit their previous discussions and the future of Greyfriars. She convinced him it would be less of an economic concern to them if they could effect a more protective relationship with their slaves. She influenced Jean to furnish all of their slaves with travel passes with the understanding that their safety was not guaranteed off of the plantation. She felt maybe they would choose to stay if they felt protected. There were planters always on the lookout for slaves suffering from the "runaway disease," ready to kill or haul them back in as examples to others thinking of wandering or running. New Orleans wasn't even as safe as it once had been for people of color, whether they were free or not.

In 1859 Clarisse and Jean were blessed again when Eleanor Hyacinthe was born. Marcel was not very happy at first but got used to having his mother's time divided between the siblings. With the twins to play with, things seemed to even out. Marguerite had Isabelle Marie in 1860, and the households were full of the sweet sounds of youth and liveliness. Marguerite and Murielle spent more time at Greyfriars now. Anne had lost her sight and could no longer function around the house. After Hubert had passed away, Kaila had moved in with her. Anne refused to stop working and pleaded for anything to do. She would scold Kaila when she felt Kaila was avoiding tasking her with anything, especially in the main house kitchen: "My eyes do not work, but my hands are still strong. I can still snap a bean, peel an onion, and fold cloth, missy!"

Kaila was just concerned about her safety, so she would have Anne sit at the kitchen table, away from the fireplace. It was her nightmare that Anne's long skirt and apron might catch an ember or spark, so she became her caretaker. She didn't mind. Anne and Hubert had always been kind to her. She knew Anne was terribly sad without Hubert. They had been working together for years and were grateful for each other's company. Kaila treated her well, hoping that one day someone would do the same for her.

More changes were soon to come. Jean and Clarisse had received word that Genny had progressed to the point of being able to return home. Jean seemed happy, but Clarisse was apprehensive, especially with two very young children roaming Greyfriars now. They would place in her the back room, Hyacinthe's old room, and hire a nurse to take the small room next to it. They hoped this would work.

Genny seemed overjoyed all the way back to Greyfriars. She had spent eleven years away from home and was returning a much older woman. Her hair was completely silver now and was in a short bob, as this was the style most appropriate for the patients, for safety and cleanliness reasons. Not having traveled for a very long time, she was amazed at everything along the way. She remarked constantly about how beautiful green everything was. How gracefully the moss draped the branches of the ancient cypress. Every now and then seeing turtles sunning themselves on logs and branches bobbing in the bayou next to the road. And the sweet sounds of the birds singing along the way. Jean Baptiste was torn. He had never told her about Jean senior dying, against the doctor's suggestions that he do so while she was under care. He just couldn't.

It was just him and Mother in the carriage. She looked across at him. "You know, your father would be just amazed at how the world has grown. And it's a shame you never got to visit me in my last room. Though an angel did bring your dear father to me every now and then. I do miss him terribly. I will grieve forever. I am so happy to be going home to my grandchildren as well. You know I shared that room with Judith, a Jewish widow from New York City, and a young lady from Sweden who did not speak Spanish or French, and very little English? But she taught me how to say 'shit' in Swedish."

While Jean sat there with his mouth open, his mother pursed her lips and said what sounded like "queeta." She then went on. "And there was Marie. She was from a Spanish island. I thought they might put the whole world in that little room with me. I wasn't happy about the ordeal at first, but they were quite pleasant ladies. Judith did not eat pork, though. And she didn't drink milk with her meat. It was very strange, but I wanted her to feel welcome, so I didn't either. It distressed her so, and it wasn't worth troubling her, so I just gave it up." She turned back to staring out the carriage window.

Jean's brow furrowed. Had he heard her correctly? She spoke of his father in the present tense and as an angel. He was starting to worry that maybe she was not ready to come home. He decided to have the doctor stop in on her when they got home. "Yes, Mother, things have changed very much, but I believe you will be happy to see Greyfriars again. Just let me know if things become uncomfortable for you, and I will set it right." He didn't quite know what to say, so he decided to keep things fairly casual.

She looked at him and cocked her head, smiling. "Oh, my Jean Baptiste. Please do not think me so unstable. I have been quite in control for some years now. And I will not be treated as a child when there are real children in the house now that need looking after. I will be fine. You will see." She reached across and patted his hand.

Their arrival at Greyfriars was met with fresh flowers in the rooms, the scent of baked bread floating through the house, and everyone standing outside when they heard the horses and carriage pulling up into the driveway. When Genny stepped down, she smiled and held her arms out for Clarisse. Clarisse handed Eleanor over to Kaila and went to her. Genny seemed truly happy. "Oh, bless you, my daughter. This is a wonderful homecoming for me. And let me see these babies. You must be Marcel." She bent down to look at Marcel as he backed up behind Kaila's skirts. "It's all right, my darling boy. There is plenty of time for us to get to know each other." She looked at Eleanor and touched her little cheek. "And you, my precious. You are too young to be afraid of Grandmother yet." Genny smiled at Kaila and winked at her.

Kaila smiled nervously. "Welcome home, Miss Genny."

Clarisse took Genny's hand and took her inside as Jean got her bags. She seemed to adjust quickly to her new room and the changes in the house. She spent a lot of time smiling.

One night when Genny asked Kaila to bring her a cup of tea with milk, Kaila was apprehensive, remembering the tea incident those many years before. Genny was sitting up in bed when Kaila entered her room. "Why, thank you." She smiled sweetly and motioned for Kaila to have a seat. She took a sip of the tea. "Mmmm. That is very good, thank you. You know, earlier at the door when I winked at you, I didn't want to give anything away. I know who you are." Kaila started to say something, but Genny raised a finger to her lips. "It's all right. I must say I am so happy that you are here with me. I thought that when I left the hospital I would never see you again. It is nice to see your hair that way, without the scarf. Although I did like that red color on you. I suppose I'll get used to it. And don't worry. I'll not tell anyone. Now I am so very tired." She handed Kaila the cup. "Good night, my dear."

"Good night, Miss Genny." Kaila left the room, stopping just outside the door after she closed it. She was afraid that if she told Miss Clarisse or Mr. Jean, there would be trouble. They might see her as scared or unreasonable. She didn't want any trouble during this time while the family was just getting back together. But she was going to watch Miss Genny very closely now—especially around the children.

Clarisse and Jean were very happy with Genny's progress at home. There were no incidences of night terrors, and they felt no need to hire a nurse for her. She seemed just fine. Even when they talked about her husband, she would smile, and she was even pleasant to Murielle and to Marguerite and her children when they visited. This was very pleasing to Murielle, who had those terrible memories from the early days in the back of her mind. When it came to grandchildren, there was always Clarisse or Kaila there too. Genny was never left alone with them. This only made it worse for Kaila. She felt as if she were the only one seeing anything wrong. Miss Genny would call her Marie under her breath and then smile as if she had some kind of secret with her.

One morning Kaila went upstairs to gather bedding and saw Genny standing at the window, singing some kind of song in a weird childlike voice, swaying back and forth to her own music. She turned around and motioned for Kaila to join her at the window. "Been waiting for you,

Marie. Come. Take my hand." She held out her hand and continued to hum.

Kaila went to her and took her hand. She smiled nervously and asked, "Who you singing to, Miss Genny?"

Genny just looked at her and said calmly, "Oh, now don't you have fun with me like that, Marie. They might hear you. They have been waiting so long now. Waiting for a freedom song. But you know that, now don't you." She turned back to the window. "Look at them, Marie. Flying around without a care in the world. How they love the hibiscus. So beautiful."

Kaila looked around in the sky and around the yard. "I don't see no birds, Miss Genny."

Genny smiled. "They are not birds. Birds are simple creatures. Remember when you first told me about them that night after the Sisters locked our door and we were having tea? Remember their names? Philippe, Ambrose, Ellie, and Jacque?" She stopped as if trying to remember more.

At that moment Kaila heard her name being called at the bottom of the stairs. It sounded like Miss Clarisse. She thanked God someone had called for her. "Well, I hear my name, Miss Genny. I must go." She backed away and then turned and walked quickly out of the room. Whatever had just happened had nothing to do with anything good or innocent. Something was very wrong. And she was sure being "touched" had nothing to do with it. Somebody had put a spell on Genny—a bad spell to make her sing to flying things that weren't there.

Kaila got to the top of the stairs, and Clarisse was at the bottom. All Kaila wanted to do was tell her what she was thinking. All she said was "Coming, Miss Clarisse." Her heart was beating hard in her chest from fear. She knew evil was here and alive in Genny. It was going to use her to harm the family. She also knew she would have to tell about what she had seen. She felt sick, and she felt scared. Their world was going to come apart again, and she was afraid this time they might not survive.

Acknowledgments

I would like to thank the perseverance of the human heart and spirit as witnessed by the genealogical journey I began researching many years ago through my own family lines full of so many tragic and beautiful human records, stories, and memories. An attendance at SummerWords Creative Writing Colloquium 2012 at American River College in Sacramento also motivated me. These experiences, Arlington Plantation in Franklin, Louisiana, a curious orange dragonfly in my own backyard, and the NaNoWriMo November Novel Writing Challenge inspired me to create this work. I am eternally grateful for the teachers, writers, historians, scientists, and genealogists without whom I could not have satiated my creative appetite. I was fortunate to have also read the following books and visited the following websites, which helped me to give my project a sense of grace, place, and times. I hope you will check them out too.

Suggested Readings

Chamberlain, Gaius. "Norbert Rillieux." November 26, 2012. Blackinventor.com/norbert-rillieux.

Faragher, John. *A Great and Noble Scheme: The Tragic Story of the Expulsion of the French Acadians from Their American Homeland.* New York: W. W. Norton & Company, 2005.

Harper, Frances E. W. *Iola Leroy: Shadows Uplifted.* Philadelphia, 2004. Project Gutenberg e-book.

Jones-Jackson, Patricia. *When Roots Die: Endangered Traditions on the Sea Islands.* Georgia: University of Georgia Press, 1987.

Kane, Harnett. *Queen New Orleans: City by the River.* New York: Bonanza Books, 1949.

Kilner, Mary Ann. *Adventures of a Pincushion: Designed Chiefly for the Use of Young Ladies.* 2 vols. London: Forgotten Books, 1815.

Kolchin, Peter. *American Slavery 1619–1877.* New York: Hill and Wang, 1993.

Louisiana State University. "Sugarcane." Accessed January 14, 2014. www.lsuagcenter.com/en/crops_livestock/crops/sugarcane.

Pons, Frank Moya. *History of the Caribbean: Plantations, Trade, and War in the Atlantic World.* Princeton: Markus Weiner Publishers, 2007.

Trammell, Camilla Davis. *Seven Pines: Its Occupants and Their Letters.* rev. ed. Dallas, Texas: SMU Press, 1987.

United States Navy. Naval History and Heritage Command page. Accessed September 8, 2014. http://www.navy.mil/local/navhist/.

University of South Carolina. "Geographer recreates 'The Great Louisiana Hurricane of 1812.'" Science Daily. February 6, 2011.

About the Author

Selene Simone possesses a bold bloodline from the bayous of southern Louisiana. She is a bibliophile with a lovely library and an old soul enchanted by the written word. Selene currently resides with her family in northern California. What the Dragonfly Saw is her debut book series.